THE UNORTHODOX ARRIVAL OF PUMPKIN ALLAN

BY
SUZIE TWINE

First published in paperback 2014

Second Edition January 2015

Third Edition June 2015

Fourth Edition May 2016

ISBN -13: 978-0-9927419-0-7

Magic Feather Publishing

Dedicated to Molly and Keith

1

Box-file labelled 'Honeysuckle' clutched tightly to her chest, Lois made her way from the flat, along numerous Islington side streets to track down her car; repeatedly contemplating the checklist she had imprinted in her head. Money transfers completed, check. Signed documents with solicitor, check. Cash from parents, with solicitor, check. Mortgage in place, check. 'Yes,' she thought, 'everything should run smoothly today.'

Tom had been anxious about her dealing with all the financial details, but now she was about to prove that, despite having a naturally carefree approach to life, she could be organised if the need arose. And everything had gone incredibly smoothly. Well, apart from thirty thousand pounds disappearing into cyberspace for several hours during that 'immediate' bank transfer, which had certainly sped up her metabolic rate. Oh, and the little hiccup with the money from her father, which had had much the same effect.

The solicitor would ring shortly to say that exchange and completion had taken place. Lois and her best friend would go and pick up the keys from the estate agent and from there she'd take Mel to see her and Tom's wonderful cottage, nestling in the Chiltern Hills.

Lois climbed into her MG convertible, slinging her large handbag behind the passenger seat. She drove, stop-start through the traffic, from Islington to Mel's flat in Finsbury Park and continued to dream of the exciting day that lay ahead. Once she'd shown Mel around Honeysuckle Cottage, she planned to make some tea, which they'd drink in the stunning back garden; revelling in the freshness of the air, the beauty of the flowers and the relaxing sounds of birds singing and bees humming. Heaven! Then, perhaps she would go and introduce herself to some of the neighbours. Lois felt excited flutters of adrenalin flow through her. She couldn't believe she and Tom were actually going to own a home of their own, and the cottage could not have been more perfect.

Lois had booked herself and Mel in for bed and breakfast at Harewood Manor, a gorgeous hotel, which stood only a few hundred yards from the cottage. She'd also arranged for some local builder-decorators to come the following day and quote for giving the inside of the house a facelift. Yes, it had to be said, her organisation on this occasion had been practically faultless.

Mel seemed almost as excited as Lois at the prospect of the next two days in the country. Being unquestionably the more fashionable and well turned-out of the two, Mel exited her flat with a suitcase for the overnight stay. She looked amazing, as always. Her long, wavy, auburn hair, shining as if she'd just been filmed for a L'Oreal advert. Designer dressed from head to toe; the white jeans and heeled sandals accentuating her long skinny legs and making Lois feel more short and dumpy than ever.

"Blimey Mel, how long are we going for?" asked Lois, as Mel struggled to get the case onto the backseat of the MG.

"I thought I did rather well. I could have brought an awful lot more, believe me. Where's your overnight bag then, Miss Minimalist?"

"A change of undies and a few toiletries in my handbag, more than enough," said Lois.

Mel laughed. "What about getting wet, the forecast's terrible for tomorrow."

"It'll be fine, I've got golfing brollies in the boot. I'm perfectly prepared."

Mel tried to persuade Lois to stop and pick up a couple of lattes prior to leaving London, convinced that quality coffee would be unobtainable outside the M25, but Lois refused. "It'll be too much of a detour, Mel. And of course you can get quality coffee in the Chilterns; we're going to Marlow, not the Outer Hebrides!"

"Well, you know me Lo, never been a one for leaving London, unless the trip culminates in getting me to warmer climes. All about to change though methinks, with my best

3

chum moving to the country. I might even invest in a pair Hunters!"

"Hunters?"

"They're three-quarter-calf-length waterproof boots Lo, don't you know anything about the country?"

Lois laughed, "Mel, normal people call them 'wellies' and I do already have a pair!"

A phone call came through on Lois's mobile just as they came off the M40. She pulled over to speak. Mel wondered what was going on. "Nothing will go wrong today," she mouthed to Mel, as a police car sped past them. It was David, the estate agent on the phone, to say the vendors were querying whether the twenty-five pounds for the cooker had been included in the final sum. Grabbing the box file from the back seat, Lois flicked through the papers anxiously until she came to her list of figures; she surely hadn't made a mistake. No, no there wasn't a mistake, that money was definitely included and she reassured David to that effect. Putting the phone down, taking a deep relaxing breath and a moments thought, she turned to Mel. "Gosh, that is unbelievable. We're paying hundreds of thousands of pounds for the house and that couple, who are about to inherit the lot, are worried about a few quid for the rubbishy old cooker, they'd otherwise have had to dump! That seems bizarre doesn't it?"

"Greed Lo, it's a symptom of the modern age. The more we have, the more we want. Anyway, at least you've done your sums right, Tom would have been most disappointed if you'd made a mistake!"

"That's true," Lois said. She was pleased to have Mel's company; she was a very good friend and if any problems were to arise, Mel would be a great support and was always good at keeping things in perspective.

A few minutes later another call came through from the estate agency, saying completion had taken place and Lois could pick up the keys.

"YES!" Shouted Lois, hanging up and passing the phone to Mel. "I knew I could do it! Would you please text Tom and let him know that I am an organisational genius!" She thought for a moment as she sped onto the dual carriageway, "Mm, actually no, don't say that, because he'll think, that I think it's a big deal to organise our finances. Best thing is probably to give the impression it was a piece of cake for a financial witch like myself. Could you just text, 'Completion completed as scheduled!'"

Arriving in Marlow, it took ages to find somewhere to park, and when they did, it was ten minutes on foot from the estate agent's office.

"Come on fatty, the exercise will do you good!" said Mel, linking arms with Lois and gently tugging her to a medium paced walk. "Oh my God!" said Mel, "I don't believe it, there's a Starbucks! Ooh, could we just nip in for a quickie?"

"Let's get the keys first, could we? Then have a celebratory little something."

"Oh okay, if it's really that important to you!" Mel gave Lois a nudge.

As they made their way along the high street, bustling with a combination of locals and summer season tourists, Mel became increasingly surprised by the number of shops that appealed to her. "Gosh, nice shops; you know this could be my kind of place after all!"

Entering the estate agency, they were welcomed by the assistant manager. He offered them both a seat, then left the office for a couple of minutes and came back with a set of keys and a hamper of goodies, including a bottle of champagne. "All the best with the move and I wish you every happiness in your new home!" Lois, grinning broadly, thanked him, asked him to pass on her thanks to Gill, the agent who'd handled their purchase and they left, Mel laden down with the hamper.

Lois had begun to wonder whether this moment would ever arrive. It was almost a year since she and Tom had first viewed Honeysuckle Cottage. Problems with probate had delayed the date for exchange three times. Yet now, here she was, walking up the garden path of their new home and it really belonged to them.

Lois grabbed Mel by the arm. With butterflies flitting

around her abdomen, her face alight with a huge smile, she asked, "Well, what do you think?"

"Lois, it's sweet!" The pair of them stood and admired the red brick cottage. "The garage is ghastly of course, but the cottage is gorgeous, and look at the flowers on that wisteria!"

Lois looked blank.

"The wisteria. That huge vine, practically covering the front of your new house." Mel felt smug. She didn't know about the country, but she did know a bit about gardening; her parent's favourite hobby must have rubbed off a little.

"Oh, is that what it's called? I did wonder. The garage is awful isn't it? I can't believe they got away with adding something so out of keeping. Anyway, it'll go when we build the extension."

Lois beamed as she lifted the rather tarnished key to the lock, carefully put it in and turned. It turned perfectly. A shudder of excitement ran through her as she pushed the door...hard, then harder, then very hard indeed. There was a loud, splintering crack, followed by a crash, as Lois and approximately two thirds of the door fell headlong into the entrance porch.

Lois landed hip and shoulder on top of the door. She thought momentarily as to whether or not she was hurt, instinctively running her hand over her enlarged belly. She was, but not physically; this was really not how she'd envisaged entering her dream home for the first time. "Bugger!" she muttered as tears welled in her eyes. Mel held out a hand and helped Lois struggle to her feet.

"Are you okay?"

Lois looked at her, expecting to find an expression of concern. But no, Mel, who was renowned for hysterical laughter in any crisis, was off. It started with a titter, then, when Lois allowed herself a smile, Mel lost control completely. She added snorting and a raucous fart into her performance, which resulted in the pair of them creased-up on the threshold of the cottage.

They didn't notice the first cough from behind them, or indeed the second. In fact, by the time they realised he was standing there, the elderly looking man was nigh on choking to get their attention. Another woman might have been embarrassed at the thought that he probably heard her fart, but exhibitionism being one of Mel's specialities, she was totally unperturbed.

Lois, ·blushing on her friend's behalf, did her best to straighten up and look dignified. Her stomach muscles ached from laughing. "Oh hi, Lois Shenfield," she announced holding out her right hand to this rather glum-looking man; probably only in his mid-sixties, but aged by his stooped posture. She assumed he must be a neighbour. Both vertically and follicularly challenged, he had an extraordinarily deep-seated frown embedded in his forehead, just above the convergence of his rather ludicrously long, grey eyebrows.

"Charles Black. I've come to lay down a few ground rules. Where's your husband?" There was a brief pause, Lois having been rendered speechless. "You are married aren't you?" he said, staring blatantly at her bump. As she tried to answer that no, she and Tom weren't yet married, but would probably tie the knot before the baby was born, he just talked over her, louder and louder. He didn't look her in the eye, but stared over her right shoulder, blinking hard every couple of seconds, screwing up his face and nodding his head slightly each time.

Lois was flabbergasted. He never did shake her hand. She self-consciously lowered it while Mr Black proceeded to tell her where she could and couldn't park, (along this idyllic, unmade road, in the middle of nowhere). He went on to demand that she must avoid Bill Riley, the farmer from the end of the lane, at all costs. "He's an interfering busybody; very odd and not to be trusted." At which point the words pot and kettle sprang to Lois's mind. "And, if you ever consider applying for planning permission you must run it by me first, so I can object."

Then, suddenly, the bizarre little man shuffled off, without so much as a goodbye.

As soon as he was out of earshot, Lois said in a low voice, "What a miserable old git!"

Mel began to snigger, but Lois was feeling a little shell shocked, what with the door needing emergency replacement and having a neighbour who was apparently an interfering nutcase. She began to wonder if this beautiful cottage was going to be the idyllic haven of which she and Tom had dreamed.

Between them, Lois and Mel managed to pull the broken part of the door into the garden. As they did so, Mel asked, "So, are you getting married before the baby's born?"

"Highly unlikely I would think. He hasn't even asked me yet and there's less than three months to go."

Having cleared the threshold, the two of them walked through the small internal porch-way and into the front room. "Wow Lois, classy wallpaper. And carpets, gosh, the giant flowers are almost matching!" Mel said, smiling.

"It is quite something isn't it? Hang on, it's a bit gloomy, let's put the lights on, so you can get the true effect."

Lois turned to where she expected the light switch to be. There was no switch by the porch; that seemed odd. Neither was there one by the door to the kitchen, nor in the dining room, or indeed anywhere at all. The only light switch she could find in the whole of the downstairs was to a strip light in the kitchen. When Lois looked up at the ceilings, she realised there were actually no light fittings in the remainder of the downstairs. The only electrical sources were old fashioned, round, two point plug sockets, into which lamps must have been plugged. How could they not have noticed this before? What's more, how could the surveyor, who'd charged them a small fortune to conduct a full survey, not have noticed the lack of electrics, or the fact that the front door was so full of woodworm that it would cave in with one or two good shoves?

Mel offered a brief grin, but could see that Lois was now well past the smiling stage.

"Oh God. I think we might have bitten off more than we can chew here," said Lois. Then, suddenly, there was a yell and a crash. Lois and Mel both jumped. "What the hell was that?" The noise sounded as if it had come from just the other side of the kitchen wall, which adjoined the next-door cottage. As they moved closer, they could clearly hear two voices - a woman, yelling unbelievable obscenities, and a man sounding as though he was trying to placate her. Then another crash that sounded as if something large and heavy had hit the other side of the wall, which seemed so paper thin, Lois wondered whether, with another good smash, this pair of semi-detached cottages might become one.

Lois gestured to Mel that it was time to go out into the back garden, away from the shouting. She needed space to process the happenings of the past fifteen minutes, hopeful that the beautiful cottage garden would help her to do this.

The back door opened like a dream, "Thank God something works," mumbled Lois as they stepped out into the garden. "I don't believe it! Where's it gone?"

"Where's what gone?"

"My beautiful garden. It's vanished!"

Lois gazed around in disbelief. What used to be the lawn now resembled a small hay crop bisected by a large fallen tree. The flowerbeds were overrun with brambles, stingers and thistles, and on the weed-ridden patio, lay a half eaten pigeon.

Lois sat on the crumbling garden wall and began to weep.

"Oh come on, Lo," said Mel, crouching to avoid dirtying her jeans and putting a reassuring hand on Lois's knee, "it'll be gorgeous when it's done, it just needs a bit of work."

"A bit of work?" sniffed Lois, starting to feel sick with anxiety. She was the one who'd been keen to move to the country and had talked Tom into buying the place; he'd wanted to stay in London. "We thought it just needed the hideous wallpaper stripping and a lick of paint; not total rewiring, new front door, complete garden overhaul and soundproofing from those horrendous neighbours!" Lois stopped abruptly as she heard voices from next-door's garden.

"Come on Stephen," came a man's voice, sounding utterly miserable, "your mother's gone berserk. Let's lie low in the garage for a while."

When Lois was sure they were out of earshot, she put her head in her hands and muttered, "What the hell am I going to tell Tom?"

9

2

Tom had been in hospital for three days when Lois and Mel collected the keys for Honeysuckle, and quite frankly, he'd had enough. He'd broken three ribs, his left wrist and had ten stitches in his chin, all due to an incredibly embarrassing mountain biking accident.

Jim, Tom's best buddy, work colleague and mountain-biking chum, had observed from behind, as Tom cycled too fast down a steep bank, without anticipating the small yet moderately muddy ditch at the bottom. His front wheel had stopped dead, causing him to summersault over the handlebars onto a muddy track, inconveniently interspersed with stones. The bike flew up in the air and crashed down, ricocheting off his chest before falling back into the ditch. "Bollocks!" he'd mumbled to himself as he lay, trying to decipher the pain messages emanating from various parts of his body.

Jim had taken a great deal of ridicule from Tom over the years for being far too much of a wuss on their mountain biking expeditions. So, seeing Tom fly through the air sans bike, Jim, who felt Tom had it coming, immediately stopped and laughed, loud and uncontrollably. It had been one of those ungainly, slow motion spectacles that would be forever etched in his memory.

When Tom didn't get up however, Jim did manage to pull himself together. He climbed down the bank, pulling the bent bike out of the ditch as he went and helped Tom, who was now moaning in pain, to ease himself into a sitting position. There was blood streaming out of Tom's chin. Jim glanced at his face; mumbled, "Oh God!" went white as a sheet, and fainted backwards into the ditch. Fortunately he still had his helmet on, or they might both have had to suffer hospital admissions.

Jim regained consciousness within a minute, by which time Tom had managed to get himself into a Quasimodo style stance. Tom mumbled something about his sunglasses as Jim crawled out of the ditch to a crunching sound under his knee. He retrieved the crumpled glasses and chuckled, "Found 'em mate!" as he looked up. He'd apparently forgotten the state of Tom's chin during his brief absence and seeing the copious amounts of blood on his friend and the fluorescent-green Lycra top he was wearing, fainted once again.

Whilst waiting for Jim to come round for a second time, Tom, in agony as he did so, managed to remove one of his socks and when Jim woke up, was dabbing his chin with it, in a futile attempt to quell the flow of blood.

Having re-regained consciousness, Jim was no longer laughing and, eyes lowered, avoiding Tom's bloody face and torso, helped him put his shoe back on. In silence, they made their way to the road, some half a mile away. Jim pushed the bikes in a slow and dazed fashion, having to lift the buckled front wheel of Tom's off the ground, to allow it to roll freely. Tom, meanwhile, tried to hold onto all his hurting places and look brave. He wondered what on earth he was going to tell Lois, a thought that actually distracted him a little from the enormity of his pain. She really hadn't wanted him to go on this New Forest trip, what with the house exchange and completion happening on Wednesday and so much to organise. She was going to have a fit when she found out.

On reaching the road, they sat for a good ten minutes without a single car passing in either direction. With neither of their phones picking up a mobile signal, when they heard a car approaching, Jim was determined to make sure it stopped. He stood in the middle of the road waving his arms frantically, and the terrified, elderly lady driver reluctantly screeched to a halt, inches in front of him.

Seeing the warped bike and Tom's injuries, she eventually put two and two together and bravely wound down her window. With an apology, a brief explanation and a bit of sweet-talking from Jim, she agreed to drive Tom to hospital in Southampton; finding some plastic bags in the boot and arranging them carefully on the passenger seat before allowing him to get into the car. She passed him a handy pack of tissues from her handbag, "Would these help dear?" she asked, gazing uncomfortably at the blood soaked sock held to his face. Tom accepted them, mustering as much gratitude as he could in his miserable state. He muttered goodbye to Jim, who said he'd return the bikes to the car and meet Tom at the hospital.

Tom spent a total of four hours lying in Casualty; the monotony only slightly relieved by having several sets of x-rays and his chin stitched up. He was given a fairly substantial dose of painkillers, but was not at all sure that the analgesic effect compensated for the pain involved in receiving the injection. Being of tall and skinny physique, there was little buttock flesh in which to insert a needle and Tom had tensed up enormously as the nurse had joked happily, "Little prick coming!" He was sure that the needle had made contact with bone. "There!" she'd smiled, "You barely felt that, did you?"

"No, hardly at all," Tom had replied in his most manly voice, as he tried to disguise a grimace.

He was eventually moved to the trauma unit, to await manipulation of his wrist under anaesthetic. His mode of transport came by way of a wheelchair that resembled a fairly typical shopping trolley, in that it was apparently virtually unsteerable. The young, gum-chewing man who was pushing him, earphones dangling between head and breast pocket, seemed oblivious to the fact that he bumped into a doorway en-route. "Ouch! You sod!" Tom hissed, to deaf, or 'heavy metalled' ears, as shooting pains shot throughout his body, creating more in the way of agony than he'd experienced all day.

The ward was dark, dingy and smelled of a combination of sick and antiseptic when he arrived. A nurse, Eve, came and introduced herself, helped Tom into bed and set up a contraption to elevate his lower arm. She took his details and asked a long list of questions, some of which were embarrassing and many, seemingly irrelevant. When she was done, Tom asked if it would be possible to have a shower to get rid of some of the mud and blood in which he was caked, and to borrow some hospital pyjamas. She said that would not be a problem and she'd be back in a minute to give him a hand. Before disappearing, Eve rummaged through Tom's belongings to find his phone. "Gosh, you're lucky that's still in one piece!" she commented, "Only use it for a few minutes Tom, mobiles aren't really allowed."

Tom located Lois's number, then paused before ringing, trying to find the best wording in his head to keep her annoyance to a minimum.

"Hi Lo, it's me."

"Hi Gorgeous, how are you? I hope you're nearly home, I'm cooking a fantastic meal!"

'Not a good start,' thought Tom. "Um, well, I'm not altogether that brilliant actually."

"Oh? Are you not hungry then?"

"No, I am hungry, but I'm afraid I won't be home in time for dinner."

"Oh really? Bad traffic?"

"Mm, no…"

"Oh Tom, you didn't?" Silence, "You did! You idiot! You fell off that flipping bike didn't you!" Tom glanced around the ward, pink with embarrassment; fortunately no one appeared to be paying any attention to the sound of his girlfriend's voice shrieking from the phone. "How could you Tom, with so much still to organise before Wednesday? I knew this would happen. You promised you'd be careful!" Tom heard Lois taking some deep breaths to calm herself down. It was rare for her to lose her temper, she was generally very level headed; but the thought of organising all the remaining financial arrangements for the house purchase, he knew would have sent her into a complete fluster.

"So, where are you and what have you done to yourself?"

"Well, I'm at Southampton General. I've…um," Tom paused, feeling irrationally nervous, "I've broken my wrist," he heard a gasp and a curt "Oh God", the eyes being raised to heaven practically making their way down the phone. Tom decided not to elaborate on his injuries any further. "That's the reason I'm having to stay in, to have it manipulated under anaesthetic. I should be out tomorrow. My parents'll come and collect me and take me home."

"So is that it, a broken wrist?"

"Yes, more or less," Tom's facial colour heightened once again. "Just the odd bruise and scratch otherwise." There was another long, drawn-out pause, in which he could sense that Lois was sceptical.

"So, do you want me to drive down to see you, bring you some things?" Lois asked, begrudgingly, as she thought of all she was now going to have to organise singlehandedly.

Tom had a moment of panic, thinking of how she would respond if she could see him now, and answered a little too quickly, "No love, please don't." Adding as an afterthought, "I don't like you driving long distances in your condition, really, not a good idea, I'll just worry."

"Mm, nice touch Tom," Lois mumbled under her breath. "Okay, well, good luck with the op. Call me later yeah? Love you."

"Love you too, and Lo, I'm really sorry." Tom could sense Lois smiling and she blew him a kiss down the phone before disconnecting the call.

After waiting at least an hour for the nurse to come back, Tom drifted off to sleep. He woke some time later, disorientated and starving hungry. When he tried to sit up, he found that he had stiffened up completely and was stuck on the bed like a beached whale. He could hear the other patients eating, and spotting the corner of a food tray overlapping his locker, felt around in vain for the call-bell. Following several painful, yet unsuccessful attempts to summon help by shouting for a nurse, he tentatively reached up to the tray.

Unable to find any cutlery, he felt his way to the plate and fingered some wet, lukewarm food. He picked up something slimy and tried to identify it by sight and smell, gravy dripping over him in the process. It was meat, origins unknown. He tore a piece off with his teeth and chewed hard. The meat was so tough that the required chewing made his injured chin throb. He returned the remainder to the plate and reached for something else. The roast potatoes he managed relatively easily. The broccoli decomposed in transit, decorating his pillow, hair and ear and causing temporary blindness in the right eye. One tiny piece of broccoli flower fell upright onto his overly prominent Adam's apple; momentarily producing a wonderful impression of a lone tree perched on a hill.

Tom did his best to retrieve some of the squishy vegetable matter and put it in his mouth. Another mistake he realised, as a combination of broccoli, blood and dried mud congealed into a foul, crunchy soup, which, too embarrassed to spit out, he forced himself to swallow.

Exhausted by such a strange dining experience, Tom drifted back off to sleep, to be woken a short time later by the beep and flash of Jim's phone camera at the end of the bed. The sight of Tom and the combination of dried mud, blood, gravy and various pieces of roast dinner pebble-dashing his face, hair and upper body, was too much for Jim to bear. His brief periods of unconsciousness and a six mile walk pushing two bikes, had taken its toll and having taken the photo, he had no strength to curb his natural emotional response; uncontrollable laughter.

3

Lois's parents had lived close to the Heath in Hampstead for the past thirty-two years, in an imposing, Edwardian, four-storey house. Irene, a not unattractive wisp of a woman, was, unlike Lois, always meticulously presented, remaining a (not so natural) blonde at sixty-five, full make-up always in place. Geoffrey, conversely, was huge, both in height and girth. His size, together with his full head of shocking white hair, small eyes and aquiline nose, created a somewhat intimidating-looking man.

Lois's father had been a barrister until his retirement three years ago, her mother an alcoholic, drinking gin in steadily increasing quantities, since Lois, and her younger brother James, were in their teens. That is, until three years ago, when the prospect of sharing his retirement with Irene in such a sorry state had been too much for Geoffrey; regretfully, he'd signed her into an expensive rehab centre for a three-month drying out programme. Regretful, in the first instance, because he loved her very much and had a fairish idea of how hard it would be for her, and in the second, because it didn't seem to be a very satisfactory way of spending one's money.

Irene's recovery, so far, had been miraculous. She'd turned to the church and the local Oxfam shop for support. She went to church on Wednesdays and Sundays and attended a variety of Bible study groups. She helped out in the Oxfam shop on Tuesdays and Thursdays, often bringing home bags full of knick-knacks to fill their oversized house. Hoarding not being a new hobby, but the habit of a lifetime.

About a year ago, Lois had told her parents that she and Tom planned to buy a house of their own, somewhere in the Home Counties. A few weeks later she received a typically formal letter from her father, saying he would like to give them a housewarming present in the form of a contribution to the deposit on a house. The sum concerned being forty thousand pounds! His astounding generosity had opened the door to the purchase of Honeysuckle Cottage, which although it had only two bedrooms, held a high price due to its, 'Rarity, charm and unparalleled location!' in the words of the estate agent.

Lois was getting on better with her father since she'd been with Tom. Geoffrey loved having a male financial expert in the family with whom he could discuss his investments. He had never felt able to do that with Lois, despite the fact that she also worked in the City. Nonetheless he seemed to have more respect for her, perhaps because she had at last developed her taste in men to meet with his approval. He didn't even seem to mind when Lois and Tom announced that there was a baby on the way. He'd cracked open a bottle of Bollinger and sat with Tom, smoking cigars and quaffing the champagne as if they were old buddies.

The announcement of the pregnancy did however send Irene into temporary shock. She had sat for at least an hour, completely lost for words. Then said, "What a shame! I gave Lois's nappies to the Oxfam shop, just last week." Much to Lois's horror however, Irene did still have her original cot, bath, potty, cardigans, hats, mittens and … well, the list went on, all safely hoarded in the loft. Lois had been busy working out how to refuse all these things without offending her mother. "The cot," she'd said to Tom after their last visit, "I'll take the cot. Paint it; get a new mattress, that'll be fine. The bath? Maybe? I'll say I don't want to be greedy; I want to leave the rest for James! Cunning eh? That'll cause some interesting discussion between him and his future partner!"

The Monday before completing on Honeysuckle Cottage, Lois took the afternoon off work and drove to her parent's house for lunch and to collect her father's generous gift. It was a stunning afternoon, so the three of them lunched in the large, perfectly manicured (by a team of gardeners), back garden. Irene had been to Waitrose that morning and bought a fantastic spread, practically all of which was to be avoided in pregnancy. Pâté, unpasteurised cheeses, prawns, coleslaw … in fact, although she didn't really believe it, it was as though Irene had purposefully bought everything that she'd been advised not to eat. She felt quite upset by this idea; hormones no doubt playing their part, Lois felt tears welling up in her eyes and as one escaped, she discreetly wiped it from her cheek before taking a mouthful of French bread and butter with lashings of lettuce. Irene didn't notice; either that Lois wasn't eating all the lovely treats that she'd provided, or that she was upset. But then, Irene never had been a great one for sensitivity.

After lunch Geoffrey disappeared into the study. This was the room of the house that he'd spent most of his time when Lois and James were growing up. He would come home from Chambers, briefly eat supper with them and then disappear to his retreat for the remainder of the evening. He seemed to have no interest in his family other than providing for them financially: both children being sent to the very best of public schools, which Geoffrey seemed to consider proof of his success as a father.

Emerging from his study on this occasion, Lois expected him to hand her a banker's draft made out to their solicitor, whose name she had emailed to him two weeks previously. But instead he handed over four large envelopes, each containing ten thousand pounds, in cash.

Lois was stunned. But her father could be unpredictable, and his sudden withdrawal of the offer this late in the proceedings would be a catastrophe. So her face flipped into enthusiastic, grateful mode while a large surge of adrenalin sent her heart thumping and her mind racing with the idea of carrying that much money in North London. She thanked him and gave him a hug. He smelled of pâté and cigars. He responded by gently patting her on the back. Then she tried to hug her mother, but felt Irene tense as she got near, so they bilaterally air kissed. Lois then tucked the envelopes as deeply as she could into her (fortunately) large handbag, thanked them both profusely and made tracks.

She thought about cancelling her coffee and cake meeting with Mel and re-arranging for a day she was lighter on cash. But they hadn't seen each other in ages and giving the matter brief consideration, she decided that, having never been mugged before, the odds of it happening on this particular occasion, were, very small.

Mel was sat waiting for her at a table on the pavement terrace outside their favourite North London café. They greeted each other and then Mel went and ordered a latte for each of them and a large slice of cake. Meanwhile, Lois surreptitiously stashed her bag under her seat, out of the way of any potential thieves.

The two of them had a great time catching up. Lois filled Mel in on recent happenings. The inappropriate lunch at her parent's house, Tom's accident, and the fact that exchange and completion on the cottage was finally due on Wednesday. "Gosh, poor old Tom. But I bet he was showing off," said Mel. "Hey, if he can't make it to pick up the keys on Wednesday, I'd love to come with you!"

"Really? Oh that would be great. I was thinking of staying the night, so it'll be a two-day trip. Can you extricate yourself from the boutique for that long?"

"I'm the boss, I can do what the hell I like!"

Lois smiled. "Fantastic. Well, provided Tom doesn't make a miraculous recovery, I'll pick you up at nine thirty on Wednesday."

Lois was just on her way to the car park, having said goodbye to Mel, when her mobile rang. She managed to yank it out of the depths of her cardigan pocket just in time to stop it switching to answerphone. It was Tom, thoroughly disgruntled; his operation had been cancelled due to emergencies that needed urgent surgery. He grumbled on for several minutes about the hospital, and how disgraceful it was that his displaced fracture was not being considered an emergency. Lois tried her best to sound sympathetic, despite feeling that he'd brought it on himself. She had not been impressed when he'd suggested going on a cycling trip this close to the completion date; now he was incapacitated for the event, she was feeling somewhat vexed. However, once again she offered to drive down to Southampton to see him. He insisted that wouldn't be necessary; his parents, who lived in Portsmouth, had visited and already brought him everything he needed.

Tom then asked how things had gone with her parents. Lois just started to launch into her mother's inability to provide a fitting lunch for her pregnant daughter, when, to her utter horror, she realised she'd left her bag, containing forty thousand pounds, in cash, at the coffee shop, on the terrace! She thought her heart would leap out of her chest. Beads of sweat came from nowhere and started dripping down her forehead, her legs feeling as if they were going to buckle under her. In a high-pitched squeak she said, "Got to run, Pet." Searching for an excuse, she added, "Traffic warden!" and disconnected the call. Tom hated slovenliness; a parking ticket would be bad enough, but losing forty thousand pounds by leaving it outside a North London coffee shop, would quite probably finish their relationship, or Tom's mental health as she knew it, or both.

Lois hurried back to the café as fast as her pregnant body could carry her. By the time she got there, flushed with worry, exhaustion and embarrassment, the terrace seating had been cleared away, the bag had gone and the shop was closed. "Oh, my, God!" she murmured aloud, as tears pooled in her eyes.

She knocked desperately on the locked door with one hand, whilst cupping the other over her eyes and peering through the tinted glass. To her relief, she could see staff inside. The teenage girl mopping the floor glanced up. Lois heard her shout to the manager, "Nathan, tha' dippy bird 'oo left 'er bag aatside's cott'ned on. Shall we give it back to 'er?" The feeling of nausea, which had accompanied Lois back to the shop, subsided slightly. The handbag was there, that was a start. Nathan gave her a wave and went behind the till, reappearing with, what she hoped, was still her astronomically valuable bag. He unlocked the door and handed it to her; Lois quickly unzipped it; to her enormous relief she saw four large envelopes, clearly untouched. She gave Nathan a huge hug and rummaged through her bag to retrieve her purse, from which she took a twenty-pound note and stuffed it into his hand.

Lois felt increasingly paranoid as she hurried to the car. Had she been too grateful for the bag's safe return? Some unscrupulous mugger might have been watching her with Nathan. She'd been too grateful. They'd know. Know the bag was valuable, *extremely* valuable. They'd push her over and snatch it at any moment. She glanced behind her to the left, then the right. The feeling of nausea returned to her throat as she realised that her anxiety in itself was probably attracting attention. "Oh for God's sake, Lois," she mumbled, "Pull yourself together! Act normal! Act normal! Act normal!" She suddenly became conscious that she was speaking out loud. She closed her mouth, stared ahead and marched as fast as she could to the car.

The feeling of relief as her beloved MG came into view was short lived as she spotted a plastic bag under the windscreen wiper, waving in the breeze. She snatched the parking ticket from under the wiper blade, unlocked the car and climbed in with a heavy sigh, locking the door behind her. Glancing from the sixty pound parking ticket to the bag containing forty thousand, Lois decided that things could have been considerably worse.

4

Annie and Dave Nutter lived in the house adjoining Honeysuckle. Both in their mid-forties, they had moved to Harewood Park from the centre of the village five years ago. They loved living in 'The Park'; it had been a perfect place for their children, Gemma and Stephen, to spend the latter parts of their childhood. Lilac Cottage was sold to them with a paddock that ran behind the pair of cottages. Gemma had loved riding and was able to have a pony during her teens. Now, she was at university in York. Stephen was in his first year of GCSEs and had the potential to follow in his sister's footsteps and make it to a good university; provided, as his dad would frequently say, he cut down on the three Fs; Facebook, football and flirting and took his homework a little more seriously.

Dave owned a main dealer franchise for a company specializing in four-wheel drives. Unfortunately, due to the combination of increased road tax for such vehicles, higher fuel prices and a country that had plummeted into recession, his once successful business was now struggling to the point where he was talking to his accountants about taking it into liquidation. He had tried to discuss his financial worries with Annie, but she always just shrugged them off. "We've a long way to go before we're on the bread line!" was her general response.

Feeling that he needed to take steps to avoid them becoming destitute, Dave had decided to get the house valued. Annie was right; they did have assets after all. The house was bigger than necessary now that Gemma was at university. The pony had been sold last year so they didn't need the paddock, which was rapidly filling with weeds. Three years ago they had built a large detached garage with a spacious loft, which Dave had christened 'The Coach House', that must have added considerably to the value of the property. Gradually, Dave talked himself around to the idea that it would actually be very sensible for them to move, he just hadn't quite plucked up the courage to discuss it with Annie.

Meanwhile, Annie had in fact, been giving a great deal of thought to their financial situation. She hadn't wanted to stress Dave by showing too much concern about the way his business was heading; she worried about his mental stability in a crisis; he'd experienced some problems with anxiety in the past and clearly suffered with an obsessive-compulsive disorder. But, she had indeed, also been considering the assets they could sell.

In Annie's opinion, it was obvious their boat should be the first thing to go. That would free up at least thirty thousand, provided they could find a buyer. The mooring on the Thames cost a small fortune and they hardly ever used it. She knew Dave had always dreamed of owning a cruiser, but if their financial situation picked up, they could always buy another one. She would sell the idea to him as, "We could always buy a bigger one."

Then there was the paddock at the back of the house. Annie was sure that there were several sets of neighbours who would jump at the chance of becoming landowners. Annie had dreamed of hosting Gemma's wedding there, in a beautiful marquee, but it had been harder to imagine recently with the paddock in the state it was. A brief Internet search of land prices gave Annie the impression that it was worth at least seventy-five thousand; now that would keep the wolves from the door for a bit. They had no mortgage on the house; fortunately they'd paid that off when Dave's business was booming.

The other asset was the loft space over the garage. Now, if they spent a bit of money converting that into a studio flat, they could let it, long-term. Annie had spent some time researching the various possibilities for that, during a particularly quiet two days temping the previous week. She had decided that if they did the work themselves, Dave being quite handy at DIY, and bought relatively cheap fittings and second-hand furniture, they could probably do the whole thing for about fifteen hundred pounds. They should be able to get a hundred pounds a week in rent, which would soon put them into profit. Annie also wondered about the more lucrative option of renting it out as a holiday let, but she needed to do some more research into that.

The day that Lois and Mel picked up the keys and fell over the threshold of Honeysuckle, was the day that Annie had planned to sit Dave down over a nice glass of Shiraz and talk through her plans.

Annie drove into Harewood Park on autopilot. She had just met with an old friend who worked as a financial advisor. After a lengthy discussion and some number crunching, Fiona had concluded that, with the sale of the boat and paddock, the renting of the garage-flat-to-be and Annie's temping, that Annie and Dave could stay in Lilac Cottage for several years. This would allow Dave time to get back on his feet again, relatively stress free.

Annie felt increasingly anxious as she passed the manor. She suddenly felt unsure about some of the figures Fiona had worked out and wanted to have them clear in her head before chatting to Dave. She started rifling through the papers on the passenger seat, searching for the information. Annie glanced back to the road just in time to swerve around Old Man Black. Unsurprisingly, he started waving his arms around wildly, shouting at her, his face turning a dark purple with rage. "Miserable old bugger!" she said under her breath as she drove away, glancing in her rear view mirror to see his hunched figure shuffling angrily down the road.

Her eyes saw Lois, Mel and what looked like part of a door, sitting in the front garden of Honeysuckle, but her brain didn't register the spectacle. She was feeling quite shaken after her brush with manslaughter, adding to her anxiety over how Dave would respond to her proposals.

She noticed Dave's car parked at the front of the house alongside a silver Mercedes, which she didn't recognise. She assumed it must belong to one of Dave's work colleagues. "Oh well, I'll just have to wait," Annie grumbled to herself, as she drove around to their second entrance and parked in front of the coach house. She walked up the external wooden staircase of the garage that led to the loft space, struggling momentarily to find the right key on her over-laden key ring, and then with the stiff lock. Once in, she found it smelt a bit musty, but not too bad considering it had barely been touched since it was built. It was full of junk, most of which should have been dumped years ago.

Annie started thinking through the possible layouts for a flat. She took a notebook out of her handbag and jotted down a few thoughts. She was convinced, as she stood there in the slightly dark, very cluttered space that it would be possible to transform it into a moderately nice place to live.

Just as Annie was contemplating the best position for a shower room, to her surprise she heard voices and footsteps coming up the stairs. It was Dave, looking somewhat taken aback to see Annie there, followed by a woman. Annie's immediate thought was, 'Oh my God he's having an affair!' and her next was, 'In the loft space!' Then she took in the appearance of the woman, who looked at least ten years older than Dave, despite wearing a thick layer of very obvious make-up and quickly concluded that she really wasn't his type. However, the colour had drained from Dave's face and his forehead and bald patch were sweating profusely. "Ah, Annie," he stammered, "um, may I introduce, Beryl Thomas-Clarke, uh, she's a, um," Dave knew that Annie would be furious that he'd gone behind her back in organising a valuation of the house; he hadn't expected her home so early. His gaze dropped from Annie's expectant face to his shoes, like an awkward schoolboy caught-in-the-act.

"Delighted Mrs Nutter," the woman butted-in, with a ridiculously pompous accent, accompanied by a toothy, somewhat arrogant smile. She reached out her hand, which Annie shook in bewilderment. "Please, just call me Beryl, I'm from BTC Estates, I'm sure you've heard of us, we sold the house next door. We'll have no trouble selling this delightful property; in fact I know of several customers straight off the top of my head who would simply adore it. I must say, I would quite like it my…"

"Get out!" Annie screamed. "Get out of here right now!"

Beryl looked only slightly affronted. "Annie, it's not her fault!" Dave called, as Annie stomped out of the door, tears welling up in her eyes. With the combination of rushing and tear-blurred vision, she missed her footing on the staircase and fell down the last three steps. Hauling herself up by the handrail, Annie ignored the fact that her ankle was really hurting and hobbled to the back door of the house, trying desperately to retain any remaining dignity. She took off her heeled work shoes, threw them into the utility room in disgust and limped over to the table, on which she leaned, taking some deep breaths. Then, feeling very slightly calmer, she made her way to the loo. As she sat there, she could hear Dave saying goodbye to Beryl, making apologies for his wife and saying he would be in touch soon, regarding when the house was to be put on the market.

Well this was too much for Annie, she yanked up her undies, sadly with the back of her skirt stuck in the top of her tights, slammed the toilet door and stormed into the kitchen, just as Dave walked in through the back door. At which point Annie lost it, properly, for the first time in her life.

"How could you? How the hell could you think of trying to sell our beautiful house without asking me, without even talking to me about it?" She felt the anger tightening across her chest, down her arms and into her fingers. Almost before she knew what was happening, she started picking up objects near to her and hurling them at Dave's head. With each throw she yelled an obscenity starting with, "You bastard!" and deteriorating from there.

The first thing she threw was a floppy chicken dog toy, which Stephen must have left on the kitchen worktop. As Annie took aim, Reaver, one of their two spaniels, prepared herself for the chase. As the toy flew, the dog skidded across the kitchen floor tiles in hot pursuit. Dave, with the lightening reactions of a karate brown belt, was able to catch the chicken before it hit the welsh dresser, and before Reaver could make a jump for it. He glanced at Annie with a 'You'll have to do better than that!' look in his eye. She yelled, she swore, she threw. Next an empty cup, which smashed against the wall, just missing the clock, this time the master of self-defence wasn't quick enough to catch it as it whizzed past his ear. Then a medium sized Le Creuset casserole lid, which she wielded like a discus thrower. Dave crouched down with his arms over his head. The lid hit the wall and the edge of the dresser simultaneously, very hard, leaving considerable dents and causing three plates and Dave's recently used coffee cup to topple off the dresser and smash. She then grabbed the casserole dish itself, containing the remains of a chicken Madras. Dave had been about to dispose of the slightly furry curry when Beryl had arrived; it had spent at least a week in the fridge. Having picked it up, Annie realised it was so heavy she would need clever tactics if she was not to lose face. She did a fast turn around where she stood, launching the casserole towards Dave, who had just stood up. The dish flew in slow motion. He decided as a damage limitation strategy, to try and catch it. But with Annie tiring, the weight of the dish and Dave's anxiety about his shoeless feet, the casserole fell well short of his reach and crashed, bottom down to the floor; cold, mouldering curry, splattering over everything in the immediate vicinity, including Dave.

There was a slam of the front door and Stephen walked in and greeted his mum matter-of-factly with a, "Hi Mum, your skirt's tucked in your knickers." He walked past Annie and said to Dave, "Dad, why've you got curry dripping down your face?" Dave stood, open-mouthed, the casserole dish and pieces of broken floor tiles in his hands. He glanced at Annie, who was bright red and shaking, tugging to free her skirt. He put the dish on the worktop, piled the bits of tile into it and grabbed a tea towel to wipe his face. "There's some on your bald patch," said Stephen, reaching up to remove a piece of slimy chicken from his Dad's head and popping it in his mouth. "Jesus, that's disgusting!" He spat it into his hand and threw it to Reaver.

"Don't give it to the dog Stephen, it'll make her ill," said Dave. He looked at Annie again, hoping for a glint of a smile, but there was nothing. Dave was not entirely sure that her outburst was over, so he walked out of the back door saying in a low voice, "Come on Stephen, your mother's gone berserk. Let's lie low in the garage for a while."

5

Adam had moved into Harewood Park six years ago, with his wife and two very young boys. He now lived alone. Tessa had left him, moved in with a work colleague and taken the boys with her. Sam and Olli came to see him every other weekend, when she allowed it. A year on, he was unattached and his anger over Tessa's behaviour continued to smoulder.

Adam had been out running for about an hour, the last mile being along the bridleway that emerged onto Harewood Park, adjacent to Honeysuckle Cottage. At the beginning of his run he'd picked up a text message from Tessa, saying the boys couldn't come to him at the weekend because she was taking them to her mother's, in Wales. He was fuming. Why did she always organise things for his weekend? As usual, she was ignoring his calls. He felt he couldn't say what he wanted to say in a text because Sam had developed a habit of practicing his reading on in-coming text messages. So Adam's pent-up anger had fuelled his run. He checked his watch as he emerged onto the road, to see that he had completed his circuit fifty per cent faster than normal. "Every cloud, blah-blah-blah," he said sarcastically, out loud. As he looked up from his watch, movement on the left caught his eye. Two women were standing in the front garden of Honeysuckle Cottage, contemplating, what looked like, the majority of the front door, which was lying on the path. They both looked up at him and probably wondered whom he was talking to. He felt mildly embarrassed and was in two minds whether to run straight past. But one of them looked very upset and presuming that they must be the new neighbours, he decided to stop and introduce himself. 'Mm, a lesbian couple,' he thought, 'now that would spice-up Harewood Park even more; if it were possible?'

Adam, standing at over six foot, lean, fit, tanned, with clean-cut features and a mop of dark curly hair, lay well within the spectrum of men of Mel's dreams. As he walked up the garden path to introduce himself and ask if he could be of any assistance, spaniel obediently at his heels, Mel's tongue was, metaphorically, lolling out.

"Hi, I'm Adam," he said, holding out his hand and grinning broadly, "I live at Primrose cottage, next door but one. You must be the new neighbours." Tears welled in Lois's eyes as she shook his hand, overcome by the sight of a friendly face.

Adam, noticing Lois's bump, was just thinking that the lesbian angle was becoming even more interesting, when Mel laughed, "No, no, no. No, this is Lois, she's moving in with her boyfriend. You'll have to excuse her, she's in a bit of a state."

Lois glared at her, "I'm quite capable of introducing myself, thanks. Hi Adam, I'm Lois, this is Mel, Tom's in hospital and…" she looked at the gap in the house where there should have been a door, "…and, this house is a disaster!"

Lois crouched down and made a fuss of the dog to hide the fact that tears were once again oozing onto her cheeks. It responded with an enthusiastic wiggling of the tail. "She's a springer isn't she or is it a he?"

"No, you were right first time, she's a she. Her name's Larch."

"Well, she's lovely." Lois eased herself back up to her full five foot three. "It's nice to see some friendly faces, isn't it Mel?"

"Ah, Old Man Black's been round already has he? That didn't take him long. Anyway, your door, can I help?"

"Oh Adam, would you?" said Lois.

"Give me five minutes, I'm sure I've got some hardboard in the shed that'll secure the house for now." And he ran off, dog at his heels.

"Whoa!" said Mel, grinning broadly, "So not all the neighbours are a disaster then!"

Lois agreed in hushed tones, "What a relief to meet someone friendly."

"Yeah and the rest!" Mel gave Lois a nudge. Lois just looked bewildered.

"Good looking?" There was still no acknowledgement from Lois. "Oh, never mind Pet, you're suffering from post traumatic stress disorder after your troubled morning. Don't worry, I've got a feeling everything's going to improve from now on."

Adam hunted through his shed for anything resembling some hardboard, but found absolutely nothing of any use at all. He started to get a bit flustered, so decided the best thing to do was to remove his own bathroom door and use that. It was old and would be replaced when he finally got round to building the extension. It was important for him to give a good impression to the new neighbours, not to mention the fact that Mel was particularly attractive and who knows, she might be single. He would have liked to have a quick shower really, he was very sweaty after his run, but he didn't want to give Lois and Mel the idea that he was more worried about his appearance than helping women in distress. So he just sprayed some deodorant over the sweat, collected his tools, then removed the door from the bathroom and set off back to Lois's house.

When he got there he found that the door was completely the wrong size for the frame, which didn't really come as a great surprise. He went home and picked up a couple of old planks that were lying behind the shed and returned.

"Bit of woodworm here then, Lois," he said, removing the remains of the old door.

"Tell me about it!"

"The doorframe looks fine though doesn't it? That's odd." Adam looked thoughtfully at the two pieces of door now on the front lawn. "You know, I'm sure this isn't the original door."

"Really?" said Lois, examining the remains herself.

"Hey, I bet those awful relatives came and took the old one. I'm sure I remember it being a really nice oak door. Yeah, I bet they took that and replaced it with this knackered old thing!" He gave the door a kick in disgust.

"Who?" asked Mel.

"Mrs Smith's relatives. Horrible pair they are, real scavengers." Having sawn the planks to size, Adam started to nail them to the front entrance. "Sorry Lois, there's going to be some holes in the door frame when all this is removed."

"Don't worry, I'm sure it won't be the biggest problem we have to face."

Adam continued working, chatting as he did so, "Yes, so Mrs Smith moved here when her husband died, she downsized from a big house on the outskirts of Henley. That was about twenty years ago. She was great; played a round of golf three times a week; drank like a fish and smoked like a chimney! Got to the age of eighty-two and suddenly found herself coughing up blood. She was diagnosed with lung cancer and died two months later." Adam paused, "I miss her actually. She was an extraordinary old girl, full of life, right to the end.

"So her nephew and his wife inherited the lot. Not the slightest bit interested in her when she was alive. They live in the next village. Swooped on this place like vultures the second she was dead. They sold everything they could via auctioneers, house sales and eBay. By all accounts, including the front door!"

Lois told Adam about the phone call she'd received that morning, regarding the cooker. "There, I rest my case!" said Adam, grinning.

It was no surprise to Adam to hear that Charles Black had already made his presence felt. He filled them in briefly on some facts about Charles. That he was a retired planning officer and parish councillor, whose wife had allegedly run off with someone she'd met at her over-fifties aerobics class a few years ago. Nobody in Harewood Park liked him; he'd upset them all one way or another.

Having secured the door, Adam wished the two women well and started to make for home, tools in hand. He hadn't gone far when Lois called to him. She looked flushed and worried as she approached. "Adam, I'm sooo sorry. Oh God, I can't believe I've done this!" She paused, plucking up the courage to confess, and then said, "The back door keys, they're in my bag," she paused again, "in the cottage!"

31

To Lois's great relief, Adam smiled convincingly. "Not a problem Lois," he said, "that's exactly the sort of thing I do myself."

Re-opening the doorway was difficult. Adam had been very generous with his use of nails. Re-sealing it, having retrieved said handbag, was a complete nightmare, with splintered pieces of planks and his poor old bathroom door falling everywhere.

When Adam had finished the re-repair, which resembled some very untidy patchwork and Lois had thanked him profusely, he invited them round to his house for a cup of tea and something to eat. They gratefully accepted, Lois was beginning to feel quite light-headed from lack of food and both of them were bursting for the loo. When they arrived, Adam directed Lois to the bathroom, which was downstairs. She reappeared almost immediately, with bright pink cheeks, "Uh…. Adam, you don't seem to have a, um, door on your bathroom?"

"Oh bollocks!" Adam blushed, firstly for forgetting there was no door to the bathroom and secondly for swearing in front of women he was trying to impress.

Lois and Mel looked at each other and smiled. "Adam," said Mel, starting to giggle, "You didn't …" Mel and Lois started laughing uncontrollably, with Adam, who looked very embarrassed, eventually joining in.

When the laughter died down he said, "I didn't expect it to matter, I don't often have adult visitors. If you can hang on for ten minutes, I'll fix it." He made his way to pick up his toolbox from the entrance porch and disappeared upstairs.

"That's so sweet," said Mel, "he sacrificed his bathroom door for you."

"Astonishing," replied Lois, "if a little odd?"

"No, not odd, just really generous."

Adam returned within minutes with another door, which, he explained he had removed from his bedroom. "I won't miss this one," he said.

Lois was the first one to start giggling this time, the others soon joining in. Adam had to lean the door against the wall, breathless with laughter, "You two must think I'm completely bonkers."

"Bonkers Adam?" cried Lois, "No, this is all perfectly normal behaviour!"

When he'd recovered himself enough, Adam took the door and fitted it to its new frame. "Ah, yes, a much better position for it. Never did look right upstairs!"

While the women made use of the facilities, Adam proceeded to brew a pot of tea and then concocted a very tasty pasta dish, which Lois and Mel wolfed down. They found out over dinner that Adam was divorced, (Mel had to try hard not to clap her hands and punch the air, yelling a loud 'YES!'). He was a self-employed roofer, having originally completed a law degree. 'Mm, nice,' thought Mel: she'd always been attracted to the unconventional.

It was nine o'clock by the time Lois and Mel made their way to Harewood Manor. They found their room to be surprisingly basic and much more modern in décor than they'd been hoping. The outside of the hotel was beautiful; old, Lois had guessed late eighteenth, or early nineteenth century. It had a classic elegance about it. She had been expecting antiques and gold leaf framed paintings inside. Instead, there was furniture that looked like it had come flat packed from IKEA and enlarged, clip-framed photos with the hotel chain's logo printed across the bottom.

Once they were settled in, sitting on the bed with a cup of tea and free biscuits, Lois phoned Tom and told him, with fingers crossed, that the day had gone well. He had at last had his operation and was still sounding a little groggy from the anaesthetic. Lois decided she wouldn't tell him any of the negatives about the house until she was face to face with him. She felt so much better about everything now anyway, having spent time with Adam, who was clearly a gem of a neighbour. Perhaps Honeysuckle Cottage was going to be the house of their dreams after all.

6

Lois woke early the next morning. She was excited about organising the work that needed to be done on the house. Mel was also excited, but in her case, it was about the possibility of bumping into Adam again.

Breakfast at the manor turned out to be as mediocre as their room. "I thought this was rated five star," said Mel, indignantly. "The food's no better than a motorway motel." She used her phone to take a photo of the pathetic, wilted rose on the breakfast table. "That should have been replaced days ago, or just taken away. What's the point in leaving a dead rose as a centrepiece?"

"Oh no, do I sense a letter of complaint brewing?"

"Quite possibly."

"About a wilting rose on the breakfast table?"

"Well about the general feel of the place, not being luxurious. That is what you expect from five stars isn't it, a bit of luxury?"

"Well, if you have nothing better to do, then good for you. But I have more important issues, like finding a fabulous builder to decorate, no, renovate my house! Coming?"

Lois rang Tom and chatted as she packed the few items she'd brought, into her bag. He sounded much better and hoped to be able to go home once the consultant had seen his X-rays. His mother was going to pick him up and drive him to London. He said how much he was looking forward to seeing his gorgeous girlfriend and hearing all about their fantastic new house. Lois went slightly red and then in the most positive tone she could muster, said that she couldn't wait to tell him all about it.

After checking out of the hotel and putting the luggage in the car, Lois and Mel returned to Honeysuckle on foot, a walk of about three hundred yards. It was a stunning, sunny day, without a hint of cloud. The birds were singing in the trees overhanging the road. Two baby rabbits shot across in front of them from under a hedge, making them jump and then laugh. Further along, there was a strong, sweet smell, which Mel identified as coming from a honeysuckle in full bloom, growing through the hedge bordering the lane. "Gosh, I feel surprisingly envious of you guys moving out here," said Mel, as the cottages came into view, "I would give anything to be in your position, Lo; lovely man, baby on the way, cottage in the country." Lois raised an eyebrow at the thought of Mel wanting to live in the country; but she did have to agree, she was very lucky. It was such a beautiful day, that the setbacks of the day before were starting to pale into insignificance.

Lois and Mel arrived at the cottage and let themselves in via the backdoor. Sunshine was pouring through the windows at the front of the house, into the living room. "Wow!" said Lois, "Now that's more like it."

Lois wrote a to-do list, while Mel made them both a cup of tea using an old saucepan that had been left in a cupboard and the only functioning electric ring on the cooker. "Hey, you'll probably get invoiced for this," she laughed, waving the emptied pan in Lois's direction.

Lois thanked Mel for the tea and took a cautious sip to test how hot it was. "Oh no, I forgot to pack sugar," she said, looking briefly annoyed before easing herself up from the floor, grinning. "Perfect, the classic opportunity to knock on a neighbour's door and introduce myself."

"You be careful which door you knock on, you don't want it to be old Mr Black's."

"Good point. Hang on, didn't Adam say he lives in Ivy Cottage?"

"Yes, that's appropriate isn't it? Poisonous old sod!"

"Anyway, that's easy, I'll not go next door, obviously, nor to Adam's, nor to Ivy". With that, Lois left, holding a small, badly chipped bowl that she'd found in a cupboard, in which to put the sugar.

She walked up the lane and did eeny, meeny, miny, moe, to decide between the fourth and fifth cottages, Rose and Bramble. Bramble won. Lois let herself through the pedestrian gate and walked up the garden path. There was a metal wheelchair ramp up to the front door. Lois felt ridiculously nervous as she approached. Would it be a family living here, a couple or another grumpy old man? No, there couldn't be more than one of those living in this idyllic spot. She tentatively rang the doorbell.

As she waited, she heard a dog bark, once, and then there was some scraping of furniture. Something banged into the front door and she could hear some indecipherable mutterings. Lois felt a twinge of guilt, wondering whether her visit was causing problems for the person who needed the ramp.

The door opened a fraction then bumped into something and stopped abruptly. "Oh bugger off!" said the voice behind the door.

"Oh no!" said Lois under her breath, the blood draining from her face, "I don't believe this!" There was a whirring sound and the door opened a bit more. Lois wondered whether to make a run for it, but a few seconds of indecision made it too awkward and she stayed rooted to the spot, heart rate increasing by the second. The door began to open wider and Lois could see that the whirring sound was coming from an electric wheelchair, manipulated by a balding man, whose remaining brown hair was heavily flecked with grey. In her anxious state, Lois had to do a double take, as the door appeared to be opening on its own. The man in the wheelchair had one hand on the joystick of the chair and the other lying limp in his lap.

"Oh bugger off!" said the man, with a cheery smile, taking his left hand off the control and holding it out for Lois to shake. Lois stood completely rigid for several seconds, her mind trying to process the ridiculously mixed messages that were being thrown at her.

"Oh bugger off!" said the man again, nodding towards his hand, with his head slightly tilted on one side and grinning, somewhat lopsidedly, but in such an endearing way that Lois took his hand and shook it firmly. "Oh buuugger off!" he nodded, enthusiastically.

Just as Lois was wondering what on earth she should do next, she heard a door closing at the back of the house and foot falls coming in their direction. "Jack, who is it?" asked a woman's voice.

"Oh bugger off!" responded the man, pointing to Lois and smiling, as the woman appeared next to him.

"Can I help you?" she asked. Lois had forgotten about the need for sugar and stumbled over her words as she tried to remember why she was there. The whole situation had taken her completely by surprise and she felt quite emotionally unsteady.

"I'm, I'm Lois, s-so sorry to disturb you. I've just moved in to Honeysuckle." At which point the woman squeezed past the wheelchair and, much to Lois's surprise, gave her, what seemed to be, a heartfelt hug.

"Oh I'm so delighted to meet you Lois, we've been wondering who our new neighbours would be, haven't we Jack?"

"Oh bugger off!" said Jack, with a determined nod.

"I'm Doreen, this is Jack and Ellie is here somewhere, where are you Ellie?" At which point Lois noticed the black Labrador sitting by the door. She dropped the rope that was in her mouth and trotted out, tail wagging, to greet Lois.

"Have you time for a cup of tea, Lois?" asked Doreen.

Lois thought about Mel, waiting for her back at the house, but was now so overcome by Doreen's offer of hospitality, she tentatively accepted, "A quick cuppa would be lovely. Oh and I've just remembered," Lois held out the bowl, "any chance I could borrow some sugar?"

Lois stayed for about twenty minutes. She felt surprisingly at ease with Doreen and Jack, but not enough to ask about Jack's problems, much as she was intrigued to find out what had caused his disabilities. So she chatted away, telling them about Tom and his accident, the baby on the way and the work that was needed on the cottage. Doreen and Jack sat listening intently. When he heard about Tom's accident, Jack covered his eyes and shook his head, saying compassionately, "Oooh buuugger off!"

The sun was still shining as Lois left Bramble Cottage. She walked down the lane smiling contentedly; 'A successful visit', she thought to herself. She started to daydream about her and Tom becoming friends with all the neighbours. Popping in for coffee, being invited to dinner and parties. Then she remembered Mr Black's grumpy face and the screaming and swearing issuing through the paper-thin walls of the next-door cottage and her smile faded.

Lois found Mel sitting on the floor of the living room, with her mobile clasped under her chin, scribbling frantically on a scrap of paper to try and get a pen to work. She glared at Lois and gesticulated for her to find another. Lois rummaged through the contents of her oversized handbag. She eventually discovered a pen, lurking beneath the ludicrous pile of papers, old programmes, books, receipts, loyalty cards, and loose change and handed it to Mel; then deciding to make some tea while Mel finished on the phone, to try and win back favour.

"Well, you leave me to make all the arrangements why don't you, while you go swanning off to have tea and cake with the neighbours!" said Mel sarcastically, as she put down the phone and stretched out her cramped legs.

"I went to Bramble," Lois said, handing Mel her tea. "The man who lived there opened the door and told me to bugger off!"

"I don't believe you! You're smiling. You're making it up!"

"It's the truth! Promise." Lois proceeded to recall her visit, which had Mel entranced, although she was still not totally convinced that Lois was telling the truth.

"This is quite an unusual little place you and Tom are moving to, isn't it?"

Lois smiled. "It does seem to be. Anyway, did you organize my life while I was out?"

Adam had said that if Lois could find a replacement door, he would fit it later in the day. He'd written down the door and hinge sizes and phone numbers of two relatively local reclamation yards, along with the best DIY stores in the area.

Mel seemed surprisingly excited to fill Lois in on her telephone inquiries. "So, this place," she said, pointing to her meticulously neat notes, "said they had a great solid oak door of similar dimensions to the original. It's in very good condition apparently and," Mel grinned, "he said you could have it for a hundred and fifty pounds and they would hang onto it for you for the rest of the day!"

"Wow, that's fantastic!" Lois gave Mel a hug. "Thanks so much."

"Yeah, it's probably the one that was here in the first place," Mel laughed.

"Well, at least we'll know it fits!"

Lois made a swift tour of the house to compile what she hoped was a comprehensive list for the builders' quotes. It included re-wiring, replacing the mustard-yellow bathroom suite, redecorating throughout, treating for woodworm and dry rot, (which had come to Lois's notice while making the list, at which point she'd started wondering about suing the surveyor). The possibilities for and approximate cost of soundproofing the party walls would also need to be discussed.

The builders came and went. There were three. The first, Eric, was a middle-aged, chin rubbing, 'Oh, you don't wanna do that!' sort of a man, who Lois didn't take to at all. Number two, John, apparently managed to walk in a pile of dog excrement, between parking his car and entering the cottage. Oblivious to this, he proceeded to make his way around the house, depositing it on the flowery carpets as he went. Lois, too embarrassed to say anything, had to stifle several retches as she showed him what needed doing. She slammed the back door after he'd gone, "What's the matter with these people?" she gasped, "are there no normal builders around?"

Builder number three, to her great relief, was apparently 'normal'. His name was Dean and he was young and energetic. When Lois apologised for the faeces on the carpet, explaining that the previous builder had trodden it through the house, he went and got some cleaning liquid and old rags from his van and scrubbed the worst of it away. By this time it hardly mattered what quote he gave, he was the builder for Lois and, since he'd had a last minute cancellation, he would be able to start on Monday.

Dean left, having promised to drop off his estimate at the cottage later in the day. Then Mel and Lois walked back to the manor car park, collected the car and drove off, down the sweeping driveway of Harewood Park, in search of a door.

Lois felt that the visit to the reclamation yard was a great success. The manager felt much the same way. True to his word, he had put a fantastic oak door to one side, which she inspected closely for woodworm. The manager, who was clearly well ahead of the game, offering the door for a hundred and fifty pounds, proceeded to sell her 'antique' door furniture and hinges for two hundred and fifty.

Having made her purchases, Lois realised that a door of this size was not going to fit into an MG convertible. She felt her cheeks grow suddenly hot with embarrassment. Thinking fast, as the manager and his sidekick carried the door out of the barn, looking for the car in which to put it, she said, "Hang on just a moment, I'll put the top down, I think it'll fit behind the front seats."

The door did fit behind the seats, but didn't look very secure. The manager offered to cut it in half, making it into a stable door effect. Lois thought better of that suggestion; he would probably try to sell her another small fortune's worth of door furnishings, as well as charging for cutting it in half. "No, it'll be fine as it is, so long as Mel puts her body weight into keeping it from flipping backwards out of the car!" Lois laughed. Mel didn't have much in the way of body weight and looked a bit dubious about the whole thing. At which point, the manager secured a length of rope around the door for Mel to hold onto from her seat, and away they went.

As the weather was now looking somewhat doubtful, they decided it would be wise to go straight back to the cottage. Indeed, as they drove towards Harewood Park, the first raindrops fell. Within a minute the intensity of the rain had increased so rapidly that Lois, Mel, the inside of the car, and Lois's beloved door, were drenched.

"What the hell are we going to do now? My lovely door's getting soaked!" Lois screeched.

"Don't panic, you've got umbrellas in the boot!" Mel shouted pointedly, remembering Lois's smug, minimalist comments of the previous day.

"Umbrellas! What are umbrellas going to be any good for, it's peeing down!" Lois grimaced, missing the point of Mel's jibe altogether.

Mel glanced over at her friend, whose short, pixie haircut was sticking to her head; she had mascara running down her cheeks and a scowl on her face. Mel, unable to help herself, said, "My word you're ugly when you're angry." This comment, unsurprisingly, did nothing to help lift Lois's mood. She pulled the car over outside the cottage, slammed her foot on the brake, wrenched on the handbrake and cut the engine. Mel got out, straight into a large, muddy puddle, which she waded through unperturbed, opened the boot and pulled out the two golfing umbrellas. She hoisted the first one and handed it to Lois, who was still sitting in the car, tears mixing with the rain that dripped down her face. The other she opened for herself. Mel, starting to feel a little peeved with Lois's sulky behaviour, said, "Bloody thing's going to get wet Lo, it's an outside door!" and went stomping off up the lane in search of a suitable man to help her lift a very heavy oak door out of the back of the car.

Mel was in luck, there was a farmer sitting in a tractor, eating his sandwiches, a bit further along the road. She reached up and tapped on the window, which seemed to spook him a bit at first, but he then opened his door and asked "Can I 'elp?" Mel quickly introduced herself and explained the situation, slightly exaggerating Lois's physical and psychological condition, in the hope of increasing his sympathy for them. "Always 'appy to 'elp ladies in distress!" he said and climbed down from his tractor. As he started to hobble, bandy-legged towards Honeysuckle, Mel began to wonder whether she'd picked the right man for the job.

When they arrived at the car Lois peered out from under the umbrella, hair soaked, eyes red, mascara trails down her cheeks; all in all, not the first impression she'd envisaged giving the neighbours. But perhaps this man wasn't a neighbour; Lois thought he looked a bit rough for someone living in these parts. He was wearing a grimy looking jacket over a shirt with the buttons done up incorrectly and the tail dangling out at the back, tatty old trousers held up with baler twine and Doc Martin's with one of his big toes poking through. He was unshaven and his mop of wavy, grey hair looked greasy and unkempt.

Mel shook her umbrella and put it in the boot, then did the same with Lois's; the rain had all but stopped. Lois seemed a lot calmer; she got out of the car and despite feeling ridiculous, held out her hand to the stranger in front of her, "Lois Shenfield, pleased to meet you," she said, in her most business-like voice. She regretted offering her hand as soon as she saw the colour of his. It was brown, manure brown. But it was too late. She cringed inwardly, trying hard not to allow her disgust to show, as he took her hand and shook it firmly.

"Bill Riley, I'm from the farm up the end o' the track, Willow Farm."

Lois thought the name sounded familiar. Then it clicked. Bill Riley was the man that Charles Black had made such a point of telling her to avoid. She wondered whether she should avoid him, he looked harmless enough. He did, however, look like the most unlikely owner of Willow Farm, which was a stunning place; she and Tom had walked past it once, when they'd driven out to admire Honeysuckle and explore the area.

Right on cue, Bill asked, "'Ave you met Old Man Black yet?"

"Um, yes I have met him," muttered Lois, noncommittally.

"'E's a right dodgy bloke 'e is. Take my advice and give 'im a wide birf!"

"Ah, right, I'll remember that." Lois decided the best thing would be to change the subject and move on. She asked Bill whether he thought he would be able to lift the door out of the car and into the garden for her, with Mel's help.

"No trouble Love, you jus' leave it t' me!" He pushed his sleeves above his elbows and was just positioning himself to lift the door when they all heard a horse approaching from the bridleway adjacent to the cottage, then heard the rider shout.

"Oi Bill, what the 'ell are you doin'? You'll 'ave another 'eart attack if you start doin' things like that again!"

The horse was huge and had foam on its neck where sweat had mixed with rain. The rider, a pretty young woman, wearing only a vest top on her upper body, was soaked through. She jumped off the horse as it pranced around. "'Ere Bill, you come and 'old 'im while I 'elp with the door."

"Oi Sissy, wot 'ave I bleedin' told ya 'bout droppin' yer H's. I spen' a fortune on tha' posh school. Now talk proper!"

Bill took the reins of the horse as the girl mumbled, "Yeah, yeah Bill, wha'ever!" Lois thought that if he had heart problems, the last thing he should be doing was holding this enormous beast, which was now jogging on the spot; but both Bill and the girl seemed totally unperturbed.

"I'm Sicily, by the way, from Willow Farm; let me give you an 'and with that. Over by the 'ouse, yeah?" And with that, the girl grabbed either side of the door, heaved it to boot level, where she rested it to rearrange her grip.

Mel hovered around, "How can I help?"

"Keep out o' the way I reck'n!" chortled Bill, as Sicily lifted the door and carried it to the front of the house, where she gently put it down and leant it against the wall.

Both Lois and Mel were practically speechless, amazed at Sicily's strength, particularly considering how skinny she was.

"Gosh Sicily, you're incredibly strong, it took two men to put it in the car," said Mel, as Sicily rescued her horse from Bill and shrugged.

"It's from working with 'orses, soon muscles you up, don't it Bill?" She glanced at Bill who was now leaning against the boot of the car, his huge beer belly busily testing the strength of his buttonholes. "Well, some of us anyway!" she laughed.

"Thanks so much for your help, Sicily; I'm Lois, by the way. I'm the one who'll be moving in, and this is Mel."

By this time the horse was totally beside itself and either the car or one of the bystanders were in danger of getting damaged. "Really nice to meet you, 'opefully see you again soon!" said Sicily, leading the horse a few yards beyond the car, then literally leaping on and trotting off up the lane.

"What a delightful girl," said Lois.

"She's the apple of me eye," Bill said, as he watched Sicily disappear from view. Then he said abruptly, "Must be gettin' on, busy, busy, busy!" and hobbled back towards his tractor.

Lois and Mel went to inspect how wet the inside of the car was. They were just contemplating whether it would be better to put the roof back up in case it rained again, or leave it open to the air to help with the drying process, when they heard the front door of the next cottage shut and footsteps scrunching across the gravel driveway. They looked at each other, Lois nodding towards the house and mouthing, "Make a run for it?" But it was too late. An unusually tall woman, with short blonde hair, appeared around the newly trimmed holly hedge and strode slowly towards them, two spaniels trotting behind her and a somewhat sheepish expression on her face.

"Hi, I'm Annie Nutter, from next door. Are you our new neighbours?"

"Hi," Lois paused, feeling slightly anxious that she was introducing herself to a psychopath, "I'm Lois, your new neighbour, myself and my partner, Tom. This is my friend Mel." Lois tried to visualise this rather gentle looking woman being responsible for all that hideous screaming and crashing they'd witnessed the previous day. 'Nutter by name, nutter by nature?' she wondered, trying desperately to keep a straight face.

"When did you arrive?" asked Annie, nonchalantly, praying that it wasn't the previous day.

Lois didn't know whether to lie about their time of arrival or about the fact that they had been able to hear, what was presumably Annie's horrendous outburst, quite clearly through the walls of Honeysuckle. Lois was just clearing her throat to speak when she heard Mel give a tiny snort, the kind that escapes when one is trying very hard not to laugh. Lois shot her a threatening glance, at which point Mel could no longer contain herself and started to titter. Then, when Annie said, "Ah, you were here yesterday," with an embarrassed smile, Mel's laughter quickly developed into nothing short of hysterical, rapidly drawing in, not just Lois, but Annie too. Soon, the three women were helpless, leaning on the car and

44

each other for support as their strength drained away and tears ran down their faces.

When they were once again able to speak, Annie offered to fetch some old towels to mop up the car and invited them to her cottage for a cup of tea. They accepted, the thoughts of a psychopathic side to Annie, from minutes previously, all but forgotten. As they walked next door, Lois noticed that Bill was still sitting in his tractor a little further up the road, which seemed odd, him having said he was so busy. He saw them and gave Lois a friendly wave. She decided he must be waiting to meet somebody and thought nothing more of it.

Annie offered Lois and Mel a shower and to put their wet clothes in the tumble dryer, an opportunity at which they both jumped. Lois went first and came down to the kitchen in a gorgeous, white, fluffy dressing gown, which Annie had given her to wear.

"That feels wonderful, thank you so much!" she said, as Annie took her wet clothes for the dryer. "I'm so sorry to be a pain."

"Oh, not at all. It's the least I can do to make my new neighbour feel welcome," she said, handing Lois a large mug of tea. "After all, you can't have thought I was very welcoming yesterday. I'm so sorry! To be honest you could not have picked a worse day to arrive. I have never, in my entire life, lost my temper. In fact I rarely get cross, I promise, I'm really quite mellow. But yesterday, I don't know, something inside me just snapped!"

When Mel arrived downstairs, Annie was explaining to Lois the predisposing factors leading to her outburst. It warmed Lois's heart to hear that she loved living in this place so much and she found Annie's strength of character and openness quite endearing. She wouldn't have believed it yesterday, but today, Lois had a strong feeling that they were going to become good friends.

Lois was tempted to start asking Annie questions about some of the neighbours she had so far encountered. But no sooner had she mentioned Bill's name, than there was a knock at the door. It was Adam, looking for Lois; he'd come to fit the replacement front door. Annie invited him in for a cup of tea, but he was eager to get on with the job.

"I'd give you a hand," said Mel, "only I've nothing to wear."

"Fine by me," Adam smiled.

Lois looked at Mel to see if she was blushing. But no, she was lapping up Adam's attention, with a broad grin on her face.

"You can borrow something of my daughter's if you like. She's about the same size as you," said Annie.

"That's really kind Annie. Oh, hang-on, I've just remembered. Unlike Lois, I came prepared for getting soaked," said Mel, "I'll go and fetch my clean, dry clothes from the boot of the car!"

Annie was delighted to have Lois stay for a bit longer, while her clothes dried; she found her very easy to talk to and was happy to have somebody different to discuss her current problems with. It seemed extraordinary how quickly the two of them had clicked and Annie felt very excited at the prospect of having a next-door neighbour with whom she got on really well. She now felt more determined than ever that she and Dave should stay in Lilac cottage.

"Anyway, enough of me and my issues, when's the baby due?" Annie asked.

"Middle of September. Not too long now. Hopefully we'll get the cottage straight in time; we had no idea so much would need doing." As they drank their tea, Lois filled Annie in on Tom's accident and the unexpected problems they had so far encountered with the house. She laughed, "Well at least it looks like the soundproofing can be crossed off my list!"

When Lois's clothes were dry, she changed back into them and Annie took her to see the garage loft-space, garden and paddock. After much discussion the previous night, she and Dave had decided that together with the boat, the paddock should be the first thing to be sold and was secretly hoping at this point, that Lois and her other half may be interested. The paddock backed onto both Annie and Lois's cottages and had direct access to the bridleway, which ran down the side of Lois's garden.

Despite the paddock being wildly over-grown, Lois loved the idea of buying it. She had always wanted to own a horse, but living in London had made the prospect not only too expensive, but too impractical to contemplate. This seemed like an opportunity not to be missed as far as Lois could see and she asked Annie what price they had in mind. Annie had apparently spoken to a couple of land agents that morning and the sort of figures they'd been throwing around, based on Annie's description and the size of the area, were in the region of one hundred thousand pounds.

Lois was astonished; she tried hard to disguise her disappointment. She'd thought the figure would be more like ten thousand for a couple of acres of overgrown land. Annie explained that the most likely thing was that they'd put it up for auction; she was sure that several of the neighbours would be keen; she just hoped Charles Black wouldn't be interested.

When they returned to the kitchen Annie made more hot drinks as they continued to chat. Lois, feeling she'd left Mel and Adam alone in each other's company for long enough, thanked her profusely for the hospitality and made her way to Honeysuckle, armed with tea for the workers, Mel's dry clothes tucked under her elbow. Annie's parting comment was that Lois and Tom could use Lilac cottage as their own while Honeysuckle was in turmoil.

Lois crossed Annie's drive smiling to herself; she couldn't believe how her opinion of Annie had changed in the last few hours. A car approached as she walked the short distance along the road to Honeysuckle. The driver opened the passenger window as he pulled up alongside Lois. A broad set man, with a seriously receding hairline and a big smile, leant over. "Hi, I'm Dave," he said, grinning broadly. "I'm assuming you're our new neighbour and that you've met my wife," he nodded at the mugs she was carrying, which he clearly recognised. "Welcome to Harewood Park; I hope you'll be as happy here as we are!"

Lois introduced herself and briefly explained why Tom wasn't with her. Dave was thrilled to hear that Tom was a mountain biking man. He said that he was thinking of taking it up as his new hobby. Then, noticing that Adam was struggling to position the new door, despite enthusiastic assistance from Mel, said he would pop home to change and then come and give a hand.

Dave was back to help Adam in no time and as a team they worked fast and effectively until the door, along with its antique hinges and lock, were fitted. Lois was delighted and relieved that the house was now secure and easily accessible.

By the time the job was finished it was seven thirty and Lois and Mel were due back in London. Annie came round to invite everyone for supper, and Lois and Mel to sleep over. This option made the idea of trekking back to the pandemonium, noise and pollution of the city, far from inviting. Lois was exhausted and starting to enjoy her new environment so much, she really didn't want to leave. Mel was bowled over by Adam, who seemed to be intelligent, kind, witty and generous on top of the good looks and amazing physique, so she was not eager to rush away, either. But, with the knowledge that poor Tom would be returning to an empty flat, with no food, and they really did both need to go to work the following day, the decision was made to, on this occasion, return to London.

Before they left, Annie invited Lois, Tom, Mel and Adam to dinner the following Saturday night. Lois, entering Annie's numbers into her phone, said she would confirm once she had seen how Tom was; then they all hugged as if they'd known each other for years; Lois and Mel settled themselves into the damp car and Annie, Dave and Adam waved them off.

7

Lois was surprised to see the state that Tom was in. He'd implied on the phone that his injuries were minor, other than the broken wrist. But in reality his chin was a horrible mess; it must have had at least ten stitches, running in a crescent shape around the left side of his dimple. He had yellow bruising which radiated from below the cut to the top of his left cheek. His temple was deep purple, from where his helmet had hit his head on impact with the ground. His broken arm was in plaster and hitched up across his chest in a sling. But the injury that seemed to be causing the most pain was his cracked ribs, of which there were apparently three. Since Lois felt it would be somewhat hypocritical to say anything about him hiding the truth, she looked him over and said as sympathetically as she could, "Well, thank God you were wearing a helmet!"

Both starving hungry, they bolted down the Indian takeaway meal-for-two that Lois had picked up from the supermarket and microwaved. Tom was still on antibiotics and Lois had been doing her best to avoid alcohol during her pregnancy, so they stuck to soft drinks.

It felt great to be back together again. Tom was surprised how excited he was when Lois started to tell him about their new home. She gave him an edited version of the previous two days, which excluded almost anything negative, other than the need for an emergency replacement front door. That, she thought, was too obvious to go unnoticed.

Tom had been feeling miserable since his accident. He had missed Lois terribly and been starting to feel quite pessimistic about their venture into property ownership. But now, hearing about the friendly, supportive environment, he couldn't wait to move and was very enthusiastic about the idea of going to Annie and Dave's for dinner on Saturday.

They went to bed, snuggling the best they could, which, following a series of "ouches" from Tom, ended up being little more than holding hands.

The next morning, Lois was up at six thirty, preparing to drag herself off to work. As she walked away having kissed Tom goodbye, completely out of the blue he called after her, "Why don't you resign, Lo? Resign today!" Lois stopped in her tracks and gazed back at him, not really understanding what he was talking about. "They'll be supervision needed on the house and then there's Pumpkin to think about. If you'd like to, resign today!" Lois didn't have time to further the discussion, she was going to miss her train; but his words repeated in her mind throughout the journey. She had never contemplated giving up work; planning to continue, if she could, to within a week of the baby's due date and then go back after six months maternity leave. But after her first two days in Harewood Park, actually, Tom's suggestion sounded very exciting.

Lois had a huge email backlog to wade through on arrival at the office. One of the first, informing her that there was to be a meeting in the boardroom at nine. "Oh God," she groaned under her breath, when she read that Ian would be heading it in place of Justin, the Floor Manager, who was on sick leave. Ian was, in Lois's, and most of her colleagues' opinions, a boring twit with next to no social skills. It wasn't going to be an experience that would enthuse her back into work that was for sure.

Lois was pleased to see that Adrienne was attending the meeting. She was a good friend and they were a great support for each other, in what was still a predominantly male environment. Adrienne, who had lived with her female partner for several years, was dark, petite and very pretty. Several of the men in the office had been extremely disappointed to discover she was gay.

Ian, however, had a problem with Adrienne. He had apparently said to one of their colleagues, that he had 'never knowingly had any contact with a gay person before and she made him a little nervous'.

Throughout the meeting, he glanced around the board table, trying to meet the gaze of as many of those present as possible, in the manner he'd been taught on his recent management-training course. However, he always skipped past Adrienne's. She wasn't bothered by it at all, she was used to his perverse ways.

Ian droned on and on for an hour and a half. Lois was finding it very difficult to stay awake, let alone concentrate, so she began contemplating whether to resign or not and if so how to word the letter. She allowed the news of various company disasters, their implications for the stock market and what should be bought and sold, to drift over her head, but when she heard Ian say, "So, in summing up…" she sat up and looked interested. He continued, "For the time being, to stop the flow of potential disasters, we must all put a finger in the dyke!"

Now this would have been fine and would probably have gone unnoticed, but for the fact that Ian turned crimson, started to sweat profusely, dropped a pile of papers on the floor in his fluster; then stuttered, "Ah, um, ah, sorry Adrienne," looking somewhere over her head. "Ok, we'll um, yes, we'll, er, call it a day then. Um…Adrienne, if you wouldn't mind waiting behind please."

As they left the boardroom Lois and her colleagues burst into hysterical laughter. When Adrienne came out several minutes later, she headed straight for the loo, with her hands up to her face shielding her expression. Lois followed. The ladies washroom had always been their own private meeting place; one advantage to being in the minority.

"What did he say?" asked Lois.

Adrienne was laughing too uncontrollably to speak for a while.

"Well," she said eventually, "he said he was sorry for drawing attention to me in such an inconsiderate way." Adrienne laughed some more, "I said, I didn't know what he was referring to, could he explain to me what he meant. At which point he stuttered and squirmed his way through where the phrase comes from, trying to explain that in no way was he referring to me or my sexuality!"

It took the two women a good twenty minutes to return to the office floor, ten of which were taken up recovering their composure and repairing their make-up; the other ten, making decisions about their futures. Lois couldn't believe how excited she felt at the prospect of resigning; and it wasn't so much the idea of being a full time mum fuelling her excitement; there was something about Harewood Park that was simply drawing her in, despite the initial hiccups. With the additional fact that Ian was soon to become their manager, his performance this morning made Lois's decision clear; the right thing for her to do at this point in her life, was to resign. For Adrienne, it wasn't so simple. Much as she would like to move on to pastures new, particularly with the knowledge that Lois would be going, jobs were hard to find in the current climate and she did at least have plenty of support from her male colleagues.

"Are you going to report him? Ian I mean," asked Lois.

Adrienne thought for a moment. "Nah, I don't think so. It'll only create more awkwardness in the department and he never really does anything wrong, other than be very uncomfortable in my presence and nobody could be reprimanded for that. And to be honest, it is very funny seeing him get himself into these situations and then trying to crawl his way out!"

Lois went back to her desk, drafted her resignation, printed it out and gave Tom a quick ring to make sure he really meant what he'd said that morning. He was delighted at the idea of her staying at home; hopefully, both of their lives would be considerably less stressful. Lois went on to tell him about the meeting, which made him laugh so much he was crying in pain. When able to speak again, he said that there was a job coming up imminently at his company that would suit Adrienne perfectly.

Lois said her goodbyes to Tom, passed the phone to Adrienne and went straight to HR to hand in her letter of resignation. She walked back into the office with the biggest smile on her face. The icing on the cake, being that Adrienne was meeting with Tom's manager after work, to discuss the vacancy.

When Lois got back to the flat that night, tired, but happy, Tom was raring to go. "Don't sit down!" he said, as Lois sat down. "Car's packed, we're off to our new house!" Lois was astonished. He'd tidied the flat, packed and loaded the car, bought food and he'd even thought to include the picnic hamper. All this, he had done with one arm in a sling and the other clutching his ribs at every given opportunity. "It took a long time!" he chuckled, slightly high from his painkillers, "I had to take it all out a handful at a time, I've made twenty-five journeys to the car. The taxi driver was very helpful and so were the staff at the supermarket. Anyway let's go, it would be good to arrive in the light."

"Ah ... yes," said Lois, cautiously, "I forgot to tell you about the lights. There is a teensy weensy problem with the downstairs lights. All in hand of course, but we will need torches at the moment."

"Don't worry," said Tom, "Mel told me all about it. Torches packed."

'Oh dear,' thought Lois, 'I wonder what else Mel's told him?'

8

The traffic was disastrous coming out of London that Friday evening. By the time Lois and Tom were driving along the rough, unmade road to the cottage, Tom was in agony, which increased with every bump. "I don't remember the road being as rough as this," he groaned, clutching his side and screwing up his face in pain. "Why've we bought a house up here?"

"Well," said Lois, curtly, "normally one wouldn't have broken ribs when being driven along it!" She was tempted to add another snide remark about the cycling accident, but instead, remembering she hadn't been completely open with him lately, said, "Nearly there. You'll feel better when you're snuggled down on the blow up rubber mattress."

"Yeah, right," grumbled Tom.

When they arrived, Lois helped Tom out of the car and they walked hand in hand up the garden path.

"Are you going to carry me over the threshold?" Lois laughed, as she rummaged in her oversized handbag for the key to the antique lock.

"Mm, maybe not today my precious. Wow, fantastic door! Quite like the one I remember being here," said Tom.

"Funny you should say that." Lois started to fill Tom in on Adam's suspicions of the original door being removed, as she located the enormous key and put it, proudly, into the lock.

"What the hell is that, Lo?" said Tom, staring in disbelief.

"It's an antique Tom, I chose it especially. I thought you'd like it, you love old things!" Tom looked at her, propped himself up against the doorframe, held tight to his broken ribs and groaned with laughter. "What? What's so funny?"

Lois hadn't given any thought to the practicalities of having such a big key. After a few moments, she laughed reluctantly. "Honestly there's no pleasing some people!" she shook her head and smiled.

Lois opened the door and walked in, Tom hobbling after her. The mid-summer sun was setting behind the back garden, bringing bright, pink tinged rays of light into the living room. They both muttered a "Wow!" and instinctively groped for the other's hand to squeeze. They made their way to the French windows and watched the large, red sun silhouetting the eucalyptus tree as it went down. Despite the state of the garden, the scene seemed absolutely perfect and they watched, mesmerised, until it had completely disappeared behind the overgrown hawthorn hedge.

"Blimey!" said Tom, "That was amazing! That makes up for the bumpy road and the giant key already."

"I don't see what's the matter with the key," said Lois, "I think it's great, it'll be much harder to lose than the key to the flat."

"How many spares did it come with?" asked Tom, in a serious tone.

"Ah yes, I see your point, might be a bit tricky getting copies made."

"Yes, and to put in the pocket of your jeans, and to have dangling off your car key fob and…"

"Okay, okay!" said Lois, "I get it! We'll have to put another lock on, but we could leave that one for decoration couldn't we?"

"Well, we could, but we'll have to stuff a sock in the key hole in winter to stop the draught!"

Tired and hungry, they unloaded the food and bedding from the car. Or more precisely, Lois unloaded the food and bedding from the car and pumped up the mattress while Tom managed, by using one hand and a good set of teeth, to open the packets of cold meats, veggie slices, cheese and salad he had bought for supper. Cutting the crusty date and walnut loaf was trickier and more painful than he'd been anticipating, so he just tore it into chunks, again, using his teeth. Then he and Lois sat on the blow-up rubber mattress in their new bedroom, which came complete with a very dirty looking and rather smelly, grey shag-pile carpet, and started to eat their supper.

"Do you think there could be fleas living in the carpet?" asked Lois, wrinkling up her nose in disgust as she pushed a large chunk of bread and cheese into her mouth.

"Oh probably. And the rest."

"And the rest?" spluttered Lois, putting her hand up to her mouth as particles of partly masticated food exploded from it. "What do you mean? Not mice surely?" Lois had an inherent phobia of small rodents, all except hamsters, which she'd kept as a child.

"It wouldn't surprise me. You'd better pick up those crumbs you just spat into our bed, they'll love those," Tom chuckled. "If you feel something furry in the night, climbing…"

"Enough Tom!" said Lois, firmly, putting up her hand to emphasise that he should stop teasing. She really was beginning to feel quite uncomfortable at the thought of sleeping there.

"We're in the country now Lo, you're going to need to cope with the odd mouse in the shag-pile if we're staying." Tom chuckled to himself, "Or is it shag in the mouse pile?"

"And how many pain-killers have you taken today?" asked Lois, raising an eyebrow.

"Oh, just the right amount my pet," Tom said. Then, in an attempt to distract his girlfriend from the thought of mice running over her face whilst sleeping, he asked her to open the quarter-size bottle of champagne he'd bought to celebrate the first night in their new home. They'd left the glasses he'd so carefully packed, in the kitchen and neither of them had the energy to go downstairs again, so they drank straight from the bottle.

Tom lay back, feeling decidedly dopey with the combination of exhaustion, strong painkillers and an eighth of a bottle of champagne. He was just getting comfortable when Lois suddenly got out of bed, "I'm sorry, I can't sleep in this room with the idea of small creatures living in the carpet. Up you get!" She gently pulled Tom, who didn't have reason or energy to protest, out of bed and started tugging at the edges of the carpet. Thankfully it was easy to pull up and having loosened all the edges, Lois rolled up one side of it, moved the mattress and Tom over the top, and rolled the remainder. She then dragged it down the spiral staircase and out of the front door. She repeated the exercise with the very old, musty, crusty underlay.

"There, that's better!" Lois said, returning to the bedroom and breathing a sigh of relief as she gazed around at the dusty, exposed floorboards. She rearranged their bed and Tom gingerly clambered back in. Lois collapsed next to him, rolled over to give him a gentle cuddle and they both fell asleep almost immediately, fully clothed and unwashed.

Within an hour, Lois was awake with a very full bladder. Moonlight was shining through the bathroom window, allowing her to make her way to the toilet without putting on the revolting and horribly bright strip-light. She thought she heard a strange noise just before she sat down, so looked around to see what it was. Something was moving in the toilet bowl. Lois screamed hysterically until Tom arrived, moaning and groaning in pain, blinking hard against the intense lighting, which Lois had now turned on.

"What is it?"

"There's something moving in the toilet," said Lois, "I can't bear to look, I think it's a rat!"

"Oh, don't be silly Lo, you're being para…" Tom, peering into the toilet, couldn't believe his eyes. There, swimming around the bowl was a frantic bedraggled creature, which wasn't a rat. It was smaller than a squirrel, with big bulging eyes. Tom swiftly grabbed its bushy tail and lifted it into the bath, where it shook violently and tried to climb out, sliding back down as soon as the curve of the bath became vertical.

"Oh, it's sweet," cooed Lois, having been brave enough to look, once Tom had said it wasn't a rat, "I wonder what it is?"

"I wonder how it got there?" said Tom. There was a knock at the door. "That's probably the neighbours, coming to see if I've murdered you." On the landing, he bent over awkwardly to pick up one of the torches they'd left in readiness, and smacking it a couple of times to make it work, slowly made his way downstairs. Lois followed, small Pingu torch in hand. It was indeed Annie and Dave standing on the doorstep in their dressing gowns, they'd come to make sure that everything was okay. Lois introduced them to Tom, prompting a brief acknowledgment and discussion of his injuries and then Lois told them about the mystery creature they'd found drowning in the loo.

"Oh, that'll be a glis glis!" said Dave, chuckling, as if it were the most natural thing in the world.

"Oh yes," said Annie, equally amused, "everyone along here's had problems with them at one time or another and I'm not surprised they're living here, with the house having been empty for so long."

Tom and Lois had no idea how to react. Could this really be true? They'd never heard of such a thing.

"It's Rothschild's fault. Old Walter, released six onto his estate in Tring, just over a hundred years ago and their descendants are doing very well!" said Dave. "Also called edible dormice, although I haven't eaten one yet. Well, not to my knowledge anyway." He winked at Annie and then asked, "What have you done with the little blighter?"

"It's in the bath," said Tom.

"I'll sort it for you if you like," said Dave, "It's illegal of course, supposed to get pest control in, or have a licence to cull them; little buggers are protected, you see. But that's an expensive business, so I usually drown them and put them out for the kites."

Tom looked completely mystified. "You put them out for the kites?" he asked, imagining the kites he often saw flying on Primrose Hill and a dead glis glis and trying to make a connection.

"The red kites," said Dave, seeing the confused expression on his face, "they're birds of prey. They're quite prolific round here; clear up anything dead in a trice. I've been thinking of knocking off old Mr Black and putting him out for them, but I'm not sure they'd get through him quickly enough to keep me out of trouble. Might need to get some pigs for that!" Dave chortled to himself.

"Oh yes, the red kites," repeated Tom; starting to laugh despite the pain it caused him. "We've got a lot to adjust to, living in the country. Red kites, glis glis in the toilet. But Mr Black, who's he?"

"Oh, didn't Lois tell you?" laughed Annie. Lois gave a sheepish shrug.

"Plenty of time for you to find out about the neighbours," said Dave, giving Tom a friendly pat on the back, while Tom suppressed a pain-induced grimace. "Anyway he's all right really, you've just got to know how to deal with him. Come on, let's go and sort out this creature of yours!"

Tom and Dave went upstairs to 'deal' with the glis glis. Lois felt very upset by the idea of it being killed but Annie took her next door for a cup of tea and explained what it was like having the little vermin living in your loft. The noise, the fact that nothing can be stored there as they will chew up and make a nest out of almost anything, and most importantly, the fire risk created by them chewing through wires. With all this information, Lois felt a little more at ease with what Dave and Tom were going to do.

"For God's sake, don't tell Black about the glis glis or how it was disposed of, he'll be forcing the council to prosecute you before you know where you are!" said Annie.

"Is he really that bad?"

"He's an evil old sod!" said Annie; giving Lois the impression that she'd had personal experience of Mr Black's nasty side. "Anyway, enough of him for now. Look Lois, it's really late; you and Tom are very welcome to come and sleep here, the bed's all made up ready for tomorrow night. I didn't realise you were coming today." Lois explained how it had been Tom's surprise for her when she'd come home from work and said that she would go and talk over the spare room offer with him.

Tom was delighted with the idea of sleeping in a proper bed. He knew the blow-up mattress would play havoc with his ribs. It had seemed such a good idea to 'camp out' at the house, but the reality hadn't been living up to his expectations. He thought Annie and Dave seemed like a nice couple and he jumped at the offer.

The next morning Tom was woken early by Lois hugging him as she slept, which created enough pain to prevent him getting off to sleep again. He could hear an unusual bird cry outside and decided, that since he was now a 'country man', he should investigate. He drew the curtains back halfway and, as his eyes adjusted to the sunlight, he was astonished by what he saw. There were two very large birds of prey dive-bombing each other. One had food in its talons and the other clearly wanted to 'share'. The flying display was unbelievable; the wonderful, graceful birds were twisting and turning, sometimes as one, screeching in defiance and occasionally looking like they'd crash to the ground. Suddenly, one of them dropped its snack and flew vertically, full pelt, re-catching the morsel before it hit the floor. When they had stopped scrapping they used their great wings, slowly and gracefully, to gain height, then glided on the air currents, subtly twisting their tails to help them manoeuvre, turning their heads from one side to the other, in search of food.

Tom was completely mesmerised by these fantastic birds. Above the two who had been feuding, he counted a further seven. He thought how amazing it was that creatures like these could be living and indeed flourishing, so close to London. He had a quick look along the shelves of the small bookcase that was in the room and, lo and behold, there was an old Observer Book of Birds. Despite the opening phrase, 'The kite is now only found in parts of Wales, except for stray appearances elsewhere,' the description was enough to leave Tom in no doubt that these magnificent and thoroughly entertaining birds, were the red kites that Annie and Dave had been talking about. He put the book back on the shelf and quietly opened the curtains right up to enable him to lie down in bed and still watch them.

By the time Lois woke up, Tom had drifted back to sleep. She went downstairs to find a note on the kitchen table from Annie, saying she had taken the dogs for a walk and for Lois and Tom to help themselves to whatever they fancied. She'd left all they needed for Lois's idea of a perfect breakfast, on the kitchen table.

Lois made tea and fresh, granary toast with 'real' butter and Marmite for her and Tom, and carried it upstairs. Tom took it from her sleepily. The toast tasted fantastic. He told Lois all about the kites he'd seen earlier. Lois couldn't think of the last time she'd seen him looking so relaxed and happy. "I've got a feeling I'm going to love this place, Lo!" he said. Lois snuggled up to him and started to feel the anxieties conjured up in the first days at the house, ebbing even further away.

It was a beautiful sunny day. When Annie and Dave got back, the four of them sat out in the garden and had coffee and biscuits.

"That'll set Pumpkin up for the day," said Lois, gently rubbing her bulging tummy, "he loves a good, strong cup of coffee!" Dave looked a little bewildered.

"Ah yes, he, or she, started off as Peanut," explained Tom, "then Orange, Melon and now Pumpkin and since pumpkins can grow quite large, I think we'll be able to stop there; until we meet him or her. Actually," he chuckled thoughtfully, "it's not a bad name."

"No!" laughed Lois, before he had time to give the idea any more thought.

Lois and Annie started discussing babies. Tom and Dave talked about business. Dave told Tom about their plans to sell the paddock and convert the garage loft into a studio flat to rent out. They went and looked at the loft and discussed possible designs that would make best use of the space.

Over a snack lunch, Tom told, for the first time in front of Lois, what had happened on his cycling trip the previous weekend. Lois, much to his amazement, found the story incredibly funny. When Tom got to the bit about him trying to eat his roast meal with his hands, Lois rushed off to the loo for fear of wetting herself.

Seeing how much pain Tom was in when he laughed, Dave said, "One of the neighbours, Richard, is a GP who practises alternative therapies. He's about to set up a private practice at home for acupuncture and homeopathy patients. He may be able to help you make a speedy recovery, Tom.

He's a really nice bloke. Would you like me to give him a ring and see if he'd see you later?"

"That would be great!" said Tom, enthusiastically. He had a very busy week ahead work-wise and was eager to get as much help as possible to enable him to cope.

Dave returned from making the call. "Richard would be delighted to see you, Tom," he said, "he's eager to test the sharpness of his new acupuncture needles!" Neither Tom nor Lois was sure who had the sense of humour, Richard or Dave.

After lunch, Dave took Tom up the lane to Richard's, Annie went shopping for the dinner she was to prepare that evening, and Lois, who was completely exhausted by the week's events, fell asleep on the sofa.

She was awoken, some hours later, by Tom giving her a gentle kiss on the cheek and telling her there was a cup of tea for her. She sat up sleepily and asked him how he'd got on with Richard.

"Yeah, nice guy, his wife seems very likeable too, maybe a bit scatty? I bet you'll get on with her."

"Are you insinuating that I'm a bit scatty?" laughed Lois.

"A bit? No, not at all Petal. Anyway, he gave me a thorough examination and an acupuncture treatment around my spine, apparently where the nerves to the ribs run, and funnily enough I'm feeling remarkably good; especially considering it's almost time for my painkillers. He also gave me a couple of homeopathic remedies to take to help the bones heal fast, oh and something for the bruising. I'll be really interested to see what a difference it makes. He didn't even charge me."

"Wow, that's generous of him!"

"He said it was all part of the Harewood Park Welcoming Committee's policy. As soon as we're sufficiently settled, I'd like to invite Richard and Debbie for dinner, what do you think?"

"That would be great and Annie and Dave, and Adam, and Sicily."

"Sounds good to me, even though I've no idea who Adam and Sicily are."

Lois went on to tell Tom what she knew about them, explaining that Adam was the one whom Mel fancied, and that they were both coming to dinner at Annie and Dave's that evening.

"You know I've been thinking," said Tom, "I'm not sure I want to wait until the house is done-up to move in. I know we've got to pay the rent on the flat for the next couple of months, but we don't have to live there if we don't want to; we could consider it a sunk cost. How would you feel about moving in a few weeks, when I'm feeling a bit better?"

Lois was delighted with the idea. "We'd have to get movers to pack for us, we'll both be working and we're usually pooped in the evenings. Actually, would it be better to wait 'till I've worked out my notice?"

"Oh yes, I've been thinking about that too. You must be owed some annual leave, which would shorten your notice period."

Lois considered this idea for a moment as she sipped her tea. "Gosh Tom, you're right, I am. I'll have to look it up, but yes, I might even be owed two weeks. Maybe even more, I've only taken two days this year and I carried some over from last year. Oh, that's really exciting, that would mean we could move in what, two weeks time? Dean the decorator said he'd start work on Monday. If we got him to sort the bathroom out first, and get the electricians in, that would all be done before we moved."

"Dean the decorator? Don't we need a plumber for the bathroom?"

"Oh he can do it all, except the electrics, he calls himself a 'jobbing builder', whatever that means. I just thought Dean the decorator scanned rather well!"

"Come on, finish your tea. Let's go next door and start making to-do lists."

Lois checked with Annie that she didn't need help with preparing dinner. Annie said she was fine, it wasn't going to be a complicated meal, that they should enjoy investigating their new home and to say hello to the remaining glis glis for her.

"Ah, talking of glis glis," said Dave, who'd been drinking his tea at the kitchen table while leafing through a DIY catalogue, "I've got a couple of humane rat traps in the garage, I'll put them up in your loft if you like. Put in a bit of fruit. Leave me with a key to the house, then I can check them each day, and when I've humanely caught any of the little buggers, I'll drown them for you!" Dave laughed to himself.

"Oh yuck," said Lois.

"That would be great, thanks," said Tom.

Dave brought the traps round to the house, along with a small stepladder. The access hatch to the loft turned out to be about half the width of a standard one, there was no way Dave would have got his belly through it. Fortunately he didn't need to get right in, he set the traps close to the door so they were easily accessible to check and retrieve when they'd done their job.

Meanwhile Tom and Lois got on with writing a to-do list. "We're going to have to choose and order the new bathroom pretty quickly if we want Dean to do that as one of his first jobs. Perhaps we'd better go DIY store visiting tomorrow," said Lois.

"I know how to help solve the time problem," said Tom, smiling, "where's your diary? Let's see how much leave you are owed, I've got a feeling it's quite a lot."

As soon as they'd found out she was pregnant, Tom and Lois had decided to save up holiday entitlement to be used after the arrival of the baby. Justin had been very pleased, as Lois had been in the middle of a major project with an important client, and her not taking leave would wrap that up all the sooner. The HR department had quibbled with him vis-à-vis allowing an employee to carry leave over from one year to the next, but eventually they'd agreed to it; the great news being that the project was now completed and she had not been assigned anything too significant since.

Lois and Tom calculated that she had enough days outstanding, to practically cover her notice period. "That's great," she beamed, "that means I only really need to go in for a day to hand over! Wow, how exciting!"

"So, have Monday off to organize what's going on here, as you'd planned and I guess you'd better call work and talk over your imminent retirement," Tom said, grinning and drawing her into a gentle hug. Then he added in a low voice, "Best ask Annie and Dave how they'd feel about having one or two house guests for the occasional night over the next two weeks?" as Dave started walking down the stairs.

"Incidentally how were you planning for Dean the Decorator to get into the house on Monday? Did he take a template of your giant key to craft over the weekend?" said Tom, smirking.

"Oh ha ha!" Lois said, sarcastically, "if you're not careful I'll tickle you!" she reached towards his ribs.

"Actually they're feeling quite a lot better."

"Well that's good. Tomorrow we'll pull the rest of these lovely carpets out of the house then shall we?"

"I doubt we'll have time for that, Lo. Not if we've got to choose a new bathroom suite, that'll probably take all day."

"Well if you do have time and need a hand, let me know," offered Dave, "I'll probably need some assistance myself at some point with some of the heavy work in the garage loft. We're all for helping each other out around here. Well most of us are anyway!" Dave winked at Lois, said he'd best get home and give Annie a hand and disappeared.

Tom and Lois spent another hour at the house, extending their original list, then making a couple more. One for the DIY stores the next day and another for Lois for Monday, when she'd be back at the flat. The first item on her list was to get the landline reconnected and a broadband connection up and running as soon as possible. Their mobile signal was more 'miss' than 'hit' in the cottage and Lois would be reliant on the Internet to source materials economically.

Just as they were drawing their list composing to a close, a face appeared at the living room window, nose pressed up against the glass. It was Mel. "Hey, cracking door!" she laughed as they let her in. "Good God, Tom, look at the state of you!" Mel blew him a kiss, not wanting to get close to any of his injuries; the look of him sent shivers down her spine.

She gave Lois a brief hug. "Come on, no time to waste. We need to be next door, celebrating your arrival!"

9

Lois returned to Annie and Dave's with Tom and Mel. She quickly got changed, then, having checked with Annie that no help was required in the kitchen, dragged Mel out into the garden to bring her up to speed with the goings on of the previous two days. Mel was astonished by Lois's decision to stop working. She had never pictured Lois as a housewife or stay-at-home mum type. She'd always given the impression of being so dynamic at work; Harewood Park was apparently having quite an effect.

Mel found the story of Adrienne and 'the finger in the dyke' hysterically funny, her laughter luring the rest of the party outside. She grinned as Adam came up and gave her a kiss on both cheeks, and Lois found herself telling the story again.

Tom and Lois had given the bottle of champagne from their good luck hamper to Dave, who arrived in the garden with the bottle and six champagne flutes on a tray. He painstakingly poured the bubbly, determined not to spill a drop. "Just enough for a toast," he announced, having handed them out, "To happiness in Harewood Park!"

"To happiness in Harewood Park!" everyone repeated.

The next topic of conversation was Tom's injuries, difficult to ignore as they were. Lois noticed that the description of his accident was somewhat elaborated on re-telling, but it provided good entertainment.

Before long, Annie beckoned the group in through the French windows, across the lounge and into the dining room. As Lois walked to her seat, she was slightly taken aback to see three stuffed animals sitting in a row on the windowsill. A stoat or a weasel - Lois wasn't sure, an owl and a green woodpecker.

Annie saw the expression on Lois's face and jumped straight into a slightly embarrassed explanation. "They're there for diplomatic reasons," she said, "They were gifts, from Richard. You know, Tom went for a treatment with him this afternoon? It's his hobby, he's an amateur taxidermist."

Tom, who was taking a sip of his champagne almost choked on hearing this news. "He's a what?"

"An amateur taxidermist," said Dave, "Really, it's no joke. He picks up road kill, takes it home and stores it in the freezer. Then, when he has a bit of spare time on his hands, he thaws it out and, well, stuffs it, in his garage. Debbie won't let him do it in the kitchen." There was raucous laughter from around the room.

"That's gross!" laughed Lois. "Remind me never to go to dinner at their house."

"Yes, good plan," said Dave, "never have been too sure what I've been eating at theirs."

"Don't be daft!" said Annie. "They're lovely people and I'm sure they've never served us anything out of the ordinary. Anyway, what he does once he's taxidermed them; taxidermed, is that a word? Oh, whatever; once he's stuffed them, he gives them to people as presents; birthday, Christmas, house warming, he's probably working on yours right now!"

There was more laughter. "I can hardly wait! Do you think telling him I'm a vegetarian would help to put him off?" asked Lois.

"He'll find out soon enough that you're lying," said Annie.

Lois put her hand to her mouth and went bright pink with embarrassment. "Oh my God, I forgot to tell you! I'm always doing that. I'm so sorry, Annie!" Tom shook his head in an, 'Oh Lois, you've let me down again!' sort of a way. "I do eat fish though, if that's any help?" Lois offered, in a vague attempt to worm her way back into favour.

"Thank the Lord for that, we'll pretend the steak is salmon and we'll be laughing!" said Annie, looking alarmingly annoyed. The memory of Annie's hideous outburst of Wednesday and the thought of her throwing a stuffed animal at her, flashed through Lois's mind. "No, just joking, can't afford steak at the moment, it's a simple pasta bake, with tuna. Lucky!"

Lois breathed a sigh of relief and reprimanded herself inwardly. 'Must remember to share non-meat-eating habits with hosts in future.'

"What is that creature anyway?" asked Tom, pointing to the weasel-stoat.

"Oh, you've got so much to learn about the country, Tom," said Adam. "It's a stoat."

"No, it's a weasel," said Annie.

"What's the difference?" asked Mel.

"Well," came back Annie and Dave, in unison, "weasels are weasely wecognised and stoats are stoataly different!" Champagne induced laughter erupted around the table.

As they sat down to enjoy their first course, Lois announced that this must surely be the point at which Annie, Dave and Adam give the low-down on Harewood Park's other residents. She was determined to get more information on the neighbours that she hadn't yet met.

"Do you know what?" said Dave, "I reckon you should find out about the rest of the neighbours yourselves. It's not good to be influenced by other people's impressions, especially Annie's."

"Thanks for that, Darling."

"Not at all Love, not at all." Dave swallowed another spoonful of soup, before adding, "It has to be said, there are some, how should I say?"

"Unusual?" offered Adam.

"Yes, unusual, that'll do; unusual characters living here."

"Oh gosh, now you're making me nervous," said Lois, frowning. "Unusual in what way?"

"Mm, let's think." Dave tore off a chunk from his slice of crusty bread and dunked it in his soup, then chewed, slowly and thoughtfully. "So many ways. I think we should leave it at that really, I wouldn't know where to start. You'll have an interesting time meeting them all though."

"So that's it? You're not even going to give us an inkling?" Lois whined, somewhat taken aback.

"An inkling might be the worst thing to give you," said Adam, smiling.

"He's right," agreed Annie, "it's always best to meet people with a blank slate and remember, never judge a book by its cover!"

"Yes, exactly," added Adam, smiling.

"Yes, yes," said Lois, still feeling slightly affronted that nobody was willing to give her any more information. "Look beyond the cover, I think I can remember that."

"They are all, how should I put it … safe though, are they?" asked Tom, starting to feel slightly concerned for Lois's welfare.

"Oh yes," said Annie reassuringly, "they're all safe enough; none of them worry me anyway."

"Well that's very comforting Annie, thanks," said Lois, sarcastically. "Anyway, Mr Black. I'm not going to knock on his door. I've had enough of him already and I've only met him once."

"Oh come on, you've got to tell me what's wrong with this Black character; what's he said to upset you?" Tom asked Lois.

"He came and introduced himself just after Lois had smashed down the front door," said Mel, "and started laying down the law, as it were. Gave the impression of being a right miserable, grumpy old sod."

"Okay," said Annie, "we'll fill you in a bit on Black. I wouldn't expect anyone to go and talk to him voluntarily; only with a gun to their head!" Annie cleared the starter plates and went to get the main course.

"So," said Dave, as he circled the table, topping up wine glasses, "dear old Charles Black. Brought up in the house he now lives in. Moved off to Windsor I think, to live and work. He was a planning officer. Married Gill; she wasn't the friendliest of souls either, although her demeanour could have been provoked by him, I suppose. Never had any children, thank God."

"Maybe that's why they're so miserable?" offered Mel.

Dave looked sceptical. "Anyway, Charles's parents both died within a few years of each other, that must have been twenty-odd years ago. They left the house to Charles and his sister, who had cared for them during their illnesses. Charles decided to buy Emily out of her half of the house and move in. Allegedly, he bribed a couple of estate agents to give low valuations, enabling him to give Emily considerably less than her half share was worth."

There were rumblings of distaste from around the table.

Annie continued with the story as she served out the main course, Dave disappearing to fetch more wine. "Having carried out this devious ploy, he and Gill came to live in Harewood Park, just as he was promoted to chief planning officer."

"What do they do that's so unpleasant?" asked Tom.

"Oh it's not 'they' any more, Tom. She left him about four years ago. It's just him now, and he's always got his nose in everybody's business," Annie grumbled.

"Yes," said Dave, "you can hardly have a shit without him taking out a tape measure to check it for size."

"Dave!" reprimanded Annie, with a smile.

"Well, it's true."

"Anyway," said Adam, "he's a busybody who regularly puts in complaints to the council. Dave, do you remember when Richard built a tree house for the kids."

"Oh yes," smirked Dave. Annie laughed and nodded knowingly.

"Can you believe, they had a knock on the door one afternoon. It was a planning officer, come to inspect the tree house, as a neighbour had reported that an illegal structure had been built and they had no record of planning consent."

"You're kidding!" said Lois, "Planning permission, for a tree house? And why the hell would he complain about it anyway?"

"Nothing better to do with his time," said Annie, "Anyway, Richard got the planning permission, even though the kids were hardly ever playing in it, on principle. He quite often goes up there himself and reads, just to annoy Black. He even takes a telescope up sometimes and pretends to be peering into the back of Black's house. He's almost as bad as Bill!"

"What's the story with Charles and Bill? They really don't like each other do they," said Mel.

Lois turned to Tom, "Bill is Sicily's dad, lives at Willow Farm at the end of the track." Tom nodded.

"All to do with planning again," Annie continued, "Bill feels it is his God given right to build what he wants on his

71

land, it is his land after all. Last time Bill started building more stables at his farm, Charles, retired by this time, must have climbed over the locked gate in the middle of the night, with Gill in tow. They probably measured the footings; which had already been laid for the new stable block. Unaware that the Alsatian guard dog roamed loose in the yard at night, he got his measurement, but lost a shoe and a piece of his trouser-leg, trying to escape over the gate. He probably disturbed it when giving a little whoop of joy having thought he'd accomplished his mission!"

Annie stood and started to clear away the plates, to compliments from around the table. Adam joined her and as they went out to the kitchen to collect the dessert, Dave continued the tale; "So, Bill found the shoe and the piece of trouser leg the next day. Had his suspicions as to who owned them and as it was winter, was able to find a socked footprint in some damp mud outside Charles's house. I saw him taking photos and measurements of it. He even made a plaster cast and of course he made plenty of noise to ensure that Charles looked out of the window and saw what he was doing, just to give him a good fright. Bill never took the matter any further, but carried on building his stables and never heard anything from the council. So now, Bill and Charles have this sort of love, hate relationship. Well, hate, hate actually. Several days a week Bill goes and sits in his tractor outside Charles's house and tries to intimidate him."

"So that's what he's doing. That's so nuts!" said Lois, "They're both behaving like children aren't they?"

"Oh yes," said Annie, sitting back down, "they are ridiculous."

Annie picked up on the story again as she served dessert, "Bert's told me some pretty strange things that Gill did when she lived here too."

"Bert, who's Bert?" asked Tom.

"Bert and Betty," replied Adam. "a dear old couple, live in the cottage between me, and Jack and Doreen. You must call in Lois, they'd be delighted to meet you." Adam winked at Annie, "Just don't have milk in your tea when you go. That's all I'm saying." Adam gesticulated zipping up his mouth, to emphasise that he would give nothing more away about those particular residents.

"Anyway," said Annie smiling, "as I was saying before I was so rudely interrupted, Tom,"

"Begging yer pardon Ma'am."

"Gill, ex-wife of Old Man Black used to complain about Bert and Betty's cat going into her garden. Bert apologized and said that he really couldn't control where the cat went. When it disappeared for twenty-four hours, Bert went to look for it and heard a loud meowing coming from the Black's garden. She had trapped the cat in a cage and left it in there without food or water. Whether her plan was to leave it 'till it died, who knows? Bert was so angry he called the police, who came and issued her a formal warning. After that, she started collecting up any dog mess she could find and throwing it into Bert and Betty's garden, as a sort of revenge, I suppose."

"Yuck, that's disgusting!" said Lois.

"So," continued Annie, "the years went by and then she disappeared! That's Gill, not the cat. One day she was here and then no one saw her again. Charles got a skip, threw all her belongings into it and that was that. One day Richard plucked up the courage to ask Charles where she was, and he said he would rather not talk about it."

"Adam, you said you thought she'd run off with some fancy man from her aerobics class, didn't you?" asked Mel.

"I did, yes. That's the rumour, but I don't know where it came from."

"I think he murdered her!" said Dave, in a determined voice. "I think he murdered her and buried her in the footings of Richard and Debbie's extension and that's why he never objected to their planning application. I think he suffocated her, dragged her to the shed, chopped her up into little bits and put them into bin liners."

"Oh Dave, stop it!" squeaked Lois.

"Well, the cement was poured late on a winters evening and I reckon, when the builders had gone and Debs and Richard were inside, he pushed the bags into the cement!"

"Mm, well done Sherlock. How are you going to gather your evidence? Knock down Richard and Debbie's house and rip out the footings?" asked Tom.

Dave sipped his wine. "Maybe I should conduct my own investigation. Hey, my new job could be as a private detective. 'The Mystery of the Disappearing Old Witch' could be my first case."

The conversation continued into the early hours, very little being given away about any of the other neighbours. Lois and Tom who were both exhausted, said their goodnights and made their way upstairs.

As they climbed into bed, Lois was very relieved to see Tom smiling. "Well, it's quite a place you've persuaded me to move to, isn't it? I hope the rest of the residents are going to be more friendly than Mr Black eh?"

10

Lois and Tom went back to London on Sunday evening, having spent a very busy day trawling around the DIY and bathroom shops, in a successful mission to order what was necessary. The good news was that their taste, in bathrooms at least, was very similar and they were both pleased with their order, an Edwardian style suite, more or less in keeping with the age of the cottage.

Once back at the flat, they sat and made yet another list. Annie had been left in charge of the giant key so she could let Dean in, enabling Lois to stay at the flat on Monday morning and make use of the computer and home phone. Lois was so excited about the cottage she could barely force herself to go to bed.

"I mustn't forget, I need to ring the office and HR tomorrow and discuss my planned retirement!"

"Don't say 'I mustn't forget', always say 'I must remember', otherwise you're sending the wrong message to your subconscious." grinned Tom.

"Oh whatever!" said Lois, "I'll write myself a note to make sure I don't forget anyway. Hey, you've done really well today, how are your ribs now?"

"Do you know, they're feeling amazingly good; there's still a dull ache, but the sharp nerve pain has gone. Interesting isn't it? I expect they would have got better by now anyway, but they do seem to have improved dramatically over the course of the weekend."

"Yes, since Saturday afternoon? Anyway, as you say, they would probably have got better anyway."

Next morning, Tom dragged himself off to work and Lois settled into ticking the items off her list. Firstly she rang Adrienne, who was happy to tie up any of Lois's loose ends at work. They arranged to meet for an early breakfast later in the week. Then she called the HR department, who agreed that she didn't have any notice to serve once her annual leave was taken into account. Only then did she ring the office. She would have felt guilty if it had been Justin that she needed to speak to, but much to her relief, Ian answered Justin's phone. Lois explained the situation and said that she would make the appropriate hand-overs. Ian sounded as disgruntled as she would have expected, but she took little notice, she was feeling very excited.

Following the call, Lois checked the phone was disconnected properly, then shouted "YES!" and started dancing round the room, rubbing her tummy and singing, "No more work for us, Pumpkin, no more work for us!"

The morning passed quickly, very quickly. Lois worked her way through her list slowly, very slowly. The telecom company's call centre in Delhi passed her from pillar to post and cut her off several times, which is something she should have taken into account before estimating how many jobs she would get done in a morning. Lois was very impressed with the fact she stayed calm. There was much controlled sighing and she ate her way through half a packet of very old bourbon biscuits; but she was totally in control of her temper, if not the phone call. The good news was that Tom had recently invested in a house phone with a loudspeaker function and a handy clip, which she attached to the top of her T-shirt. This meant that she could deal with the telecom company whilst simultaneously attempting to encourage her pixie haircut to look more pixie, less hedgehog, putting on her make-up, making tea, opening biscuit packets and looking up information on the Internet, without getting a crick in the neck.

Organising a 'man with a van' to move them, proved to be much easier. She tried two phone numbers she found on the Internet and two from the local free paper that had been posted through the door on Friday. Ed was the least complicated of the four. He popped in at eleven o'clock and made a quick assessment of what the job involved. Opening the road map he'd brought with him to plan a route, he said he'd 'come a week Fursday wiv free blokes and do the packin'. It would only take a few 'ours. Den come back first fing Friday and load up de van.' He reckoned they'd be all moved in and unpacked by lunchtime. Ed suggested four hundred pounds in cash and Lois said that would be great and she'd see him on Thursday. After he'd gone, Lois thought she probably should have taken some credentials from him; Tom wouldn't be overly impressed if he and his chums loaded up the van and then disappeared with all their belongings. "Oh well, hey ho!" she said out loud, shrugging her shoulders.

By the end of the morning Lois felt an urgent need to go to the cottage and see how Dean was getting on. She packed a large suitcase with clothes, toiletries, hairdryer, phone, (just in case the telecom company got its act together), mobile, laptop, camera, and a multitude of chargers. She finished packing the case, managed to force it shut, went to take it to the front door and realised it was far too heavy for her to manoeuvre. She found another bag to empty the heavier stuff into and congratulated herself on, once again, being very well organised.

She was about to leave the flat when Tom rang, "Hi Lo, just a quickie. Did you remember to pack me some clothes, so I can go straight to the cottage from work?"

"Yes, yes, just finished packing your case," Lois lied, "Everything pretty well under control here, just about to leave!"

They said their goodbyes and just as Lois was about to hang-up, Tom said quietly, "Remember to pack my bag Lo!" and disconnected the call. Lois smiled, how did he know? She returned to the bedroom, dragged a small suitcase out of the wardrobe and quickly packed what she felt would be necessary for him for the next few days. She took one case at a time out to the car, which fortunately, was parked unusually close to the flat. It was a bit of a struggle, fitting everything into the MG, but eventually she was away. She smiled all the way from Islington to Harewood Park.

By the time Lois arrived, it was half past three. There was a skip on the front drive, already containing several carpets and the Lino from both the kitchen and bathroom. As Lois came into the house she was surprised to hear radio four blaring from a small radio tucked behind the stairs. She heard Dean shouting instructions to two men, who were carrying the old bath down the spiral staircase. Lois briefly introduced herself to them. They managed to pant out their names. They were both apparently called Martin. One of them chuckled breathlessly, "We're the House Martins!"

As soon as they were out of the way, Lois went upstairs to see how much progress had been made. The toilet and basin had been disconnected and in no time the House Martins were back upstairs to remove them. The floorboards throughout the upstairs were all in good condition and amazingly, no woodworm in sight. Dean was really excited by this; he liked the idea of sanding down and varnishing them. Lois wasn't so sure. In London, in a flat, it was a great idea. But in a cottage, bare floorboards didn't seem cosy enough and Lois didn't like the thought of a baby crawling on them. But she just told Dean she thought leaving them exposed sounded like a great idea and she'd talk it through with Tom – she could then disagree by proxy.

Lois suggested making tea. Both the Martins asked for a cup of hot water for their herbal bags, of which they had brought a selection, and Dean asked for a pint of water. Lois was astonished. She hid the kilo of granulated sugar that she'd bought to cope with the needs of the builders at the back of the cupboard and briefly contemplated giving up sugar herself. She shrugged, put two rounded teaspoons into her large cup of strong tea, and then added another one for luck.

The four of them sat in the garden and discussed progress. Dean told Lois he had delegated the tiling to a friend, whom he'd arranged to come the following Monday to tile the kitchen and dining room floors, and the bathroom floor and necessary walls; he explained that it was a job best left to a specialist. He'd also organised an electrician with whom he'd worked before, to come and quote for rewiring the cottage; telling Lois that although a little expensive, this chap was very good and that electrics were definitely not something to skimp on. He then handed her an approximate cost that Danny the electrician had come up with. Lois was horrified, five thousand pounds, for such a small cottage? She felt it was far too much.

"When can he start?" Lois asked, tentatively.

"Tomorrow, he's between jobs at the moment and would just have time to fit it in. I doubt you'll find a much better quote Lois; electrics are expensive."

Lois wasn't surprised the man was between jobs, charging prices like that. Her intuition was to give Danny a miss, or at least get some more prices for the rewiring job. She told Dean that she would see if she could use Annie's computer to organise some more quotes, at which point Dean offered to make a couple more phone calls to people he knew.

Lois phoned Annie at work to explain the problem and ask if she could use the computer. "No need!" said Annie, chirpily, "I know just the man. I'll call him now and see if he can pop round, I'll let you know. His name's George by the way; lives in the village."

At five o'clock, George, a man in his sixties, arrived. He'd done all the electrical work for Richard and Debbie's extension and was the electrician at the manor. He and his son would work in the evenings, starting the next day, from four 'til seven and Saturday if necessary, and his quote was less than half that of Danny's. Lois felt very smug and jokingly wondered how to spend the money she'd saved.

George gave her a list of items to buy and told her where to go for them. She felt surprisingly relieved to have a defined task for the next morning. No sooner had George left, than Dean gave her a list of plumbing fittings that he would need for the following day.

"The other thing is paint for the bathroom. I presume you're not renewing the skirting and architrave, are you?"

"Gosh, I haven't given that any thought, would it look okay if it was just painted over?"

"Yeah, that'll be fine. But the window ledge, you've got some rot in there. Are you planning to change the windows, get some proper double glazing in?" The cottage had wooden, Georgian style windows, which had seen better days. Some of them were secondary 'glazed' with sheets of Perspex.

They both went upstairs and did an inspection of all the wood in the bathroom. The window ledge was definitely rotten and would have to be replaced. Lois and Tom had discussed a budget within which to keep this first renovation;

they planned to extend the cottage later and luxuries like double glazing would have to wait until then, it was bad enough adding the electrics into the current equation.

"We'll just repaint the skirting and bits," said Lois, "The windowsill, I'll have a think about. Tom's Dad's very good at woodwork, maybe he'd be able to do something with it."

"Oh, I've just remembered, Lois. There was a scratching coming from the loft earlier. I had a look and found you'd caught a glis glis. Very naughty!" Lois blushed; worried that Dean might report them for setting a trap. "So I whacked it on the head, put it out for the kites and reset the trap for you, okay?"

"Thanks Dean," said Lois, relieved.

They discussed the paints that Lois needed to buy, at which point she began to realise that she was going to be very busy over the next few weeks, just shopping for materials.

Tom arrived at the cottage as Dean left. He'd picked up a takeaway on the way home, which they sat and ate on the floor of the living room, propped up against the wall. They filled each other in on the day's events, then Tom cautiously slipped into the conversation that Pippa and Chris, his parents, were coming for a visit to help out, tomorrow.

"Tomorrow!" wailed Lois, turning white, "Oh God, how am I going to feed them? Entertain them? I'll be out shopping for most of the morning. Oh Tom, I really wish you hadn't invited them without asking me!"

"Well, they sort of invited themselves, actually. It'll be fine Lo, Crapper will bring enough lunch for the whole street and Piss'll work in the garden. They'll be a great asset, you'll see!"

"And please, stop calling them that, one of these days…"

"I know, I know, one of these days you will accidentally call them Crapper and Piss to their faces and it will all be frightfully embarrassing! I think not actually Lo, the most casual you've been in addressing my parents is calling them Mr and Mrs A"

"Well maybe not, but imagine how awful it would be!"

"Oh, they've heard it all before. Joe used to call them that all the time, in front of his friends, and theirs very often. They sort of got used to it."

Joe was Tom's older brother, who, having been a bit of a wild youth, was now, allegedly, growing up. He was married, living in St Albans, working as an estate agent and had a baby due within a couple of months.

"Well can you please ring them and let them know they'll have to take care of themselves, for the morning at least."

Lois and Tom had decided to stay at their own cottage that night, despite Annie kindly offering for them to sleep next door. Annie had looked stressed that morning and Dave, having said he would call round and check the glis glis trap, had not materialised. He had apparently been meeting with his accountants during the afternoon. Lois felt they probably needed their own space; anyway they would be fine in Honeysuckle now Tom's ribs were feeling so much better.

As there was no usable bathroom, they used the outside toilet, which was attached to the utility room, accessible from the yard by the back door. Then they washed at the kitchen sink.

In the middle of the night, Lois tried desperately to ignore the need to go for a wee. Getting up in the night had become an ever-increasing habit over the past few weeks of the pregnancy. She really didn't want to have to make her way to the outside loo. She contemplated crouching over the open pipe that was left where the bathroom toilet had been, but decided it was probably going to cause more problems than it would solve. So, torch in hand, she made her way down the wooden treads of the spiral staircase, through the kitchen, out of the back door and into the toilet. She left the door open to let the three-quarter moon shine in. From where she sat, she had a perfect view of the garden and watched, in disbelief, as a barn owl swooped down into the long grass of the 'lawn', disappeared momentarily, then flew off to the silver birch in the centre of the garden with a mouse in its beak and proceeded to eat it.

Lois sat for some time, absolutely mesmerised, to start with by the owl, then once it had flown away, by the sheer beauty of the night. She could hear Tom calling to see if she was all right. He'd also got up to pee and of course had

81

managed very well with just a pipe, but was wondering what was taking her so long. Lois called him down, she wouldn't have woken him to see it, what with having to go to work the next day, but since he was awake anyway …

The pair of them sat on the small, crumbling, garden wall for about twenty minutes, until cloud had partially hidden the moon and the first drops of rain started to fall. They didn't talk; they just watched, listened and absorbed the beauty and tranquillity of the night.

As they climbed back into bed, Tom suggested perhaps they should leave the lawn long to encourage wildlife. Lois laughed and told him he wasn't going to get out of his gardening jobs that easily and pre-empted his next question by saying no, they didn't need, nor could they afford, a ride on lawnmower.

11

The next morning, Lois and Tom both woke early and had a strip wash at the kitchen sink, standing on one of Annie's old towels that Lois had, thus far, failed to return. Tom seemed to be adapting very well to having his arm in plaster. It was much easier to get on with everyday routines now that he had jettisoned the sling. Lois helped him wash the bits that were too painful for him to reach, admiring the various shades of bruising interspersed about his torso.

Tom went off to work, wishing her luck with his parents, which made Lois scowl her goodbye. She tidied up as well as she could, left the back door open for Dean and made for the electrical and plumbing wholesalers, as instructed.

She got back at ten o'clock to find Chris and Pippa's estate car parked on the lane outside the cottage, the boot of which had been left open. On seeing this, Lois was reminded that Pippa would have brought countless bits of tat for her and Tom and expect her to examine them all at length, despite the fact that she had a million things to sort out.

Lois took a deep breath, got out of the car and made her way to the house, reminding herself what helpful, loving and caring people they were. She said how lovely it was to see them, hugged Chris and tried to hug Pippa, but she was too busy thrusting a large plastic crate, overflowing with newspaper articles and old magazines at her.

The first three articles Lois glanced at had the headlines, 'Don't Invest in Property Now!' 'Moving to the Country is so Last Year!' and 'The Curse of the Chiltern Glis Glis.' Well that was enough for Lois; she firmly put the basket in the corner of the room and told Pippa she would read them all later. At which point Pippa handed over her next 'presents', gardening gloves, a trowel and a pair of secateurs. Now, under other circumstances, Lois would have taken these gifts as a personal affront; she had a habit of translating Pippa's acts of kindness into a criticism of her own ability to function as a grown-up; so bringing some gardening tools would be pointedly indicating that Lois knew nothing about gardening.

But, since she did know absolutely nothing about gardening and, more importantly, these items might just keep Pippa out of her hair for the afternoon, Lois thanked her warmly.

"And," said Pippa walking towards the front door, "I've made a lovely quiche for lun… ah, get away, get away you horrible dogs!" she shrilled. Lois and Chris followed her out to see Annie's dogs Reaver and Rupert just finishing up the remains of the 'lovely quiche' in the boot of the car. As Pippa ran towards them, waving her arms and yelling, the dogs jumped nonchalantly out; Rupert burped his appreciation, while Reaver slunk off with a knowing look of 'Oops I think we're in trouble.' Raucous laughter emanated from the open bedroom window where the House Martins were lapping up the entertainment.

At that moment Annie emerged from her driveway and walked towards the car, with the dogs peering out sheepishly from behind her. Lois didn't know what to say, so decided to introduce everyone as if nothing untoward had happened. But before she had opened her mouth, Pippa said, very accusingly, "Are they yours?" Annie nodded, assuming she was going to be complimented on her lovely dogs. "They ate my quiche!"

"I'm sorry?" said Annie, looking confused.

"They climbed into the back of our car and they ate my quiche!" Annie, seeing the House Martins leaning out of the bedroom window laughing, thought it must be a joke and started to smile. Then she saw the look of disgust on Pippa's face, apologised profusely and said she would drive to the village and buy a replacement.

Pippa turned away sulkily; clearly nothing shop-bought was going to be a match for her homemade dish. She never had liked dogs. Lois mouthed to Annie not to worry, but Annie said she would go to the village straight away.

On returning to the house, Lois decided it was time to get Pippa involved in the garden. "Mrs A, how would you feel about making a start on tackling the jungle at the back of the house?"

"Yes, I can do that for you Lois," said Pippa, smugly. "Come and tell me where you'd like me to make a start." The two of them walked out into the back garden. Pippa looked quite taken aback by the state of it, "Oh my, it's lucky I like a challenge! I'm not sure the trowel's going to be too useful at this stage, eh Lois?" she chuckled. "What tools have you got here?"

"Do you know Mrs A, I'm not sure we've got anything other than what you've brought with you, but let's go and check the garden shed and see if anything's been left."

The two women waded through the long, thick grass, interspersed with the odd nettle and thistle, to the shed. Lois trampled down the smaller weeds around the door and opened it gingerly, praying she wasn't going to come face to face with rodents of any description. She gazed in silent astonishment. She'd hoped that there might be a few rusty old garden implements, enough to keep Mrs A busy for the remainder of the day. But what she actually found was a shed full of brightly coloured, pristine looking tools and garden machinery, and a shelf, upon which sat four garden gnomes, a packet of Rizlas and a box of matches.

"Wow! That's amazing! Mrs Smith's relatives must have forgotten this lot when they came to clear out."

"Let's make the most of it shall we?" said Pippa, donning the gardening gloves and grabbing a big branch lopper. "Okay Lois, you get on with your jobs, leave the garden to me!"

Lois walked back towards the house, surprisingly impressed with Pippa's gung-ho attitude. En-route, she decided to make a detour to the outside loo. As she sat, she puzzled over the shed full of goodies. The tools and machinery, she sort of understood, an oversight on the part of the greedy relatives. But the gnomes were a bit odd, they looked brand new; why would anyone buy four garden gnomes and leave them in a shed? She decided the most likely explanation was an unwanted gift and decided not to give them any more thought.

Emerging from the toilet, Lois could see Pippa giving the brambles at the bottom of the garden hell. Seeing Lois out of the corner of her eye, Pippa called out to her, asking if she'd noticed if there was a scythe. Lois walked back across the grass, meeting Pippa by the shed door. "No, I don't think so," she said, glancing around, "there's a petrol strimmer though and a chainsaw … would you like to have a go with those?" she gave her mother-in-law a joking nudge.

"Oh yes!" came the response, Pippa looking more animated than Lois had ever seen her, "I've always fancied trying out some decent garden machinery."

Lois hoped she was joking, but wasn't sure, so decided the best thing to do was to send Chris out to keep things under control. Returning to the house, Lois was delighted to find him squatting on the floor, with what looked very much like a cardboard template for a windowsill in front of him. Dean had apparently shown him the problem in the bathroom and Chris had taken it upon himself to sort it out.

"Hope you don't mind me taking this job on board Lois, you know how I love a bit of woodworking."

"That's great Mr A, thanks. But I would also be very grateful if you would go out in the garden and supervise your wife with the garden machinery; I'm a bit worried she's going to bite off more than she can chew." The proverb made Lois feel sick as one of Pippa's limbs being mangled up in the chainsaw sprang to her mind.

"Oh God. Well it wouldn't be the first time." Chris got up and marched out to the garden with an uncharacteristic look of determination on his face.

Lois went into the front garden with the paint colour charts and shortlisted the paints she liked. She was planning an escape for the afternoon. Buying paints for the entire house could keep her out for some time.

Mel had suggested one particular paint manufacturer, saying the paint was expensive, but worth the extra cost. Lois looked at their chart first, but seeing paint names like 'Dead Trout', 'Rhinoceros Breath' and 'Churlish Taupe', she decided to give them a miss. She couldn't imagine telling her friends they'd painted the dining room in Dead Trout.

She looked at all the charts at length, wanting to be daring with colour, but feeling that perhaps she wasn't quite brave enough. She called Tom, to get his opinion. He was in the middle of an important meeting and was quite cross that Lois had asked his PA to call him out. "We can discuss this later Lo, I can't do it now. Anyway Dean's not going to be painting the rest of the house until next week, why the need to buy the paints today? …Oh, I get it; you want to go out. Well you'll have to find something else to go out for; leave the paints for today. Love you!" and he was gone.

Lois felt momentarily despondent, but was quickly distracted by the sound of a loud mechanical noise coming from the back garden and went to investigate. There, was sixty-five year old Pippa, all five foot three of her, wielding an enormous strimmer at anything and everything that got in her way. As Chris walked past, he said, "I tried Lois, I tried, but she is a very determined woman, Tom's mother. I'm going in, I can't bear to watch! Oh and Lois, don't go within ten foot of her, will you." Lois decided she really couldn't watch either and as she couldn't buy paints today, she would instead, go and register with the local GP. She would be due for her next antenatal appointment in a couple of weeks, so it was something she needed to do. She told Chris and Dean where she was going, said she wouldn't be long and disappeared.

Lois returned an hour later to find everyone out in the back garden, about to have a picnic. Pippa had, much to everyone's amazement, successfully strimmed a large area of the lawn and raked the trimmings into a pile for burning. Annie had delivered the most fantastic assortment of picnic food, bought from the deli in town, presumably at great expense, as a peace offering for Pippa. Lois pulled her to one side. "Annie, this must have cost a fortune, you didn't have to do this; she would have forgiven you…eventually!" The two of them started laughing.

"I can't believe the dogs did that, they don't usually steal."

"I don't suppose they usually have a meal left so accessible to them either," said Lois, as she squeezed a twenty-pound note from her purse into Annie's hand. Annie tried half-heartedly to refuse, but Lois insisted she take it, much to Annie's relief; she really was trying to hang on to every penny.

"Come along Lois, Annie, do come and eat!" called Pippa, adopting an exaggerated upper class accent. She seemed to be brimming over with enthusiasm generated by her successful morning of gardening. "Look, sit on one of the rugs I brought with me, I knew they'd come in useful. Are you all right on the floor Lois, or would you prefer a chair? Of course I never made a fuss about being pregnant, but you never know how other people deal with such situations," she said, giving Annie a knowing glance. As she looked away, Annie and Lois looked at each other, both raised their eyes to heaven and stifled giggles while Chris shook his head, which he'd buried in his hands.

The lunch was delicious. Lois and Annie cleared away as quickly as possible and Pippa went straight back to strimming. Dean called to Lois as Annie left, wanting to discuss what she wanted doing, if anything, with the spiral staircase.

Lois had already expressed her opinion of the staircase to Dean. It was the one thing about the cottage, other than the bathroom suite and the décor, which she really didn't like. "I've looked into replacing it with a conventional staircase, but under present day regulations there isn't space for one," Dean said, as the two of them stood contemplating the sixties monstrosity. Lois's face dropped with this news. "But I do have an idea," said Dean, looking uncharacteristically excited.

"Go on," said Lois, not convinced that anything could transform the hideous thing stood before her into something she'd like. The staircase consisted of a cream coloured metal central pole, stair supports and uprights supporting the handrail. The handrail itself was covered in black plastic; the stair treads were wooden with large 'ornamental' bolts on the underside and, to top it all, there were huge gaps between the uprights, making it a potential death trap for children.

"Well, first we take the plastic off the hand rail, then paint the whole thing matt black, including the steps. Then I get this special metallic powder paint and scumble glaze, dab it all over, varnish over the top and Bob's your uncle, you've got a cracking centre piece for your living room. Oh, and I think I can get some swirly fillers very reasonably too, we'll decorate them the same way and weld them in place."

"I can't imagine it'll transform it that much, but I'll leave it to you Dean, whatever you think. Give me a list and I'll go shopping."

"Eager to get out the house again, are we Lois?" Dean laughed, glancing out of the window at Pippa, who was trying her best to start up the chainsaw.

"No, whatever gave you that idea?" Lois smiled, thrusting a note pad and pen into his hand and gesticulated for him to get writing. The moment he put the pen down, she thanked him, grabbed the list and her bag and quickly exited the house. As she went out of the front door, Pippa came in through the back, asking where Lois was - she needed petrol for the chainsaw. Lois's MG flew down the bumpy track just as Dean was apologising for the fact that Pippa had just missed her.

Whilst in town, Lois got a phone call from Tom, "Hi Lo, I'm so sorry about earlier, I was in a really stressful meeting." Lois was quite surprised; Tom generally wasn't one for apologies. He went on to say, "And for leaving you to deal with my parents single-handedly. I left the office early, so I'll be home within half an hour and able to give you some support."

"Okay, that's great," Lois paused, still feeling slightly taken aback, "I'm just finishing off the shopping, see you there." She hung up and slipped the phone into her pocket. As she ambled around the DIY shop, it suddenly occurred to Lois that Pippa might have borrowed some petrol from one of the neighbours. She was struck by a hideous vision of Tom arriving home to a scene resembling the Texas Chainsaw Massacre, blood and limbs scattered over the back lawn and her being to blame. She gathered the last two items on Dean's list and raced to the checkouts, where the queues were long. Lois started to tap her foot impatiently as she waited. She heard an ambulance siren outside and immediately imagined it was on the way to their house to collect up the limbs and torsos of Pippa and her accidental victims. She huffed and puffed, wondering whether to abandon the shopping to another time. As the manager passed by, she said, "Would Madam care to use one of the self check-outs, if Madam's in a hurry?"

"Oh, yes," said Lois, feeling somewhat embarrassed, "I hadn't noticed them."

For once, she managed to make the checkout machine beep first time for all her items, paid and made for home. Ridiculous images of the disaster awaiting her pounded her mind. Tom, blaming her for the death of his parents; their life together finished; being alone for the birth of the baby; a single mum.

In tears as she passed the manor, Lois rounded the bend to see Tom in the distance, attempting to hug his mother and then shaking hands with his father. She breathed an enormous sigh of relief, delved into her bag for a tissue and carefully dabbed her eyes.

The remainder of the afternoon was spent with Lois, Tom and his parents doing what they could with the back garden. Tom wasn't at all worried about his mother with the strimmer from the point of view of injuries, either to herself or to others; he was more concerned that in her enthusiasm she would damage the machine. He thought it was great that she was tough enough to handle it, and Lois had to admit that Pippa had made a huge impact on the garden. Lois and Chris had a go at tackling the brambles while Tom supervised and occasionally pulled out a weed. Lois snuck into the shed early on, when no one was looking, removed the chainsaw and hid it between the back of the shed and a large shrub. She had a horrible feeling that Tom would be desperate for a go with it, despite his injuries.

Late in the afternoon, Pippa and Lois between them raked the rest of the grass cuttings onto the existing heap, and Tom went and borrowed some petrol and matches from Dave. "It's a bit gusty for that, guv'nor!" George called as he walked around the back of the house, just as Tom was removing the cap from the petrol can.

"Do you think so?" Tom licked his finger, boy-scout style, to test the direction of the wind. Thinking that George was meaning the fire might damage the silver birch, he ignored the comment; the wind was blowing in completely the opposite direction. As he chucked petrol onto the heap of grass, a fair gust blew some back, significantly spattering Tom's trousers and the ground between him and the heap. 'Oh well, I've got a change of clothes upstairs,' he thought; lit a match and threw it onto the fire. In a flash, the petrol caught alight, as did the grass on the heap, the grass still attached to the ground, and Tom's trousers.

"Help!" Tom shouted, and, adrenalin-fuelled, started running towards the house shouting, "Help, I'm on fire!" Fortunately, George, who'd had a similar experience as a youth, had been watching from the kitchen window, he'd already found a bucket and filled it with water, just in case. On seeing Tom, flames licking up towards his crotch, George shot from the kitchen with the bucket and threw its contents at Tom, successfully drowning the flames.

Lois, who had run faster up the garden than she would have thought possible, stood looking at Tom in disbelief, her heart pounding. "Bloody hell, Tom!" was all she could say at first. Then she managed, "Are you okay?" he nodded, looking very shocked. Chris retrieved the bucket from George, filled it from the outside tap and went and stood over the bonfire in an attempt to make sure nothing else went wrong. Pippa who had been strimming throughout the entire crisis, carried on, blissfully unaware.

When Lois had calmed down, she thanked George for his quick response and led Tom by the hand into the kitchen, where she made him take off his dripping trousers and toss them into the sink. Then she took him upstairs, looked his legs over closely and was astonished to see that they looked fine. "Are you in pain?" she asked. Tom was still in shock and just shook his head, numbly. "And to think it was your mum I was worried about…" Lois said, shaking her head in amazement that he would do something so stupid.

Unfortunately, although he had apparently suffered no burns, the dousing had turned Tom's plaster into a soggy mess, resulting in a trip to casualty.

The department was hideously busy, but as Tom only needed a cast replacement, the plaster technician managed to fit him in almost straight away. "How did you manage to get it so wet?"

Tom went red and glanced at Lois. "Uh, someone accidentally threw a bucket of water at me?"

"Yeah right, whatever," said the technician, knowing from Tom's tone and the lingering smell of petrol, that he wasn't telling the whole story; but he didn't delve any further. As he finished applying the new cast, he said, "Well, whatever happened, don't do it again!"

"Don't worry," said Tom smirking, "I won't."

By the time Lois and Tom got back to the cottage, George and son had left. Pippa and Chris, who'd been resting on the blow-up mattress, got up to welcome them home. "Perfect timing," said Chris, "just booked a table at the restaurant in the village, Chez somebody or other. I was hoping you wouldn't be long; we're starving! So, a nice meal and we'll be off home."

"Perfect!" said Lois and Tom in unison.

12

Tuesday had a very much more relaxed feel about it, without Pippa and Chris being there. Dean had put the first coat of black paint on the staircase by mid-morning. The House Martins had completed the wallpaper stripping upstairs and prepared the walls for painting. There were several areas in all the rooms which appeared to have needed patches of re-plastering, Lois didn't ask why, she suspected it was due to the House Martins over enthusiasm in their wall paper scrapings. Anyway, it all looked fine now.

Lois went out and bought the paints that she and Tom had decided on the previous evening, tucked up in their blow-up bed. Having presented them to one of the Martins, she decided that her priority for the rest of the day should be to meet one of the previously unmet sets of neighbours.

Lois was not born gregarious, but during her working life she had gradually increased in confidence, to the extent that she felt able, with a small amount of internal coaxing, to go and knock on the door of one of the houses and introduce herself. Which one to choose though, that was tricky? Lois had written down the names of all the cottages in a little notebook and had filled in any details she knew about the residents living in them.

"Rose, Bramble or Holly?" she called to Dean.

"Rose."

"Right, Rose it is!" and off she went, Dean completely oblivious as to what was going on.

It was a beautiful sunny day. Lois was wearing a pair of lightweight cotton shorts and a vest top stretched over her bump and was still very hot as she walked up the lane. Rupert and Reaver caught sight of her and came trotting up, both curling their bodies to the left as they wiggled a greeting. Lois fussed them briefly, and then told them she had to get on; she was on a mission.

On arrival at Rose Cottage, Lois impatiently negotiated the ancient garden gate, which looked as if it could well be the same age as the Victorian cottage to which it was the portal. Struggling with the rusted latch, she pushed and kicked to gain entry. The gate looked even more warped when she attempted to close it. She guiltily stroked it in an unconscious attempt to make it better. Then, realising what she was doing, glanced round to see if anyone was watching and hurried off towards the house.

The cottage looked tiny from the front, squashed between Bramble and Primrose. It had an ancient looking rose creeping up the brickwork by the front door and covering most of the front of the cottage. Lois thought how nice it was to have the namesake of the house so obvious and made a mental note to plant a honeysuckle in their front garden. A passageway ran to the left of the house, giving access to the garden. Lois knocked enthusiastically on the rather tired-looking front door using the tarnished doorknocker. She felt far less anxious than she'd been when calling to introduce herself to Doreen and Jack; having had Bert and Betty described as 'a sweet elderly couple' … there couldn't be too many surprises behind this door.

After a few moments, Lois heard a loud man's voice issuing from some way behind the door. "Come in, come in, door's open; give i' a shove!"

Lois tentatively pushed the door, wondering, as she did so, whether Bert and Betty were also disabled. The door opened a little way, then stopped, as if something, or someone, was blocking it. The voice returned, "Come on in, give it a good push, who are you?"

She pushed the door harder and poked her head around it, calling out, "Hello there! I'm Lois, I've just moved into…" But, as her eyes saw what was in front of her, Lois's mouth momentarily seized up. The front door opened straight into, what presumably would have been the living room, but cardboard boxes and crammed bin-liners filled the space, more-or-less from floor to ceiling. That is, except for a tiny passageway down the side, less than two feet wide. Even that was flanked with piles of books to hip height; papers, magazines, old milk cartons and all sorts of other rubbish littered the space, mounding up to a couple of feet high at one point. Lois pulled herself together on noticing the little man, presumably Bert, standing at the other end of the passage, "ummm…into Honeysuckle, I've, we've, that's me and Tom, my boyfriend," Lois, suddenly worried that co-habiting might offend him, said, "husband, yes, husband, we've just moved in, wanted to come and introduce myself." Lois stopped, realising she was having acute verbal diarrhoea.

"Come on in love," called Bert, "steady as you go." With that, he turned and walked in the opposite direction. Lois pushed the door open a bit further to allow her body to follow her head and wondered how best to tackle the obstacle course that lay before her.

She was relieved that there was enough light coming through the glass panels of the front door for her to see the brown banana skin and the hole created by a missing floorboard, before they caused her a problem. Slowly and carefully she scaled the mountain of papers, supporting herself with her right hand on the wall and her left on the surprisingly solid barricade of boxes and bin liners.

As she approached, what appeared to be the kitchen, Lois heard a little voice call out, "Hello dear, come on in."

The kitchen floor, much to Lois's relief, was not strewn with debris. There were however, mounds of pots and pans covering the surfaces, interspersed by cutlery and crockery. Bluebottles were lazily buzzing around the unwashed utensils heaped up in the sink. When the smell of rancid milk hit Lois, she thought she was going to be sick; but determination not to embarrass herself, or her hosts, took over and she forcefully swallowed it back down.

"Where are you Love?" called the little voice. Lois turned to see a tiny lady sitting in a small alcove, set to the side of the kitchen. She was holding out her hands towards Lois, her eyes milky white with cataracts. Lois introduced herself, taking the waiting, cold hands in her own. Bert meanwhile, struggled to pull a fold-up chair from between the fridge and dresser, then using it as a walking support he hobbled over to where Lois stood and unfolded it for her.

"Here you are love, you sit opposite Betty, she'll 'ear you better then." Lois thanked him and sat down. "Right, I'll get the kettle on. Nice cuppa tea?"

Lois, remembering the advice Adam had given her at the dinner party and the stench that had hit her as she came into the kitchen, which amazingly, she seemed to be growing accustomed to, requested a black tea.

"You youngsters, always worryin' about yer figures. Nearly all our guests have their tea black, don't they Betty? I don't know, really I don't." Bert said, as he shuffled away towards the stove.

Lois turned the best of her attention to Betty, trying not to worry about the cleanliness of the cups. The old lady reminded Lois of a baby dormouse, tiny, curled up and blind; fine wisps of white hair adorned her head and chin. Betty continued to clasp Lois's hands, as if her visitor would vanish if she were to let go. "Now sweet 'eart, what did you say your name was?"

Lois introduced herself again and briefly told Betty about her and Tom's purchase of Honeysuckle, the ensuing renovations and their plan to move in prior to the baby's arrival. On hearing that Lois was pregnant, Betty became very excited. "Oh, such a shame I can't still knit dear."

"Bert!" she called, "when you've made the tea, would you get me old shoebox, so as I can show, sorry love, what did you say your name was?"

"Lois. Sorry, it's quite unusual isn't it?"

"It is love, quite unusual, but I'll get Bertie to write it down, then he can remind me what it is."

Bert arrived with two cups of tea, about a third of each one, sloshing around in its saucer. He put them down on Betty's table, then, one by one, emptied the contents of the saucers back into the cups. Lois got a whiff of the rancid milk from Betty's tea and had to, once again, swallow hard to block the feeling of nausea rising in her throat. She thanked Bert and off he shuffled to find the shoebox.

"He's such a good soul, my Bertie." Betty whispered to Lois. "He looks after me all by 'imself you know. 'E does all the 'ousework and everything." Lois didn't quite know how to respond to that comment, so decided to change the subject.

"So, how did you two meet?"

Betty chuckled. "Well, we met at a dance in the village rooms and got married the following year. I took on a job as a cleaner at the manor, so we worked together an' all, 'cause Bertie was the butler. That was when the big 'ouse was in proper ownership, you know, a family lived there; lovely they were, the Crowthornes. That's 'ow come we live 'ere you see Dear. This was the butler's cottage. These were all worker's cottages, 'oneysuckle was the gardener's."

"Oh wow," said Lois, "I had no idea they were linked to the manor; but of course they were, how stupid of me not to realise."

Betty patted Lois's hand. "Well, it was love at first sight for me and Bert, you know. Married within the year and here we are still, seven'y-odd years later."

"Seventy-odd? Gosh! Do you mind me asking how old you are Betty?"

"Not at all dear. Bert and I are both ninety, give or take; I forget exactly."

"Ninety, gosh, you are both remarkable."

Bert arrived back in the kitchen with the box, which he put down on the table for Betty. "'Ere you are Pet."

"I was just telling the young lady how we met, Bertie."

Bert chuckled as he shuffled out of the room again, "Oh aye, that's goin' back a bit."

"So, you were able to stay on in the cottage when the manor was sold?" asked Lois.

"No; we'd 'ave 'ad to move out. All the cottages were sold when the big 'ouse was. But Bertie, bless 'im, 'ad been puttin' away savings ever since 'e started work. 'E stored a lot of it in paper bags in the loft! 'E saved really 'ard and, much to everyone up the manor's surprise, we bought our little cottage!" Betty smiled broadly, displaying her few remaining teeth.

"Do you mind me asking what you've got in the box Betty?" asked Lois, curiosity getting the better of her.

"Not at all dear." Betty felt for the shoebox in front of her, carefully took off the lid and placed it under the box. Then she slowly felt her way around its contents, smiling as she went. "For a doll's house," said Betty, as she took out a tiny baby's carrycot with the hood up, the inside covered with a minute crocheted blanket. "Bert and I star'ed makin' when we were hoping to 'ave children of our own. He made the 'ouses, beau'iful they were; we've still got one somewhere. Then I'd make the little furnishin's. Course, I could see in them days."

"Ah, it's gorgeous," said Lois, as Betty handed it to her. "How did you make it? It's exquisite."

Betty chuckled to herself, "It's made from a walnut shell. I cut a quarter of it off and then varnished it, looks sweet, don't it?"

"Oh Betty it's beautiful, how clever you are!"

Betty trawled slowly through the box, showing Lois furnishings she'd made from lollipop sticks and toothpicks. Tiny vases with dried flowers in them; although a little squashed, they still looked very sweet. Bert sat himself down next to them and watched the proceedings, looking a little sad. He knew how much Betty missed being able to make things and he missed watching her create such beauty out of so little.

The box was finally packed away. Lois, glancing at her watch, was amazed by how late it was. She made her excuses to leave, adding, "Would you mind me calling in again?"

"We'd be deligh'ed love," said Betty, shaking Lois's hands.

"Okay if I go out through the back door?"

"Of course," said Bert, "and if you come again, you'd best use that one…we'll hear you better."

Arriving back at Honeysuckle, Lois found George and son, getting stuck into sorting out the electrics. She had a quick look around to see what progress had been made. Seeing that the house was now practically uninhabitable, Lois decided to go and beg a bed from Annie and Dave for the next night or two.

Lois knocked at the front door and was greeted by Annie, brandishing a glass of champagne.

"Ah, Lois, good timing! Come on in and help us celebrate." Lois was surprised; she'd been expecting to be encouraging Annie out of an impending poverty-stricken gloom.

"What are we celebrating?" Lois asked, as she gesticulated to Dave that an inch of champagne in the flute was plenty.

"Dave has just been offered a chain of dealerships to manage!" Annie's face was alight with excitement as she grabbed Dave from behind and gave him a bear hug, almost causing him to drop the bottle and glass that he was holding.

"Dave that's amazing, well done. Congratulations!" Lois held up her champagne and the three of them clinked glasses. "Where are they? When do you start?" Annie beckoned Lois out to the garden, grabbing a bowl of cashews on her way. They sat on the patio, Dave filling both the women in on the most interesting details of the offer.

"So, does this mean you don't have to go ahead with selling the paddock and converting the loft?" asked Lois.

"We haven't got as far as discussing that yet," said Dave, still smiling broadly.

"I think it would be good to do the conversion anyway," said Annie. "It'll be an investment for the future ... one never knows what's around the corner."

"That's a good thought," said Dave. "Yes, you're right, let's go for it. You'll have to be in charge though Annie, I won't have much time for organising stuff; I'm going to be far too busy!"

Annie gave Lois a wink, "Oh, I think I'll manage; you'll help me with designs won't you Lois? Perhaps Dean would be able to give a hand with the major work when he's finished your place."

"It'll take time to sort out plans and planning permission though won't it?" asked Lois.

"Planning permission, what planning permission? I think mum'll be the word on that one." Annie tapped the side of her nose.

"What about old Charlie-boy? He's bound to get wind of it and cause problems."

"Oh Lois, where's your sense of adventure? It's all a game you see. I bet you fifty pounds he'll know nothing about it, even when there's a tenant living there."

"You're on!" said Lois. Annie and Lois shook hands, both confident they would win the bet.

13

On Thursday morning Lois was woken at six by sunlight pouring through the window of Annie and Dave's spare-room. Tom was perched on the edge of the bed, supporting his chin in his hands, elbows on the window ledge, gazing out at the view.

"Morning," Lois said, joining him on his perch.

"Good morning to you too, the soon to be Mrs Allan and Master or Miss Allan." He stroked Lois's tummy, Pumpkin responded with a little kick. "Incidentally, when are we getting married?"

"'Incidentally', what sort of an attitude is that?" Lois said, giving Tom a gentle poke. "You have to get down on one knee and beg me first!"

"Oh, is that all?" To Lois's astonishment, Tom proceeded to slowly lower himself onto one knee. She felt her cheeks start to glow red, anticipating the question she'd recently been hoping he'd ask. Unfortunately, Tom was squashed between the bed and radiator; his ribs were better, but not that much better; "Ow!" he grimaced, as he took Lois's hand. "Lois, Lois, will you, please," he paused, "move to the other side of the bed so I can do this properly?"

Lois laughed, "That was a bit of an anti-climax, Tom!"

She moved to the other side, grinning broadly and sat on the edge. Tom lowered himself, once again onto one knee. "Lois, I love you more than pie! Would you do me the honour of becoming my wife, as soon as we can get an appointment at the registry office?"

"Tom you are *so* romantic! How could I refuse? Yes of course I'll marry you, and shall we have the reception at McDonald's?" Lois laughed, "And the ring Tom, I expect you've bought me a beautiful ring?" she added sarcastically, convinced that the thought would not have crossed Tom's mind.

"Now it's funny you should say that Lo," he said, easing himself up and fumbling in the pocket of his jacket, which was hanging over the back of a chair. Lois's heart started to race as he took out a black velvet box and opened it to reveal...a child's ring, silver coloured with a large red stone. Lois didn't know whether to laugh or cry as Tom took her left hand in his plastered one and pushed the ring as far as it would go, which was the first knuckle on her little finger.

"Tom, I'm speechless!"

"Well, Mel and I discussed this. I asked her if she would come and help me choose, but in the end, we both decided you would probably rather make the choice yourself. So I've booked us an appointment at Le Posh Jewellers in Hatton Garden on Saturday, just in case you said yes."

"Wow!" said Lois, amazed. She lay back down in bed, grinning inanely, as Tom started to dress. "So, when are we going to do the deed?"

"Before the Pumpkin's due date I think. Don't you?"

"Sounds good to me!" said Lois, beaming.

Having breakfasted together, Lois and Tom agreed to meet at the flat that evening and Lois waved Tom off. She returned to Annie and Dave's spare room, propped herself up in bed with a note pad and pen and wrote a list for the day, which was of course extended, now that she and Tom were getting married! She practised saying 'Lois Allan' out loud a few times and then tried her new signature, smiling to herself. She and Tom had agreed they were committed to each other about a year after they met, when they decided to move in together. Then Lois had fallen pregnant the month after they'd started trying for a baby and she hadn't, until recently, given a great deal of thought to getting married; the commitment was there after all, what did a piece of paper and a ring mean anyway? But now that Tom had asked her, she was, very excited. "Mrs Allan," she said out loud, just as Annie knocked on the door with a cup of tea in her hand.

Annie looked mystified, "Who were you talking to, Lois? I thought you must be on the phone."

"No, I'm practising my new name. Tom proposed this morning!"

"Oh, congratulations!" Annie gave her a hug, "Actually, I didn't realise you two weren't married. Big white wedding?"

"Well, I'll be big!" Lois smiled, looking at her ever-expanding midriff, "No, it'll be small, just family and close friends."

"Well, if you need help with anything, let me know."

Lois told Annie how Tom had produced the ring box, taking her by surprise, and how it had had a toy ring inside. She laughed as she recalled the story. Annie started to look pensive.

"I remember Dave and I having fun like that, not taking life too seriously. It's sad that things have changed so much."

"What's changed?" asked Lois.

"Well, I suppose I've turned into the proverbial nagging wife and he's responded by becoming a down-trodden husband."

"I can't believe that Annie, you seem to get on fine, you were both great fun at the dinner party."

"Yes, I know, we can be fun and perhaps I'm exaggerating a bit, but, seeing how light hearted you and Tom are, just reminds me of how we used to be. We used to have such a laugh, then the stresses of children, mortgages and money. I don't know, things just slowly change, until, before you know where you are, almost all the fun has gone. I think it's time for me to change my attitude and hopefully if I can stop being so negative, Dave will be more fun again."

"Well, they say being aware is the first step," Lois smiled.

"Yes, perhaps we could start a support group. 'Hello, I'm Annie. I'm a nag. I haven't nagged my husband for twenty-two days.'" They both laughed.

"Good plan and I will always be fun, respectful and never nag, because I will have joined a support group before getting married!"

Annie suddenly noticed the time, said she had to dash and as she left said, "Gosh, I almost forgot, we've all been invited to Debbie and Richard's for dinner on Saturday night. Seven thirty. Hope you can make it!"

Annie disappeared, and Lois finished writing her morning to-do list, which consisted mainly of making phone calls; chasing up the telecoms company, organising a service for the boiler, ordering central heating oil and finding a roofer to come and sort out some loose tiles. She suddenly realised she had a roofer for a neighbour and thought Adam would be sure to do it for her, and maybe not even charge too much. During the afternoon, her plan was to start investigating getting married!

Lois decided she had to approach the dull tasks in a determined fashion, procrastinating was only going to depress her. Positive thinking worked a treat and having successfully completed her list, she locked up Annie's house and went next door to see how things were progressing. She walked through the back door to find the interior of the cottage looking more shambolic than ever; there was a thick layer of dust everywhere and holes in the walls where George and son had been drilling for the new wiring. She walked around checking they had noticed all her wall scribbling, earmarking where she wanted sockets and switches. She was pleased to see that George had added a few, in places she'd overlooked.

The House Martins were busy wallpaper stripping in the dining room. As Lois walked into the lounge, she gasped. Dean was halfway up the stairs, scrutinising his work of the previous afternoon, when he had applied the bronze effect glaze, which had fortunately dried before George had started drilling. The staircase was looking amazing.

"Dean, it looks incredible! Wow, I can't believe it's the same staircase!"

"Yeah, I'm pretty pleased with it myself. Wasn't sure it would work, bit of a gamble, but I think it's going to pay off. I've just got to varnish it now. Best do that when the dust's gone though eh?"

"Good thinking. Thanks so much Dean, it's really great!"

He pointed out a shopping list that George had left. Having perused it briefly, Lois decided to go straight into town. While she was there she made her way to the registry office and organised a meeting to discuss and set a date for the wedding.

She was as high as a kite when she arrived back at the house and decided to pop round and see Doreen and Jack.

Lois walked up the metal ramp to the front door and rang the bell to Bramble Cottage, remembering how apprehensive she'd felt on her first visit. She could hear a lot of shuffling behind the door, which was eventually opened by Jack with help from Ellie, who wiggled her welcome.

"Oh bugger off!" said Jack in enthusiastic recognition, gesticulating to her to come in. He had a lovely smile, albeit a little one sided and his welcome was so heart-felt; Lois felt she may laugh or cry at any moment.

Jack ushered her through to the kitchen. "Oh bugger off?" he asked, air drawing a T shape with his index finger.

"Yes please," said Lois, hoping she'd understood correctly, "Milk, two sugars please. Can I help you make it?"

"Oh bugger off!" said Jack, shaking his head as he skilfully manipulated the electric wheelchair. He pulled a chair part way out from the small kitchen table and offered it to Lois, using his hand and eyes to gesture. The kitchen had been redesigned for Jack's benefit; one of the work surfaces lowered, with a sink, and small hob installed; a kettle, mug rack, and tea and coffee caddies lined up neatly at the back.

Jack put the kettle on, then went to the back door. He unlatched it and without him saying anything, Ellie pulled on a short piece of rope that was tied to the door handle and opened it while Jack used his only functioning hand to manipulate his wheelchair. Once part way through the door, he called out, "Oh bugger off!" in the singsong way one uses to call someone's name. He must have then gesticulated T again, as Doreen's voice came back from the garden, "Ooh, yes please Jack, that would be lovely. I'll be there in one minute." Jack moved away from the door and went to make three cups of tea, while the dog nosed the door shut.

Doreen came in just as Jack was transporting the drinks to the table on a tray attached to his wheelchair.

"Oh hello Lois!" she said, enthusiastically. "How's it going at the cottage?"

Lois brought Jack and Doreen up to speed on the progress at Honeysuckle. She felt very touched that they seemed to have a genuine interest in what was happening in her life.

"We've been so looking forward to an update on the Honeysuckle goings on, haven't we Jack?" said Doreen, with Jack nodding eagerly. "But we don't like to intrude."

"Well, you're both welcome at any time, although, it has to be said, you might not want to call in for the next couple of weeks, the house really is in turmoil and dust everywhere!"

Ellie nosed up to Lois for a stroke, "How long have you had her?" she asked Jack.

"Oh bugger off!" he said, as he held up one finger, then three fingers.

"One year and three months?" asked Lois, hoping she'd interpreted his signals correctly. Jack smiled, nodded and pointed his finger at Lois, to let her know that she'd got it right. Lois felt a huge sense of relief that she was able to understand him, so far anyway.

"And she's specially trained is she, to help you around the house?"

"Oh bugger off!" Jack nodded, enthusiastically.

As they sat and drank their tea, Ellie lay down beside the wheelchair, watching Jack attentively.

"She's changed your life, hasn't she Jack," said Doreen,

"Oooh buugger off!" said Jack, again nodding enthusiastically.

"She looks after Jack, picks things up for him, opens doors, is a constant companion, and in return Jack looks after her, feeds, grooms and walks her. All in all it's a wonderfully symbiotic relationship. You were quite down, weren't you Jack, before Ellie came along,"

"Oh bugger off!" Jack said, tossing his head back and giving a small tut in agreement.

"Then I read in a Sunday supplement about Ability Dogs for Disabled people. There was a whole article on the benefits and what a difference they can make to a person's life. So I rang the charity, not really expecting any joy, what with Jack's communication difficulties;" Jack shook his head with a smile, "but they said that shouldn't be an issue, provided they could find him a dog that could respond to hand gestures and, she does. She's brilliant, aren't you Ellie!" Ellie got up and wiggled her whole body as she approached Doreen for some fuss. "It must be almost time for your walk, Ellie," Doreen said, as she scratched behind the dog's ears. Jack glanced up at the kitchen clock, then, in a similar tone to somebody saying 'Walkies!' said a high-pitched, 'Oh bugger off!' He then waved goodbye, reversed his wheelchair and headed for the backdoor, which Ellie opened, and away they went.

"What an amazing pair they are!" said Lois to Doreen. She paused, and then added, "Do you mind me asking what's wrong with Jack?"

"Not at all, Lois. He had a stroke; let me think, must be nearly three years ago now. We'd not long since retired. He was quite overweight then. He'd been a civil engineer based up in London. It was a stressful job, especially the last five years or so. He smoked a bit, just a few a day … and there you have it Lois, the recipe for an unmitigated disaster. He went shopping in town; I never really got to the bottom of exactly what happened, but received a call from the hospital to say he'd had a stroke and could I come to casualty."

"Oh my God, that must have been awful!" said Lois. But intrigued to learn more, she added, "So, then what happened?"

"Do you want the short or the long version?"

Lois glanced at her watch. Unusually, she was not in a rush and having little knowledge of the effects of stroke, yet being aware that her father was a prime candidate to have one, she was eager for more information. "The long one, if you've got time."

"I have - Jack and Ellie will be out for at least an hour."

Doreen proceeded to explain to Lois, at length, the trauma she experienced in the days, weeks and months following Jack's stroke. She compacted into an hour, Jack's journey through unconsciousness; waking to find he had no function in his left arm, little in his left leg and the horror of being able to utter only one phrase, and that being something he would never have said in his previous life. She recapped on the anger and frustration he suffered, followed by weeks of depression; his rehabilitation and his eventual change in attitude, to make the best of what he had, having seen some patients in the hospital considerably worse off than himself.

107

She finished by telling Lois what modifications to the house had been needed; then suddenly a broad smile stretched across her face.

"This'll make you laugh Lois. Charles Black wrote a letter of complaint to the council saying that the ramp was unsightly and not in keeping with the cottages, miserable old fool. Such a nice man came from the council. He said the ramp was fine and not to worry. On his way out, he went and looked over at Mr Black's property and noticed some severe tree surgery had been done in the front garden. He rang me later to let me know that apparently, Mr Black had not applied for permission to work on the trees and since this is a conservation area, could be fined up to twenty thousand pounds and he would be taking the matter further! Oh I did laugh; I shouldn't I know, but it's not easy, living next door to such a moaner. You're very lucky having Annie and Dave."

As Lois was agreeing with Doreen that she was indeed, very lucky with her neighbours, she glanced at the clock. Astonished to see the time, she thanked Doreen for her tea and said she must get back and check the builders had everything they needed. Doreen apologised for keeping her so long and thanked her for listening.

"Well it's great for me to feel I'm getting to know you both better," said Lois. She hugged Doreen goodbye and walked away contemplating what an extraordinary couple Jack and Doreen were.

A car was approaching as Lois walked towards Honeysuckle. It was a somewhat battered looking, old Peugeot estate. The window opened and the driver, a woman in her fifties, beamed at Lois. She was hugely overweight. Her hair was in a neat bun with grey at the well grown out roots. She had large, baby-pink, plastic rimmed glasses with thick lenses, perched on the end of her nose.

"Hi," said the woman in a higher than expected voice, "are you Lois?" Lois nodded. "Ah, I've been dying to meet you. Heard all about you from Debbie and Richard. I'm Margaret; I live at Holly Cottage, last one in the row. Welcome!" Margaret held out a hand that looked like it was made of Pillsbury dough, and Lois shook it, smiling.

108

"Nice to meet you Margaret, I've been planning to pop up and introduce myself."

Lois thought how uncomfortable she looked in the car. Her short stature necessitating the seat to be forward, wedging her enormous breasts and tummy against the steering wheel. Lois was intrigued to know how she managed to steer.

"You must come round for tea! Are you free now?" said Margaret enthusiastically, as a small red van approached. She glanced in her rear view mirror as Lois was desperately trying to decide whether she could possibly make time for more visiting. "Chazzy!" squealed Margaret. "My husband, oh what good timing Lois!"

Chaz got out of his van just as a horse and rider emerged from the bridleway. The sudden, loud scrunching of hooves on the stony road, making Lois jump. When the girl on the horse called out "Watcher Mate!" Lois realised it was Sicily. She rode up to Chaz, whose stature resembled a very small beanpole and held out her hand for a high five, which Chaz responded to with a hard slap.

"Hi Chazzy," squeaked Margaret from her wedged position. Sicily stopped the horse adjacent to the car. "Hi Sissy, this is Lois, the new neighbour!"

"We've met," said Sicily, grinning at Lois and giving her an encouraging wink.

"Watcha Lo!" bellowed Chaz, with a voice surprisingly deep for a man of his size. "Ow yer doin' Mate, settled in all right 'av yer."

Lois, taken aback by Chaz's accent, responded, "Yes, thank you, we simply love it here." Turning red when she realised how pompous she must have sounded, and Sicily had started to giggle.

"I was just inviting Lois round for tea Chazzy, I've bought a delicious lemon drizzle from Waitrose; you will come won't you Lois?"

As Lois took a breath to speak, Sicily butted in, "No sorry, she can't, Maureen's invited 'er for tea, 'asn't she Lois? In fact, you'd better get goin', she's expectin' you at five." Sicily winked at her again.

109

Confused, Lois paused, "Oh…yes."

Sicily pointed to her watch, "It's quar'er to Lois, you'd better get a wiggle on!"

Lois, not having a clue why Sicily was behaving like this, decided to go along with it anyway, "Gosh, I had no idea it was so late! Well it's been lovely to meet you both, another time for tea perhaps?"

"Oh super!" smiled Margaret, "Tomorrow then, five o'clock. Must dash now, TTFN!" and she wound up her window before Lois could respond and drove slowly up the lane.

"See you 'morrow then Lo, and you Sis, you commin' an' all?"

"Will there be enough cake?" asked Sicily, cheekily.

"Funny!" said Chaz, winking at Sicily, "Very funny!"

As Chaz drove off, Lois said, "What was all that about Sicily, I didn't have a clue what you were talking about, or am I going senile?"

"I wan'ed to warn you about Chaz, I thought it was only fair."

"Warn me about what? I could tell he's a bit, well, you know…" Lois suddenly realised she was digging herself into a hole. She was about to say 'common', then realised that Sicily and her father were hardly well spoken. She turned red again. Sicily laughed.

"I'm not as bad as Chaz, am I?"

"No, not at all. Anyway, moving swiftly on, what did you need to warn me about?"

Sicily glanced around her then leant down, gesticulating for Lois to move nearer the horse. In hushed tones she said, "'E's a drug dealer."

Lois laughed, "Yeah, yeah. Course he is Sicily!"

"No. Straight up. 'E's done a couple of long prison terms. Anyway, pop up the farm for tea, quick as you can and I'll fill you in. I'll just put 'er away," she nodded at the horse, which looked as if it had fallen asleep, "I'll be ready in twen'y."

"Okay," said Lois, looking stunned and a little confused as she watched Sicily take up her reins and gently encourage the horse to pick up some forward momentum.

110

Lois called into Honeysuckle to check on progress. All appeared to be going well and none of the workmen looked like they wanted any interference. As Lois was going to drive straight from Sicily's to London, she stripped the dusty bed linen to wash at the flat, stuffed the pillows and duvet into bin liners and put them in the wardrobe in an attempt to keep them dust free. Then she went and collected the rest of her washing and overnight bag from Annie's house, loaded it all into the car and made her way to Willow Farm.

14

Lois had to drive extremely slowly along the lane as it became increasingly dilapidated the further she went. She began to think it would have been quicker and much better for her poor MG, its exhaust repeatedly grounding, if she'd walked to Sicily's.

Lois could see the farm a couple of hundred yards ahead, when she came across a large brown puddle, which was about twenty yards long and stretched right across the road. It smelt, as her mother would have said, 'very countrified'. She would have liked to turn the car around at this point, left it somewhere safe and walked the rest of the way. But the road was too narrow to turn back and she had no wellies with her, so she very slowly started to ease the car through; as she did so, the cause of the puddle became clear; a huge muckheap on the verge, until this point curtained by brambles. Lois felt her head, in a 'touch wood' gesture, hoping that the little car wouldn't give up on her. The thought of having to wade through it in sandals turned her stomach.

As the car emerged, Lois gave it a little pat on the dashboard, "Good car!" she said, feeling relieved and a little smug having negotiated such an obstacle successfully.

She drove down the farm drive and parked her car alongside half a dozen others; three of which were very new looking Range Rovers, complete with personalized number plates. As she got out, Sicily appeared from the stable yard.

"Ah, you've been through Bill's manuur 'eap in an MG, I bet that was interestin'. Your lucky 'e didn't 'ave to come and tow you out with the tractor; it wouldn't 'ave been the first time."

"What did you call it?"

"The manuur 'eap. Ask Bill about it when you next see 'im, 'e can't say manure…or so 'e says."

"So all that," Lois paused, "manuur, comes from here does it? Why does he put it by the side of the road, why not pile it up on the farm somewhere, there's plenty of land here isn't there?"

"Oh yeah, he could do that, but 'e likes winding people up. Particularly Charles Black. 'E thinks it discourages Black from venturing down 'ere. It doesn't o' course, but it keeps Bill 'appy. Come on, let's go in and 'ave a cup o' tea, Maureen must be out, 'er car's not 'ere and Bill's out in 'is tractor."

"If Maureen's not here, who owns all these cars?"

"Oh they're not ours, my family all drive old bangers. These belong to owners of ridiculously expensive horses. More money than sense most of 'em!"

Sicily and Lois made their way to the farmhouse; a stunning brick and flint building, apparently seventeenth century and listed. There was a large dog kennel outside the back door with a huge Alsatian lying in its doorway. On seeing them approach, much to Lois's concern, he got up and idly walked towards them. "Is he safe?" she asked Sicily, having never been a fan of German shepherds.

"Oh, don't worry about Boot, 'e's fine, so long as you're with me. Don't come into the garden on your own though, 'e'll eat you."

"Ah, now I'm reassured … not."

They made their way through the back door and into the kitchen via a boot room. Sicily made the tea in an exquisite china teapot and got out a matching jug of milk, sugar bowl, plates, cups and saucers. She then produced a homemade cake, which Lois was surprised to learn she had baked herself. Lois felt a bit guilty that she found this whole set up very unexpected.

"So come on Sicily, give me the full story on Chaz."

"Mm, where to start?" Sicily paused briefly. "Well, 'e and Mags live in the last cottage in 'The Park', next to Richard and Debbie. They moved in about three years ago. She's a lecturer up the university. This'll tickle you, she works in 'ealth promotion, specialisin' in diet! That's a laugh innit, I should think she weighs about eighteen stone!"

"Oh my God, that's hilarious! Appalling, but hilarious. Hang on a minute, are you kidding me?"

"Would I? No, straigh' up Lois, everything I tell you this afternoon will be the truth, promise! Anyway, Mags, as you know, very well spoken, well educa'ed, parents allegedly live in a mansion in Yorkshire. Then there's Chaz: says he runs a," Sicily gesticulated inverted commas as she said, "'distribution business'. Well, I suppose that's the truth.

"Anyway, they moved in and all seemed fine. Everyone thought they were NFHP, that's normal for Harewood Park." Lois laughed. "Some of the snobs in the park didn't take to Chaz in a big way, but that was about it; until Richard's sister came to visit. She and 'er 'usband arrived for a barbecue and bumped into Chaz and Mags as they were gettin' out the car. As they walked into the 'ouse, they slammed the door and burst into hysterical laughter. When they were finally able to speak, Ellen, the sister, said, "Nice neighbours guys, good to see the place is going up market!" Well, this comment got Debs' back right up and she star'ed going on about not judging books by their covers and all that. But it turned out Ellen and 'er 'ubby knew 'em from Ealing. Neighbours, funny enough. Ellen gave Mags a lot o' support while Chaz was inside. Anyway, she broke the news to Debs and Richard, what it was his distribution company distributed; 'eroin and coke mainly; and that was that. I wish I'd been there to see Debs' face."

Lois sat quietly, unsure whether to grin or be appalled.

"Apparently Hannah, Debs' eldest, thought this was well cool and ran straight up to 'er room to start texting 'er friends; Ben star'ed asking questions about class A drugs and what effect they 'ad on you and since he couldn't get any answers off of 'is parents, who were in a combined state of shock and disbelief, went to the study to look it up on the Internet. At which point, this being eleven-thir'y in the morning, Debbie went and opened a bottle of wine to steady 'er nerves.

"Richard said that Debs refused to go out in the garden while he fired up the barbecue, as 'they' might be listening to the conversation. She needed more facts, so she stayed inside until she was sure she 'ad all the information she needed to deal with the horror of 'aving a master criminal living next door.

"Apparently, not long after she'd been told all this, Debs saw Chaz, from Lisa's window, sneakin' round to Charles

Black's green'ouse whilst 'e was away. Unaware that she was watching, 'e put a briefcase inside. She couldn't report it though; Chaz would have known it was 'er; their 'ouse is the only one that overlooks tha' part of the garden."

"Hey Sicily, our house has been empty for ages. You don't think he would have hidden anything in our shed do you?"

"It wouldn't surprise me. 'Ave you looked in it?"

"Yes," said Lois slowly, looking thoughtful.

"Anything unusual?"

Lois pondered for a few seconds. "Four brand new, identical garden gnomes, they seemed a bit odd."

"Did any of them look 'igh?"

"Well, they were all up on a shelf. Oh ha ha," Lois said, as she got the joke.

"So anyway, time moves on. We all know 'ow Chaz makes 'is money, but pretend we don't. It's quite su'ink really innit Lois?"

Lois, feeling she knew Sicily well enough now to tease her a little, responded, "Yer Sis, it is su'ink innit!"

"Oh, I know I don't speak well. I blame Bill. 'E was brought up in Slough. But I'm gonna make an effort to talk posh like you, Lois. I'll start tomorra. Anyway, goin' back to what I was sayin', before bein' so rudely interrupted," they both laughed, "another funny thing, was that Richard and Debbie 'ad watched a film the night before Ellen and 'er 'usband came and broke the news. It was 'The Whole Nine Yards' about 'aving a contract killer movin' in next-door!"

Lois laughed, shaking her head. "Gosh, you know I was hoping to meet some interesting characters by moving to the country, but so many, in such a small place? Talking of which, it sounds like your family isn't exactly run-of-the-mill." Sicily laughed as she poured the tea.

"Now, what can I tell you?" Sicily thought for a moment as she passed Lois a dainty cup and saucer. "Bill did very well for 'imself, marrying Maureen. She's, well, you'll meet 'er soon enough, she's very different to 'im. Nothing much fazes Maureen and it's 'er who runs the farm. She organises everyone, keeps us all in order, staff, liveries and Bill alike. Bill you've met. 'E's responsible for all the jobs around the

115

farm that need a man or a tractor, but nothing too 'eavy, those are saved up for Norman, my brother. Bill gets angina, had an 'eart attack a few years back, so 'e's gotta be careful."

Sicily cut them both enormous pieces of cake, which she placed carefully on the china plates and got out two small silver cake forks and linen napkins rolled up in silver rings. "Bill's daily routine consists of gettin' any jobs done around the farm; then 'e hitches the cart to the tractor and takes the muck to the manuur heap. After that, 'e usually carries on to Charles Black's 'ouse and parks outside."

"He sits there for hours doesn't he? I heard it's all part of a long term feud between him and Charles."

"Yep; all down to old Black bein' an interfering old nosey parker and Bill's inability to abide by the rules. They're like a couple o' kids really; but what can you do?

"Anyway, depending on how vindictive he's feelin', how cold it is and whether his gout's playin' 'im up, 'e stays there for sometimes four or five hours, Mum thinks 'e's at the pub! 'E takes sandwiches, a flask of coffee and the MP3 player I gave 'im; I put all 'is favourite country and western music on it. Then he sits staring in to Black's front room and kitchen windows as constantly as 'e can. 'E don't do weekends though," Sicily laughed, "'e feels 'e's entitled to a couple o' days off; besides 'e quite often drives me to riding events at the weekends, gives old man Black a bit of a reprieve!"

"Has he never called the police? Charles I mean."

"Yeah, on several occasions. They came out and talked to Bill after the first complaint, but Bill said it was a pretty place to sit and eat lunch and since there were no parking restrictions what was the problem? When Charlie Boy said that Bill had been starin' in, intimidatin' 'im through his windows, Bill laughed so 'ard, 'e inhaled a piece of the salami 'e was eatin', which came down 'is nose and got stuck. 'E 'ad to go to casualty eventually and 'ave it removed! Anyway, the policeman just laughed along with Bill, or so 'e says. Bill reckoned the policeman said 'e didn't look very intimidatin' and didn't even give 'im a warning.

"About a year after it all began, Charles 'ired a mini digger which 'e used to dig a trench. Then 'e 'ad some big

Leylandii trees planted to block out Bill's view, must 'ave cost 'im a fortune. Bill, determined that Black wouldn't get the better of 'im that easily, snuck up to Charles's 'ouse in the dead of night and fixed cheese wire round the trunks. As the trees grew over the next few months, the wire dug into the bark and they died.

"Well, Black seems to have given up since then. I'd like to say he's stopped interfering, but I don't suppose for a minute 'e 'as. 'E's just accepted that he has an old boy in a tractor staring in at 'im every day; but I'm sure 'e's on the lookout for someone else to badger."

Lois jumped when an owl started hooting, directly above her head. Sicily laughed. "My, you are jumpy! That was just the clock. Different birdcall every hour, that's six o'clock."

"Gosh I'd better get going Sicily, I've got to drive back to London tonight."

"Oh, 'ere's me Mum!"

Maureen struggled her way through the back door, with several bags of shopping dangling off each wrist. Sicily went to relieve her of half of them, simultaneously introducing Lois, who was desperately trying not to look too amazed. Maureen was a very attractive, glamorous looking fifty-something; smartly dressed, beautifully made-up; in fact, about as unlike Bill as it was possible to be.

"Oh, hi Lois, Sissy said she'd met you. How are you settling in?"

"Well, we've not properly moved in yet. We're just having some work done. We move officially a week Friday."

"I'm sure you're going to love it, it's a great place, Harewood Park. It's a shame not everyone appreciates what a fantastic area it is. Do you ride?"

"I used to, as a child, but not very much since."

"Well, once you've recovered from having the baby, which I'm sure won't take you long, you'll have to come and have a ride. Sis'll find you something nice and quiet and you can get back into it again. What do you think?"

"Sounds great, that's very kind."

"Not kind at all, always on the lookout for free help exercising too many horses, that's all, eh Sis?" Maureen winked at Sicily.

"Anyway Ma, Lois 'as gotta rush."

"Bye Lois, lovely to meet you!"

"And you Maureen. Bye!"

"I'll take you to your car, it's almost Boot's dinner time." said Sicily, grinning.

"I see what you mean about your Mum and Dad being very different from each other. Where did they meet?"

"Ballroom dancing."

Lois looked at Sicily, askance. "You're pulling my leg Sicily! I mean Maureen, yes, I can see that, but Bill, ballroom dancing? You're having a laugh!"

"No, straigh' up! They won loads o' competitions."

"Well, I've thought it more than once this week," said Lois, shaking her head and smiling, as she climbed carefully into the MG, "you should never judge a book by its cover!"

"I don't," said Sicily, as she shut the car door, tapped the roof twice and walked towards the yard. "See you soon Lois!"

15

Lois arrived back at the flat late in the evening. Tom found Sicily's claim of Harewood Park having its own resident drug dealer somewhat far-fetched and accused Lois of being far too gullible. She didn't even bother to argue, knowing that when he'd spent some more time in their new home, he'd understand.

The next morning Lois put in a load of washing, then left the flat with Tom and caught the tube to Clerkenwell with a small, wheeled suitcase in tow. She met Adrienne for breakfast and to hand over the few bits of outstanding business that needed to be followed up. They had a really good catch-up. Adrienne only had a few weeks left to work for the company and was very excited about her move to Tom's firm.

When they'd finished a ridiculously large breakfast, they went to the office together, where Lois handed in her work laptop, cleared her desk and said goodbyes to the team. As she walked out through the main doors and onto the street, laden with a suitcase full of stuff, a bouquet of flowers and a gift for the baby, wrapped in teddy bear paper and tucked into her handbag, Lois beamed with anticipation for the next phase in her life.

Arriving back at the flat, she threw the washing in the dryer and collected up various bits and pieces to take to the cottage. Cleaning equipment, hoover, wireless router, the spare printer. The list went on until the MG was packed so tightly that there was only just room for her. She'd just opened a can of soup for lunch and found some slightly soft rye crackers in the cupboard, when Mel phoned. They hadn't spoken since the weekend, when Adam had very kindly offered Mel a bed in one of his children's rooms; allegedly, so that she didn't have to worry about driving home.

"So, how was sleeping at Adam's?" asked Lois.

"Oh, fine. We just said goodnight and went to bed."

"You did? That sounds a bit dull."

"Yes, I know. But he did ask me to go out to dinner with him, tonight actually. What are you up to today, where are you?"

"I'm at the flat. I've packed the car with heaps of stuff. I'm heading off in about twenty minutes. How about you?"

"I've taken the afternoon off work. Adam thought we could go for a walk, so I'm supposed to be there by two thirty. Can I cadge a lift please, the train journey is really slow … and I've missed you, obviously!"

"Well I'll have to make some space in the car, but yes, that would be great."

Lois finished her lunch and re-organised the car to make space for Mel, taking out a few of the less important items. Just as she was pulling away, she realised she'd left the washing, which included the bed linen, in the dryer and nipped back to retrieve it.

When Lois picked her up, Mel looked momentarily taken aback. There were boxes in the foot-well and a large sack on the passenger seat.

"Sorry," said Lois, taking the sack so Mel could get in. "You'll probably do best to put your feet up on the dashboard." Mel sat on the seat and swung her legs straight up. She could just fit her holdall, which fortunately was remarkably small for Mel, under her legs. Then Lois put the sack of clean washing on her lap. She could just see over the top. "There, comfy?" said Lois.

"Luxurious!" smiled Mel.

"So," said Mel, as Lois manoeuvred the MG out of a particularly tight parking space. "Getting married eh? That's sooo exciting!"

Lois grinned.

"When are we going to start organising the wedding? I trust I am invited!"

"Invited, of course you're invited. You're maid of honour! I'm going to make you wear a pink frilly dress and have your hair all bouffant!"

"Okay, I'll wear pink frills, if you wear white frills, how about that?"

"All right, you win. I'll let you choose what you want to wear. Gosh, it's quite exciting isn't it?"

"You'd better get a wiggle on if you want to have done the deed before Pumpkin shows his or her face. When's it due?"

"'Fifteenth of September, that's…" Lois used her fingers to calculate.

"Hey Lo, I can see why the City's going to struggle without you and your financial wizardry. Did you always use your fingers when making multimillion pound deals on the stock market?"

"Always. Now where was I?" As the traffic had eased and she'd started driving again, Lois tapped her fingers against her leg, "Gosh, that's less than eight weeks to go, that's a bit scary isn't it?"

"What, for time to organise a wedding, house renovation, house move, and prepare for the birth of your baby? I don't see why. Or were you referring to going through the most painful ordeal of your life?"

"What getting married?"

"No. Giving birth!"

"Thanks for that. Remember I'll be able to worry you too when your time comes. Anyway, I meant both."

"Yeah, I don't suppose my time will ever come at this rate. I thought Adam might have ravished me the other night, but not a sausage, as it were. Oh, and the fact he had no bedroom door made him a bit embarrassed!"

As they continued on their journey, Lois described her second meeting with Doreen and Jack, and then told Mel about Bert and Betty. "Oh God, I forgot to tell you, I'm going to tea with Chaz and Margaret later!"

"Are those names supposed to mean something to me?"

Lois laughed, "Now, this you really won't believe!" She proceeded to relay Sicily's story of Debbie and Richard discovering the real occupation of their next-door neighbour.

"Are you sure she wasn't winding you up?"

"She said not. I'm pleased to say Sicily's coming with me this afternoon; she seems quite chummy with them. I think I would be somewhat anxious if I was going alone."

"Blimey Lois; I know I've said it before, but it's quite a place you've found, isn't it?"

As they entered the sweeping driveway of Harewood Park, which led first to the manor and then the cottages, the beauty that lay ahead of them, once again, amazed Mel and Lois. At the beginning of the drive, post and rail fences bordered the lane, as it sloped down to a dip, with horses grazing in the fields on either side. The manor stood majestically on top of the facing hill, surrounded by spectacular, meticulously kept gardens, with the lake at the front glistening in the sunlight.

When they arrived at Honeysuckle, Lois persuaded Mel to pop in before going to Adam's, to admire the progress that had been made. Even Lois was surprised by the changes made since the previous day. It looked like the rewiring was finished. All the holes around the sockets and switches had been plastered over. Dean said George was coming later to mount and connect the fuse and meter boxes. The staircase was finished and looked amazing. The bathroom suite was fully functioning and the whole of the upstairs had had a coat of paint.

"Wow," said Mel, "it's fantastic! I can't believe the staircase; it looks stunning! The whole place is really taking shape, Lo."

"You guys have been very busy today, it's looking fab? When do you think you'll be done?" Lois asked Dean.

"Middle of next week should do it."

"Perfect!" said Lois, grinning broadly.

Mel went off to find Adam, with Lois calling after her to have a great time. Then she looked at her watch. Ten to five; Sicily was due to appear at any moment. She nipped upstairs to the bathroom, briefly luxuriating in the comfort of the new loo and as she was walking down her incredibly beautiful staircase, there was a knock at the door.

"You ready?" asked Sicily, whom Lois thought had an unusual smell about her.

"Ready as I'll ever be."

"Oh it'll be fine. Pretend nobody's told you what Chaz does; take 'em as you find 'em and decide whether you like 'em or not. I get on quite well with 'em as it goes."

"I say, aren't you supposed to be talking posh today?"

"Oh yeah. Mm, maybe I'll start tomorrow."

"Gosh, what is that smell?" asked Lois, as Sicily turned to walk down the garden path. Then, noticing that the back of her jacket and hair were covered in, what looked and smelt very much like manuur puddle, added, "Um, Sicily, how did you get here?"

"On me dirt bike, why d'you ask?"

"You seem to have half of Bill's 'manuur' heap up your back and in your pony tail."

"Oh crap!"

"Exactly!" Lois laughed. "Look, do you want to borrow some leggings and a T-shirt, I've just brought some clothes from the flat. I tell you what, go up to our newly installed bathroom and give the shower a test run." Lois rummaged in the holdall she'd brought in from the car and found a towel and clothes for Sicily to change into. "Here you go. The leggings are somewhat stretched out of shape and will be too short, but at least you won't smell so bad! Oh, hang on just a sec," she went through to the kitchen and found a bin bag, some soap and a small bottle of shampoo. "There you go, now make it snappy, I don't want to get off on the wrong foot by being late!"

"You can go up there on your own if you like, I'll meet you there."

"Ha ha! Hurry up, pleeeease!"

"By the way, did you find any of Chaz's class As in yer shed?"

"Oh gosh, I completely forgot to look. I'll go now, while you're in the shower."

Lois searched the shed for suspicious packages. Then, lifting the gnomes off the shelf one by one, she found a hole underneath them and hollow bodies. She felt slightly disappointed in a strange way. It would have made a great dinner party story, finding gnomes full of heroin in the shed.

The moment Sicily arrived downstairs Lois rushed her out of the house and up the lane to the last cottage. In the event, they were only five minutes late. The lady of the house opened the door, and Lois saw her in her entirety for the first time. Even though she had an idea of what Margaret looked like, Lois was still shocked by her appearance and had to concentrate hard on not letting her jaw drop. Seeing her standing, it became apparent that the woman was more or less as wide as she was high. Margaret gave Sicily an enthusiastic hug, and then reached for Lois's hand and kissed her on both cheeks. 'Like kissing a couple of dough balls,' Lois thought to herself. She was relieved not to have come with Mel; she would never have kept a straight face.

"Thanks so much for the invitation Margaret, it's awfully kind of you." Lois found herself putting on her upper-class accent, causing Sicily to turn and raise her eyes to heaven, as if to say 'Not again!'

"Oh please, call me Mags, all my friends do."

Lois felt like saying, 'Steady on there Margaret, lets not be too presumptuous!' But actually said, "Okay Mags." And, as if she had read Lois's mind, Sicily, once again, raised her eyes to heaven.

Margaret waddled towards the kitchen; Lois noticing how tiny her slippered feet were and wondering how on earth she managed to keep her balance. It reminded her of Chinese foot binding. Then she realised that if Margaret had been of average weight for her height, her feet would probably not look so small.

As they were about to go into the kitchen, Lois stopped so abruptly that Sicily walked into her. She was staring at a wedding photo on the wall. Chaz was recognisable enough, but Margaret, where was she? Surely Chaz wasn't keeping a photo of a previous wedding on display.

Before Lois could draw her eyes away, Margaret had retraced her steps to see what the hold up was. "Ah, yes, I look a bit different there, don't I?" Lois, for a change, was rendered speechless; astonished by the transformation Margaret had gone through. Sicily came to her rescue.

"You'll 'ave to cut down on them cakes, Mags!"

"I know, I know and I will, tomorrow, I promise!"

"Yeah right, I've 'eard that one before. You know better than any of us 'ow bad it is for your 'ealth. Look at poor ol' Jack, you don't wanna end up like 'im do you?"

"No, you're right Sissy. You do have a remarkably sensible head on very young shoulders. I will try hard, I promise. It's just that when you've got so much to lose, it's very disheartening you know."

"Yeah I'm sure, but you'll lose your job soon, they've warned you 'aven't they?"

"Yes, yes. Okay, I'll start now." Margaret ushered Lois and Sicily into the kitchen and indicated for them to sit down at the table, which was covered in all sorts of wonderful looking treats. Lois hadn't been offered a tea like this for a very long time and she scanned the display trying to decide which of the glorious items to sample first.

"Sissy," said Margaret, thoughtfully, "would you like to be my personal trainer? I really need someone to keep me in line; be firm. I'll pay you well."

Sicily didn't look at all surprised by this suggestion, she just said, "Sounds great, we'll start now." Then, went to the cupboard under the sink, took out a bin liner, and to both Lois and Margaret's astonishment, and horror, emptied each plate from the table into the bag; sandwiches, scones, malt loaf, a fantastic looking coffee cake, chocolate cake and a plate full of iced fairy cakes. Then she got a spoon out of the drawer, scooped the cream and jam back into their containers, which Margaret had left on the side, and threw them into the bin liner as well. She tied up the handles of the bag, marched out of the front door, up the garden path and slung it into the wheelie bin.

"Well," said Margaret, sitting down to get over the shock, "well that, I suppose, is a start." She sat in silence, looking completely bewildered for some time. Lois thought she could see tears welling up in her eyes. Then she said, "Sorry Lois, perhaps I should have mentioned the personal training idea after tea."

Lois felt sorry for her, she looked lost, as if she didn't know what to do or say without the presence of food on the table. "I'll put the kettle on," said Lois.

"Right Mags, don't look so surprised, this is 'ow it's gunna have to be from now on. Tea means cup of, not 'enough cakes to feed a village.' If you're 'ungry, 'ave some fruit. Where's Chaz by the way, we'd better let 'im know you're on a mission."

Margaret still looked very much as though she was in shock. "He's out in the back garden, doing some weeding."

"Oh, he likes gardening?" Lois said, naively.

"No, Lois. If Mags says he's doing some weeding or some potting, trust me, it's got nothing to do with gardenin', 'as it Mags?"

"No love, it hasn't. Oh, Lois, I'm so sorry, you must think we're a right old pair, him smoking dope and me eating cakes. But, I, for one, am going to change!" Lois thought she could see a slight hint of determination in Margaret's face. "Sissy, perhaps you could help Chaz too?"

"Steady on Mags! I might be tough but I ain't a miracle worker!"

A few minutes later, Chaz came in, sat down with them at the table and had a cup of tea. Sicily gave him an explanation as to why there was nothing left to eat, while Chaz roared with laughter. "Cor, bloody 'ell Sis! Good fir you mate, good fir you!"

Chaz asked Lois where they had been living and what had made her and Tom want to move out of London. To which she replied, that she had always wanted to live in the country and now that the baby was on the way, it just seemed like the right time. She kept her answers short; she didn't feel comfortable with him knowing personal details about her.

"Good fir you Lo. I's a great environment out 'ere. D'ya know wha' I mean? It ain't rough like whaddit is up London. Ain't that right Sis?" Once again, Lois was pleased that Mel wasn't with her.

At six o'clock, Lois excused herself, saying she was expecting Tom home any minute and he wouldn't know where she was. She thanked Margaret very much and wished her luck with her diet.

"She'll need it!" laughed Chaz.

"Yeah, and a bit o' support from you wouldn't go amiss," said Sicily, giving Chaz a friendly, yet hard, punch on the arm as she left. "I'll call in tomorrow mornin' and we'll go through a programme. Ten o'clock Mags, okay?"

"All right Sissy, see you then," said Margaret, misery causing her normally high-pitched voice to drop several tones.

When Sicily got to the wheelie bin, she opened it up and yanked out the bin liner. "Just to remove the temptation!" she called back to Margaret, who was waiting forlornly in the porch. "Oh, and by the way Mags, I've got your car keys, just until tomorrow. If you need su'ink from the shop, you can always walk to get i'!"

As they made their way down the lane, Lois asked Sicily, "Where on earth did you get the confidence to talk to people, indeed treat people in that way. Throwing ALL the cakes in the bin!"

"Oh, I know them pretty well. I know that Mags would love to look like she used to. She star'ed puttin' on weight ten years ago apparently, and 'aving put on a stone it was just a slippery slope. The bigger she gets, the more she needs to eat because 'er size depresses 'er. It's a vicious circle innit?"

"Seems to me you should be a psychologist or something, not messing about with horses."

"Lois, it's them that keeps me level 'eaded!"

When Lois and Sicily arrived back at Honeysuckle, Tom was just pulling up. He got out of the car and gave Lois a hug. "How's my favourite fiancée? Not been kidnapped by an evil, drug dealing neighbour, I'm pleased to see!" and turning to Sicily, added, "And who's this? I bet it's the famous Sicily."

"It is indeed," said Lois, "Sicily, Tom. Tom, Sicily."

"Delighted," said Tom as they shook hands, "I've heard so much about you."

"Oh yeah, Lois said. You think I've been winding 'er up."

"And haven't you?" Tom asked, as he reached into the car to remove a bag of takeaway food.

"No, not yet," Sicily said, smiling.

"Ah, well you must tell me more. Bought enough food for an army Sicily, would you like to join us?"

"Sounds great. I'll just phone me mum and let 'er know what I'm up to. There's plen'y o' cake for pudding too, eh Lois?"

As Sicily walked away a little to make her phone call, Lois explained, "Margaret, we went for tea, remember? But Sicily, having been offered the post of personal trainer, confiscated the entire spread and put it in a bin-liner!" Lois pointed to the bag slung over Sicily's shoulder. "We'll fill you in later. Come on, I'm dying to show you the house."

Tom and Lois went inside. Tom was astonished to see how much progress had been made since Wednesday. Lois went and got the vacuum from the car and started hoovering. The place was so near to being liveable-in, it seemed a shame not to have a quick clean up before dinner. While Tom was putting the takeaway in the oven to keep it warm, Sicily came in carrying the box of cleaning equipment, which she'd noticed when Lois got the hoover out of the car. She went through to the kitchen, collected a bowl of water and washing up liquid, took a rag from the box and proceeded to wash down all the dust covered surfaces and the windows in the lounge; polishing up afterwards using a couple of microfibre cloths.

By the time Lois and Sicily had finished, half an hour later, the effect was amazing. The evening sun poured through the French doors, the amount of light entering the house appearing to have doubled.

Lois found the rugs that Pippa had brought and laid them on the floor in the corner of the living room. Tom had painstakingly served up the takeaway. He made five journeys to carry the plates, a bottle of wine and three glasses through to the lounge. He wasn't worried about driving his automatic car with one hand in plaster, but dropping an Indian meal was another matter.

Tom and Lois sat propped against the wall, Sicily opposite them in the lotus position, her back perfectly straight. They were all very hungry, Sicily in particular. She hadn't eaten lunch, pending a feast of cake at Margaret's house. The three of them sat in silence, munching their way through large platefuls of food.

Eventually, the urgent need to get food to mouth subsided and they all, suddenly felt very full.

"So Sicily, Lois tells me you live at Willow Farm and are in charge of exercising the client's horses. Do you enjoy it?" asked Tom.

"Oh yeah, it's all right. But I wanna go travellin' soon as I'm eighteen."

"How old are you now?" Tom asked. He and Lois were both surprised she wasn't well beyond eighteen. Lois had tried to put an age to her and decided, since she seemed so competent, she must be in her early to mid-twenties.

"Sixteen."

Lois nearly choked on a piece of onion bhaji she was trying to stuff down, because she couldn't bear to see it go to waste. "You can't be!" she spluttered.

"Seventeen in October; can't wait! Bill's bought me a car already, an old banger, I've been drivin' it round the fields on the farm. It was really funny; the first time I did it on my own, Bill came to find me afterwards. 'E was ranting on about me 'aving run over Diana. I 'ad a real panic, thought I'd hit one o' the livery's dogs or a chicken. But turned out I'd run over some old door that was lyin' in the yard. 'E'd called it Diana, Diana Doors." Lois, mouth still full, almost blew her nose into her remaining curry and had to excuse herself and go and fetch some kitchen roll.

"Blimey, it sounds like you lot are nuts!" said Tom, laughing.

"Tom, don't be so rude, you've only just met her," Lois said, sitting back down.

"Oh God, don't worry Lois, 'e's not the first person to call my family nuts, I can assure you!"

"Anyway Sicily, where is it you want to travel to, have you made any plans yet?"

"Oh yeah, on my first trip I want to go to India, to study yoga."

Had Lois been eating anything at this point, she would undoubtedly have choked. This young girl, who seemed so tough and really, Lois had thought, a bit rough around the edges, was very unusual.

"That sounds very exciting. Have you investigated where and how yet?" Tom asked.

"Yeah, top of me list for yoga is the Ashtanga Institute in Mysore. But I wanna travel around India and Sri Lanka as well."

"What do your parents think about you going travelling?" asked Tom.

"Me Mum's in two minds. She thinks it'll help me mature. Thinks I should take the opportunity while I'm young; but she doesn't know how she'll cope with runnin' the yard without me. Bill," Sicily looked up from the plate she was polishing with a piece of naan bread, to Tom, "Bill's me Dad. 'E's not s' keen. 'E's never been abroad in 'is life, 'e don't trust foreigners and will probably do everything 'e can to stop me goin'!"

"Oh, you'll be able to talk him round, I'm sure. I bet you can wind him round your little finger. I did some travelling around India, when I was young, free, single and happy. Ow!" said Tom, as Lois elbowed him in the ribs, forgetting all about his injuries. Fortunately, she was not sitting on Tom's broken side. "I'm very careful which side of Lois I sit!" he said, smiling.

"How did you injure yourself, Tom?" Sicily asked.

"Oh, have you not heard? Mountain biking accident, very dramatic!"

"Oh, I love mountain biking!" said Sicily, becoming very animated. We normally go to Wales, which mountain were you on?"

Lois laughed so much; she had to stand up to relieve the pressure caused by baby, curry and laughter on her abdomen. She propped herself against the wall. "Yes, which mountain was it Tom?"

"Oh yes, you can laugh, it can be pretty treacherous in the New Forest, you know!"

"Ah, the New Forest," said Sicily, feeling a bit sorry for Tom at this point, she hadn't meant to mock him. "Yeah, it can be pretty rough, a friend of mine had a nasty crash down there."

"Thank you!" said Tom, looking at Lois with a 'see' look on his face, but Lois continued to titter.

"Imagine what you'd look like now if you'd been on a mountain! I don't think you should ever do that, Tom. Well not before we sort out your life insurance anyway."

Sicily decided that this was probably a good time to clear up the plates, Tom and Lois joining her. She used the bag the food had come in to collect up the empty, plastic takeaway boxes. "Do you want these?" she asked Lois, showing her the containers. "Just that Maureen collects 'em, always finds something handy to do with 'em."

"Yes, you take them. Sounds like Maureen might be like my mum; is she a bit of a hoarder?"

"Yeah, you could say that, or she likes recycling anyway. Right, hope you guys have got room for cake. Sorry it's a bit squashed!"

Lois and Sicily explained to Tom in more detail, what had happened at Margaret's house.

"Gosh, I can't wait to meet all these characters, I feel I've been missing out! And her husband's a drug dealer Sicily, really? Straight up?"

"Straigh' up Tom, straigh' up!"

Lois and Tom both got up early on Saturday morning. The weather forecast had predicted a sunny start, with winds increasing during the day, culminating in a thunderstorm late afternoon or early evening. Since they wanted to fit in a walk, going before making their way to the jewellers seemed like the sensible thing to do.

Annie was at the front of her house doing some gardening as they passed. Rupert and Reaver came trotting up in their usual wiggling way, to say hello.

"Hi Annie, would the dogs like a walk?" asked Tom, much to Lois's surprise.

"I'm sure they'd love it," said Annie, "where are you going?"

"To the woods, for about an hour." Tom sounded as if he knew where he was going, which made Lois smile; as far as she was concerned they were exploring.

"I'll fetch their leads," Annie said, returning moments later with the leads and a small bag of treats. "Now, regular treats are the key to keeping them close. They are generally fine, unless they see a deer, then Reaver in particular, tends to disappear for some time."

"Great!" said Tom, forcing a smile. As they walked away with both dogs tugging at their leashes, Lois put her finger to her lips to try and stop him moaning within Annie's earshot. Ten yards further on he said, "Well she could have told us that before we were committed, we've got to leave at ten thirty to get to Hatton Garden."

"We could keep them on the leads," suggested Lois.

"No we couldn't," said Tom, unclipping Reaver, "Bloody dog's already hurting my ribs." He called her back, giving a couple of treats as a reward when she responded. After being dragged even harder by Rupert now that Reaver was ahead, Lois released him too.

"And what's with, 'we're going to the woods for an hour,' it makes it sound like you know what we're doing." At which point, Tom removed a sheet of A4 from his pocket.

"I was bored in the office yesterday, so I worked out a one hour route around the woods." He showed Lois the way on the map he'd printed out, then called both the dogs back and gave them each a treat.

"You see! I am a natural for living in the country!"

Lois and Tom settled into their stride, which was by no means brisk. They followed the well-trodden footpath across two fields, from which hay crops had been recently taken. The second field was large and dipped down towards the woods. As they moved out of the sunshine into the relative darkness of deciduous woodland, it took a few seconds for their eyes to adjust. Ten yards in, they stopped abruptly, hearing a rustling in the undergrowth, which seemed to be coming from behind a holly bush. Both the dogs put their hackles up and barked. Tom, thinking there might be a deer, grabbed Reaver by the collar. As the rustling got louder, they all realised it was a person. Tom released Reaver and she went wiggling into the bush.

"Hello Reaver," came a high voice, "I'm so glad to see you!"

"Margaret, is that you?" Lois asked, before Margaret eventually emerged from behind the bush, looking somewhat the worse for wear. She had bits of foliage in her hair, which had been half pulled out of its, usually, neat bun. She was wearing an enormous, no, colossal, cream jogging suit, which was smeared with mud, both top and bottom. She had scratches on her face and hands. Yet, she was grinning from one dough-ball to the other.

Seeing Tom, Margaret immediately started to brush herself off and fiddle with her hair, embarrassed that she was meeting him for the first time, in such a state.

"Margaret, whatever happened to you?" asked Lois.

"You must be Tom, I'm so sorry," she said, ignoring Lois's question and straightening her glasses, "you must think me very strange, out in the woods and looking so dishevelled!" Margaret rubbed her muddy hand on her jogging bottoms and offered it to Tom to shake. "Welcome to Harewood Tom, I hope you'll both be very happy. Now," Margaret glanced around her, "which way's home?"

133

Tom guided Margaret to the edge of the wood and pointed out the path. She thanked him and stumbled onto it.

"Do you think we ought to go with her?" Lois asked Tom, "I'm not sure she's herself."

"She looks like she's herself and several other people to me!"

"Tom, shush, she might hear you."

"Yes, you might be right," he whispered, "She doesn't travel very fast, does she? What's she doing out here anyway, she doesn't really look like the walking type."

"It must be part of Sicily's training regime. Why do you think she was so muddy? And she smelt of wee, did you notice?"

"I reckon she went into the bushes to pee, lost her balance and rolled down a hill."

"Stop it, don't be mean!" Lois nudged Tom, then added, "But I suppose it's possible." And at this point, Lois decided she'd better duck behind a bush herself, three cups of tea at breakfast were now taking their toll. Emerging, fully relieved, she asked Tom if he knew where the dogs were.

"They're right … " Tom looked around him, not a dog in sight.

Lois raised her eyes to heaven. "Oh God, I knew this would happen!" she said, looking indignantly at Tom.

"Don't blame me!"

Lois didn't respond, although she was sorely tempted, but started to call the dogs. When there was no response, she tried, unsuccessfully, to whistle them…whistling never had been one of her strong points. A minute or so passed, with no sign of either of them. Lois was starting to feel sick. What would she say to Annie? Then Tom, put his thumb and middle finger in his mouth and gave an almighty whistle. Lois, who was only a metre away, put her hands over her ears and shouted, "Tom, that really hurt and I'm sure they won't…" she stopped, mid sentence. Both the dogs were careering towards them. They then sat down at Tom's feet and looked up at him. "Wow, now that was impressive!"

Tom gave them a treat and a pat. "Well, looks like I've got a hidden talent, doesn't it Lo? Dog whisperer."

"Well you've certainly got something!"

Tom checked his watch, half an hour had already past. "You know, I think we'd better head back before anything else happens to make us late."

Making their way out of the wood, they could see Margaret going through the gate at the end of the first field. It looked as if she was holding it open for someone.

"So, is Sicily going to try and kill her do you think?" asked Tom, indicating Margaret with a nod of his head.

"No, I'm sure she'll be very sensible. It'll be interesting to see how much her input helps. Oh look, here come Jack and Ellie; more neighbours for you to meet."

"Ellie's the dog I take it and Jack, oh yes Jack, can only swear. What is it he says, 'Oh bugger off!'?"...Tom had found a lot of what Lois had told him about the neighbours difficult to believe.

Jack trundled up towards them, the wheelchair bumping effortlessly over the stones and large tufts of grass on the path. When he spoke, his voice vibrated with the movement of the chair. "Oh bugger off!" he said, before stopping and touching hand to forehead, in a greeting gesture.

"Jack, lovely to see you! How are you?"

"Oh, bugger off!" he said, nodding slowly, tilting his head slightly from one side to the other, and pushing out his bottom lip, signalling 'so-so'. Then he pointed to Tom. "Oh bugger off?" he asked.

"Oh, sorry Jack, yes, this is Tom, my boyfriend, no, fiancé." Tom, quick to notice the man's right hand lying limp in his lap, went to use his left hand to shake Jack's, and then realising his plaster cast was in the way, swapped to his right. They both chuckled at the complexity of such a basic greeting. "Pleased to meet you Jack, I've heard a lot about you."

Jack smiled and raised his eyes to heaven as if to say, 'Yes, who hasn't.' He then pointed to the plaster on Tom's arm. "Oh bugger off?" he asked.

"Silly accident," said Tom, "came off my mountain bike; a ditch got in the way."

"Oooh buugger off!" said Jack, looking like he was trying to look concerned, but struggling not to laugh.

Jack glanced at his watch and gave a wave, "Oh bugger off!"

"Nice to meet you Jack, see you again!"

"Bye Jack," called Lois, as he pulled away. Ellie sniffed the ground as she trotted along in front of him, having her 'free time'.

Lois was relieved to see that Annie's dogs had remained with them while they'd been talking; she'd been completely distracted and if they'd disappeared, she probably wouldn't have noticed. They walked across the final field and down the lane. Sicily was outside Margaret's house, with a very dirty looking mountain bike.

"Sicily, you're surely not thinking of getting her on that are you?" said Lois, cringing at the thought of what might happen if Margaret were to try to mount it.

"Don't be daft! No, I've come to give Mags her first lesson: Eatin' for one."

"We'll let you get on," said Tom, smiling as he dragged Lois away. "Come on, we've got an appointment!"

Lois and Tom arrived at the jewellers bang on time, which was unusual. For all Tom's stickling for precision in life, he was remarkably bad at timekeeping. Lois had started to secretly change the time on the clocks and their watches, in an attempt to overcome this problem. Setting them all ten minutes fast, on this particular occasion, had worked like a charm.

"Good morning Sir, Madam. I'm Piers and I will be your personal jeweller this morning," said a very 'shiny', somewhat camp-looking, middle-aged man at the desk where they'd confirmed their arrival.

"Oh God," whispered Tom, under his breath, as Piers went to get the keys for the engagement ring cabinet from the safe. "I'm not sure I can be doing with all this."

"Oh come on you grumpy old sod, it'll be a laugh. Look, I like that one," said Lois, pointing to a platinum ring with five small diamonds set into it. "There's no price on it, do you think that's a bad sign?"

"Definitely," said Tom, as Piers flounced back in.

"Now, engagement rings. Why don't you give me an inkling into your style."

"Well, I like that one." Lois indicated the platinum ring.

"Oh *wonderful* choice sweetie, *wonderful* choice! Let's get that out for you and see if it fits!" Lois thought Piers sounded so excited, anyone would have thought it was he who'd just got engaged. He unlocked the cabinet, took the tray out and slowly and carefully placed it on the top. He then removed the ring as if it were a crucial part of an unexploded bomb, took a cloth from his top pocket, which he flicked open with a flourish and gave the ring a thorough polish before gently handing it to Lois.

"Before I try it on, I'd like to know how much it is please."

"Ah," Piers' face fell, just a minuscule amount, but enough to tell Lois it was going to be bad news. "This particular ring retails at just five thousand pounds."

"Oh." Lois paused, handed the ring back to Piers and said, "Please give us a moment."

"Certainly madam," he said, looking slightly despondent, "I'll be over here if you need me, just give me a call!"

"Bloody hell, Tom. Why did you make an appointment at somewhere so expensive? We're not going to buy anything here!"

"Sorry, it was Mel's suggestion. She said they have a fantastic selection; that you'd love the rings here and we'd be sure to find something. I just wanted it to be romantic, to be honest I didn't give much thought to cost."

"Oh bless you!" Lois stroked his cheek, and then reaching up to give him a kiss, said, "I really love you!"

"I love you too!"

Lois turned around to talk to Piers, who had his head tilted to one side and his hand up to his mouth. "Oh I'm sorry, it almost brings a tear to my eye, seeing you two looking so happy. I see a lot of couples in here, some look like a good match and some don't. You two look perfect together!"

"Well that's very nice of you, but I'm afraid it's not going to make you a sale," said Lois.

"Don't you worry, just go and be happy!"

Lois and Tom said goodbye; Piers kissing them both flamboyantly on both cheeks and then, holding the door open for them, he said, "I wish you every happiness in your life together!"

They wandered through Hatton Garden, hand in hand. "You know what Tom, perhaps we shouldn't get a ring."

"But you'd love to have a ring, Mel said she'd had long discussions with you over what sort you'd like."

"Well, yes, we have talked about it, that's what girls do. But actually, the quality of a relationship can't be judged by the value of a ring, or indeed, by the fact a ring's being worn. I thought I wanted you to wear a wedding ring, to show that you're 'taken' I suppose. But a relationship is so much more. The deep trust that we need to have in each other, it makes rings seem, I don't know, rather," Lois paused, searching for the right word, "irrelevant?" She thought for a few moments. "Perhaps we should earn a ring, spend money on a special ring when we've been married a long time. Maybe after ten years, something like that."

"Ten years? Bloody hell Lo, I wasn't planning on staying married to you for that long!" teased Tom, moving away as he said it, to narrowly avoid a poke in the ribs.

"Ha, ha! But really, what do you think. We could put that money towards things we really need at the moment. And, if we don't make the ten years, we've made a five grand saving."

"Well I'm happy with that. So, if we're saving five grand today, can we have lunch somewhere posh."

"No Tom! We're saving five grand today. We'll eat in a pub as we'd planned. The money can stay in the bank until we need to buy something, like, oh I don't know, the piece of land behind our house?"

"Oh yes? Is this the reason you're declining my engagement ring, you want to buy land so you can get yourself a pony?"

"No, no, no," said Lois rubbing her face lovingly on Tom's shoulder, "I was just thinking what we'd need to spend a large sum of money on and that was the only thing that came to me. Mind you, five thousand wouldn't go very far towards buying it."

"Why, how much do they want?"

"A hundred."

"A hundred thousand for that bit of scrubland?"

"I know; it's a lot isn't it? But that's what it's been valued at. I bet they'll get it as well. God, I hope old Black doesn't buy it!"

17

Lois and Tom had a leisurely lunch, discussing all sorts of issues that they hadn't found time for before. The progress of the house came first, but didn't need much input as, surprisingly, all the work seemed to be well ahead of schedule. Dean and his chums had been doing a great job. Adam had been to replace the missing roof tiles the previous day. The electrics were sorted. Even the landline and broadband were functioning. By Friday, the likelihood was that all the interior work would be complete, just in time for them moving in.

"Ah, curtains. I haven't done anything about curtains yet. Off the rail or get them made up?"

"Up to you my treasure, that's woman's work," joked Tom, moving away from Lois slightly, to avoid a physical rebuke.

"Ok, suits me. So you don't want any input into colour, style or pattern then?"

"Ah, that's not what I said. Well, that's not what I meant," Tom said, backtracking fast, he was actually very particular about décor.

The next subject was the wedding: where and when. Lois told Tom about the appointment at the registry office. "Registry office?" Tom looked surprised. "Can't you get married pretty much anywhere these days? Wouldn't you prefer to do it in a nice stately home, or church? Hey, is there something you haven't told me; have you been married before?"

"Stop it, Tom," Lois said, laughing, "I can hardly walk down the aisle eight months pregnant can I?" she paused, "But maybe a stately home?" Lois sat and thought about this for a couple of minutes, munching her way through an enormous plate of cheddar ploughman's. "Hey, what about Harewood Manor, I wonder if they do wedding ceremonies there? I bet they do. It's a bit tacky inside mind you; Mel won't be impressed. But the grounds are beautiful and it's so convenient."

"Sounds good to me."

Lois got out her phone and put in an alarmed note to remind her to make enquiries on Monday.

The next thing Lois wanted to discuss was the birth of the baby. Attending her antenatal appointment the previous week, she had talked with the midwife about the possibility of a home delivery. Much to Lois's surprise, the midwife had been very enthusiastic. She said they tried to encourage as many fit, healthy women as possible to have home births. She had given Lois some web links, so that she and Tom could make an informed decision, but Lois wanted to sound Tom out before spending time researching the idea.

Tom sat for a moment thinking it through, and then said, "Well, I'm not averse to reading the research to see why they encourage it."

"Great! I'll look into it next week. The other thing I wanted to mention is a birthing pool, apparently you can hire them to have at home. Do you remember we saw that documentary on babies being born in water? I'll do some research into that too, if you're that open minded?" Lois gave Tom her most spectacular smile, showing off her orthodontically perfected teeth and the dimples in her cheeks.

"Okay, but I won't be happy unless the research is very positive. I don't want you or Pumpkin to be at unnecessary risk."

"Of course!"

After lunch, they made their way back to Harewood Park with plenty of time for a rest before going to Richard and Debbie's for dinner. Just as they both settled down to what they had started to call their 'rehabilitatory nap', Tom's phone rang. He wasn't happy to be disturbed. Seeing that it was his mother, he pulled a face and was about to put the phone back on the floor, but Lois was peering over his shoulder.

"Go on, answer it, Mr Grumpy!"

Tom grunted, then pressed the answer button, "Pippa! How nice to hear from you! How are you?" he said in a loud, bold voice, with a forced smile on his face. As his mother talked, he managed to push himself into an upright position and made his way downstairs, so at least Lois could have some shut-eye.

When the phone call had finished, Tom returned to the bedroom and eased himself, as quietly as he could, back into bed. His weight on the rubber mattress tilted Lois, disturbing her. She opened one eye. "How's Pippa?"

"Yes, she's fine," Tom said thoughtfully. "Apparently she and Chris want to give us some money as a sort of house warming, wedding present."

"That's nice," Lois said, still half asleep.

"Yes; the figure she mentioned was fifty."

"How lovely, we could put it towards the curtains."

"No Lo, not fifty pounds, fifty thousand pounds!"

Lois sat bolt upright in bed, "Bloody hell Tom; fifty thousand pounds! I had no idea they had that sort of money."

"Me neither. I reckon they - I mean she, Pippa, is in competition with your mum and dad. Never been a one to be upstaged, my mother. She's probably persuaded Chris to re-mortgage the house."

"Mm, hope your dad's okay with it." Lois thought briefly before adding, "Hey, at this rate, we could end up with that paddock after all!"

"Yeah, right!" said Tom; looking disappointed that Lois could seriously be thinking that buying a paddock was a good idea. "I think any money we have post renovation will have to go towards the eventual extension Lois, don't you?"

After the phone call, it took some time for them to fall asleep, their minds, both very active: Tom, worrying about his parents, and Lois, feeling guilty for her selfish suggestion, which had clearly annoyed Tom. When Lois eventually did fall asleep, she dreamed of a birthing pool, which she was desperate to get into, but couldn't, because it was full of diamonds.

Tom and Lois woke to a hard hammering on the door. Tom dragged himself downstairs to open it and found Annie and Dave standing in the rain.

"Are you ready?" asked Dave, shaking his umbrella outside as he backed into the house after Annie.

"Ready?" responded a very bleary eyed Tom.

"Dinner, Debbie and Richard's?"

"Oh no! What's the time?"

"Seven thirty."

"Whoops! We only went upstairs for a little snooze at four o'clock," Tom explained, ushering Annie and Dave further into the living room and then realising there was nowhere for them to sit.

"Oh, perhaps you'd prefer to go on ahead and we'll meet you up there?"

Annie pointed to the rugs on the floor, "No, no, we'll wait. We'll make ourselves comfy, won't we Dave?"

"I doubt that," Dave chortled, "but we'll wait anyway."

Hearing the voices downstairs, Lois had woken, looked at the time, had a minor panic attack and started to change as fast as she could. When Tom reappeared she was just resurrecting her make-up. "I'm ready," she said, "how about you?"

"Ready as I'll ever be!" said Tom, spraying on some deodorant. He looked reasonably smart from the trip to London that morning, if a little crumpled. They grabbed the bottle of red wine they'd bought in town and the orchid that Lois had carefully chosen for Debbie. Dave, who had decided to wait standing-up, heaved Annie to her feet, pretending she was much heavier than she really was.

"You'll need your waterproofs or a brolly," said Dave, "it's foul out there."

Tom gave Lois his 'You know where everything is!' look. "It's in the car, the brolly," said Lois, tossing him the keys. "Go, be gallant good knight, save me from this dreaded downpour!"

"Good night!" said Tom, as he ventured out into the rain.

Making their way up the lane, brollies aloft, Dave said to Annie, "Now, are you sure you locked the door properly? Should I check?"

"Yes, I locked it properly and no, you shouldn't check!" Annie said curtly, grabbing Dave by the elbow with one hand, whilst taking the umbrella from him with the other, pre-empting his retreat to double, triple, quadruple check the door, and dragging him forward.

143

"It won't take a second, just one push." Dave jerked away from Annie's grasp and went running towards the front door. When he got there, he pushed it with as much force as he could muster and called back to Annie, "Did you check the oven and hob?"

"Dave, for God's sake, we've been through this already! Stephen's in anyway, he'll be using the cooker in a minute."

"Even so," said Dave, taking the house keys from his pocket and opening the door, "you go ahead, I'll catch you up!"

Lois could see Annie's face reddening and her forehead becoming increasingly wrinkled during this performance. Indeed by the time they started to walk on, she looked like she was about to blow a gasket. But she didn't. She took three long breaths, muttering "In through the nose, out through the mouth," and visibly started to relax again. "Yoga," said Annie, "I've started going with Sicily, she's really into it, you know. I've found it very useful in helping me to cope with life. Well, more precisely, my husband. Honestly, leaving the house is a nightmare with him. As for going on holiday, it takes what feels like hours to get him in the car and finally drive away! Every plug in the house has to be removed from its socket, then he stands looking at the empty sockets for ages, contemplating whether they are really empty. The windows and external doors have to be checked and double checked and treble checked, until I'm just about tearing my hair out. He returns to the cooker endless times to make sure it's off. He actually stands with his hand underneath each tap in turn, for at least a minute, then having walked away he invariably goes back again, to make sure that not one, single, drip, is going to escape from the tap while we're away."

"He can't be that bad, surely?" said Lois.

Annie nodded as she continued, "Then of course, there's the locking of the front door. He checks it at least five times, pushing it with all his strength to make sure it's shut. He then walks a few yards from the house, goes back and pushes it again…and again…and again! Then he asks me to check it!" They walked through the gate to Debbie and Richard's house. "One of these days, I swear I'll go on holiday without him!"

Annie reached up and rang the doorbell, just as they heard footsteps running up behind them.

"There, that only took a minute, didn't it?" said Dave, grinning. Then, the grin suddenly disappeared, "Oh bugger, I can't remember whether I shut the door properly." This time it was Lois and Tom who grabbed an elbow each and frog marched him through the front door, which Debbie had just opened. Richard appeared almost immediately, followed by two of the children, shivering in dripping swimming costumes, eager to catch sight of the new neighbours. Annie introduced everybody who didn't already know each other. The children, twelve-year-old Lisa, and eight-year-old Luke, said a brief hello on being introduced to Lois and Tom and then disappeared back out to the garden. "Only another ten minutes in the pool!" Debbie called after them, in a voice that seemed amazingly loud for somebody so petite; in fact, for a woman who'd had four children, Lois's first impression, was not only how trim, but how vibrant she seemed.

Tom and Lois handed over the gifts to their hosts. Debbie, who seemed very pleased with the orchid, ushered the four of them into the living room, where Adam and Mel were already sitting. The first thing that struck Lois about the room was its size; they really had managed to add an enormous extension to this cottage; the second was the number of orchids that were sitting on every available surface. Lois felt embarrassed to have bought another one. But as Debbie saw Lois's face drop slightly on seeing the other plants, she grabbed her by the arm with both hands and said, "I love them; you couldn't have bought me a more perfect present, honestly!"

"Ah yes," boomed Richard, "talking of presents, I have your house warming gift in the garage, I'll just get it. Sorry, it's not wrapped."

Lois felt slightly sick as Richard walked through the French doors and out towards the garage. She really couldn't imagine having a stuffed animal on her windowsill.

Debbie asked her newly arrived guests what they would like to drink. Lois felt like asking for a large gin and tonic to settle her nerves, but didn't want to give the wrong

145

impression to the doctor and his wife, so requested an orange juice.

She glanced around the room to see if there were any dead animals on display. She couldn't see any. What would she say to Richard? How could she respond without looking disgusted? As she heard the garage door slam, Lois firmly fixed a grin onto her face in readiness for expressing enthusiastic praise and gratitude. She was pleased that Debbie had not yet returned to the room when the huge sigh of relief escaped her. Richard had come into view, pushing a wheelbarrow containing a sweet little tree, which Lois later learned, from a surreptitious glance at the label, was a miniature weeping willow. She went over to the French windows to see it more closely.

"Oh Richard, it's beautiful! Thank you so much; what a lovely surprise! But come on in, you're getting soaked."

"I don't know why you're looking so amazed. What were you expecting? A couple of stuffed glis glis or something?" Richard left the barrow where it was and came back in, shutting the rain out behind him.

"Well," said Lois, cautiously, "I did wonder."

"Are you disappointed? I have almost finished a pair. Very fiddly they were too. I've never done anything quite so small before. Debbie said I couldn't give them to you because you're a veggie, but if you'd like them? Do you want to come and see?" He ushered Lois towards the door. She felt unable to refuse the offer, he seemed really sweet, the willow was lovely and she didn't want to, or indeed feel a need to refuse. As they walked out of the door, Debbie came in with the drinks.

"Richard!" she shouted, firmly, "Please, don't take Lois out to your little house of horrors!"

"I'm fine Debbie, don't worry." Lois decided not to add, 'as long as I don't have to have any of them sitting on my mantelpiece!'

"Well if we hear a scream, we'll come and get you."

At this point, Mel and Tom decided they didn't want to miss out on the intrigue of Richard's garage and followed Lois out into the soggy garden.

"It's not really a house of horrors, the wife doth exaggerate," Richard said, walking them over the wet lawn to the garage, which, like Dave and Annie's, was detached with loft space above. The children were still in the pool. Richard called to them that it was time to get out as he opened the side door of the garage, and Lois followed him in. The strip light flickered and as it did so, Lois could see the most incredible form of a barn owl in flight in the centre of the garage. The light settled and it became clear that the bird was hanging from the ceiling. Lois, Mel and Tom, stared at it in awe. It looked so alive.

"Wow Richard, did you do this one?" asked Mel.

"It's great, isn't it? Friend of mine hit him late one night. Went back to see if he was repairable, but he'd had it. Then he thought I might like to preserve him and of course, I jumped at the chance."

"Gosh, you've done an incredible job," said Tom as he walked around the owl, studying it in detail.

Richard showed them a woodpecker that he had also recently finished and was waiting to re-home. Then, he reached up to a high shelf and brought down the pair of glis glis. Perhaps he really had stuffed them for her and Tom. Lois wasn't sure what to say.

"What do you think?" asked Richard, "Actually, I think they're finished."

"Well," Lois paused, trying to find the right words, without offending him.

"I love them!" said Mel, taking them from him and studying them closely, "They're real little characters, aren't they?"

"Well, they were." said Tom.

Mel was stroking one of the strange looking little animals behind the ears. "Do you sell them Richard? I'd love to…"

Richard laughed, "Sell them, God no, I have enough trouble giving them away. Are you saying you'd like them?" Richard asked, tentatively.

"Oh yes please, I'd love them! To be honest, I prefer dead animals; you never know quite where you are with live ones. They'll look fab on my mantelpiece and nobody in London will have a clue what they are … great for breaking the ice at dinner parties."

"That tells you a lot about Mel's friends!" chuckled Tom.

Lois felt a swell of relief that Mel appeared to be getting her off the hook and wondered whether she really wanted them, or was doing Lois a favour, realising that Richard would never know if she disposed of them.

They returned to the house, Mel grinning as she carried her new acquisition into the lounge and showed Adam. "Lovely!" he responded, in a tone that may or may not have been sarcastic, cautiously stroking one of the bushy tails. Mel sat with them on her lap, caressing them gently. Lois began to realise that Mel genuinely liked them. 'Weird!' she thought.

There were drinks and nibbles waiting for them by their seats. Richard picked up his gin and tonic and went to the kitchen to give Debbie a hand. Lois decided she needed the loo, for which Annie pointed her in the right direction. She walked past, what appeared to be a playroom or kids TV lounge, where six children were huddled together on the sofa, watching the current "find a pop star" competition. There were toys and wet towels littering the floor. Lois smiled. She liked this house, it had a relaxed, bordering on the chaotic feel about it. She thought how nice it would be to have so many children and have their friends eager to sleep over.

Lois backtracked and went into the room. She casually introduced herself to the children she hadn't met, Hannah, sixteen, Ben, fourteen and their two school friends.

"Do you ever vote?" Lois asked, pointing to the TV.

"Ten times a week for the same person," said Hannah, "but don't tell Mum, she'd go ballistic!"

"Mum's the word," said Lois, tapping the side of her nose.

The adverts started and Luke, the youngest, completely out of the blue, said, "Lisa nearly drowned today!" and he and Lisa started to giggle.

"Gosh, what happened? Was it really that funny?" Lois sat herself down on a pouffe with a look of concern.

Lisa pulled herself together and said, "We were playing fifty ways to kill yourself in a swimming pool, it's our new game." Hannah raised her eyes to heaven as her sister

148

continued, "I put on a rubber ring, which was quite, like, tight and went into the pool head first, so my legs were up in the air. It seemed funny to start with, that I couldn't, like, get myself the right way up. Then I thought I was, so gonna die! Anyway, I got to the side of the pool in the end and managed to pull myself up."

Lois had a hand up to her mouth, flabbergasted that the children could find this funny. "God, that's awful Lisa. You must have been really scared."

"Yeah. I'm not gonna do it again, that's for sure. We're not gonna play that game anymore, are we Luke?"

"No, too dodgy."

"I'm relieved to hear it," Lois said, getting up, to continue making her way to the toilet, then she paused to ask, "Luke, didn't you try and help?"

"No, I couldn't. I'd put armbands round my ankles, I was having trouble staying above the water myself!"

Lois shuddered. "Perhaps you should get rid of some of this, so called, safety equipment, it sounds much too dangerous!" As Lois walked through the door, Lisa called to her, "Oh Lois, please don't…" Lois and Lisa tapped their noses simultaneously and smiled at each other.

"But," said Lois, "only, if you promise never to play that game again!"

"Pinky promise!" said Lisa and Luke together and both held up their little fingers. Lois walked back and shook pinkies, which according to Luke was enforcing an unbreakable agreement.

"When's your baby due?" asked Hannah.

"Middle of September."

"Wow, that's so exciting! Can I babysit for you?"

"Yes, I'm sure you'll be able to, when he, or she, is big enough to be left."

"Woah, luckyyy!" exclaimed Lisa. Then their favourite contestant appeared on the TV and they all, once again, became engrossed.

By the time Lois got back, everyone had left the lounge, made their way to the dining room and were sitting around the large oak dining table. A space had been left for her between Richard and Adam.

During the first course the conversational focus was very much on Tom and Lois. Where they'd been living, which professions they were in, where they worked. Debbie and Richard were intrigued to find out about their plans for Honeysuckle; to which Tom replied that they wanted to live there for a while and get a feel for the house, before they decided what major changes should be made. Lois noticed that he kept very quiet about the fact that they'd run out of money, and then she remembered Tom's parent's offer.

"Lois? Penny for them?" said Richard.

"Oh, sorry I just…" Lois daren't say what she was thinking out loud, Tom would not be happy if she talked about anything to do with their finances in public. She decided it would be best to change the subject altogether. "…So, Richard, you're a GP?"

"Yes, that's me," he said, then took a large glug of wine.

"And a homeopath and an acupuncturist!" exclaimed Dave, as Debbie got up and started to clear away the plates, refusing Annie's offer of help.

"Yes. It sounds quite impressive doesn't it? But it's the homeopathy that I enjoy the most. We've just kitted out our study as a consulting room, so I can see private patients here instead of at work. It was becoming a little, shall we say, awkward?"

"Go on Richard, tell them what happened," said Debbie, as she returned from the kitchen with three of the children helping her carry plates and the dishes of the main course. "It is a very funny story!"

"Oh really, I feel a bit too sober for divulging that one."

"I'll tell it then," said Debbie, emptying her glass of wine, which Adam refilled for her immediately. She served up the food as she spoke. "One day, Richard had rushed to fit in an acupuncture treatment in between his GP consultations. He'd used a spare consulting room. I can't remember what was wrong with him now Richard?"

"I was treating him for migraine."

"So where did you have to put the needles?"

Richard paused; he wasn't at all sure about telling this story to people who were relative strangers; but Debbie seemed to be luring him into it. He took another slug of wine, "I put two here, under his nose, two to the sides of his nose and the remaining six at various points on his forehead. He did look quite funny it has to be said; a bit like a plump, bald porcupine!" Richard laughed at the thought. "I asked him to stay on the couch and relax and said I would be back in half an hour to remove the needles."

Richard looked at Debbie, waiting for her to continue with the story. "No, go on Rick, its much funnier coming from you."

"Well, by this time I was late for my next NHS patient, which flustered me a bit, I don't like running late and had to play catch-up for the rest of evening surgery. Even then, I finished later than I should have and still had paperwork to do. Lindsey, the receptionist, knocked to say she was off home and that, as I was last to leave, would I set the alarm. I glanced at my watch, it was seven thirty, even later than I'd thought. I'd promised to get home early that night, so, I grabbed my coat and bundled my paperwork and laptop into my bag and made for the door. As I left my consulting room I heard some muffled sounds coming from the room next door, which seemed odd, after Lindsey saying I would be the last to leave." Richard paused and took another gulp of wine. "My first thought, was whether there was an intruder in the building and as I approached the door, my second thought was, should I be going into the room unarmed? The only potential weapon I could think of, which happened to be in my bag, was my tendon hammer. I listened at the door, yes somebody was definitely in there, Lindsey must have forgotten to lock the door behind her.

"A tendon hammer? That sounds like a dangerous weapon to be wielding!" said Mel, astonished.

Richard laughed, "Hang on a minute, I'll fetch it." He disappeared briefly to his study, returning with his tendon hammer behind his back. Mel looked suspicious, while Debbie started giggling.

"Okay," said Richard, "a demonstration of me wielding a tendon hammer. I approached the door of the room containing the 'intruder', thus." He lifted a tiny wooden hammer, resembling a child's toy, above his head. At which point Mel and the rest of the party, joined in with Debbie's laughter. "Giving the impression of brave defender of property or complete prat? I leave you to decide. Anyway, I gently opened the door and walked in, heart racing, hands shaking. A man turned towards me, 'Oh my God it's Frankenstein!' I thought. Then I realised it was my poor patient, needles still in place, looking very concerned.

"'I thought you'd forgotten all about me Doc,' he said, his forehead wrinkling, making the needles point in different directions. I lowered the hammer.

"'Forgotten you Mr Smith! No, I would never forget about you!' He was looking at the tendon hammer enquiringly, so I continued, 'No, I was just coming in with my tendon hammer to, er,' I had to think fast. I could of course have said, 'to check your tendon reflexes,' but no, what came out was, 'to just give some of those needles a little tap before I take them out. It's fairly standard practice you know.' God, saying those words made me cringe! I was also beginning to wonder whether I could be struck off for malpractice. I decided that if I went ahead with tapping the needles with a hammer, I probably could. So I asked him how he was feeling. He replied that he was a bit stiff after lying on a couch for two hours, but otherwise, okay. So I said, that in that case, no need to use the tapping method, I'd just remove the needles."

Laughter filled the room. Mel was laughing so much at the idea of the poor old bloke with a face full of needles, she could barely breathe. "Hence, the reason I want to start seeing my private patients at home, I'm hoping to be more focused! Anyone wishing to book an appointment?"

"I have every confidence in you Richard," said Tom, "I seemed to make a remarkable recovery after coming to see you."

"Did you, Tom?" said Debbie, sounding very excited, "That's great news! I have to say we use homeopathy a lot, especially for the children and very often it has a staggering effect. I think Richard ought to start doing some official research into the results he gets. I'm sick of reading in the papers about these doctors who are too closed-minded to accept that there might be a place for homeopathy and acupuncture. It reminds me of all the academics who believed the world was flat and refused to believe otherwise until it was proven to them. Just because they can't understand something scientifically, it doesn't mean that it doesn't work."

"All right Debs, don't get on your high horse," Richard said, smiling; looking like he was loving every second of Debbie's rant.

"Go on Debbie, I'm enjoying it, I reckon you could take on all the sceptics singlehandedly!" said Tom.

"Well, it seems downright pompous to me to consider, homeopathy for example, as 'hocus pocus', I bet most of them have never even tried it, not properly. As for all this rubbish about it being the psychological effect of having an hour's chat to somebody, how come it works on children; babies; animals? Sicily and Maureen have been using it on their horses with great success, on ailments that conventional veterinary medicine struggles with." Debbie sat back in her chair and downed the remainder of her wine. "There, I'm done!"

"Come on, let's change the subject," said Richard, knowing that he and Debbie could very easily monopolise the evening talking about alternative medicine, such was their passion.

"Before we move on," said Mel, "we have to know, your patient, did he respond well? To the acupuncture I mean, not the incompetent care and near assault!"

"He did, fortunately. He responded very well. When he came back for his follow-up, he brought a fantastic bottle of scotch as a present! Talking of which, can I tempt anyone?"

All the men's eyes lit up, as did Mel's. Richard went to fetch the bottle, while Mel, Lois and Annie cleared the table ready for dessert. Lois and Mel were most impressed to see Debbie produce two fantastic looking puddings from the fridge. "Tiramisu, sorry Lois, that's not for you."

"No, that's for me!" said Annie, who had quietly polished off the best part of a bottle of wine and a couple of G&Ts since arriving. She took the dish from Debbie and walked out of the kitchen.

"Here's yours Lois," said Debbie, "lemon tart."

"Wow Debbie, that looks amazing! And will do me very nicely, thank you." Lois carried it through to the dining room and was surprised to find no sign of Annie, or the tiramisu. "Anyone seen Annie and a pudding?"

"Oh no, not again!" said Dave. "She's done this before. She gets a bit pissed and the next thing you know, she's stolen a pudding! Come on, we'd better go and find her, before she finishes it."

"Are you serious, Dave? She surely isn't going to lock herself away somewhere and eat that whole thing!"

"That Lois, is exactly what she is likely to be doing, as we speak!" Dave left the dining room and went to the TV lounge, where he enlisted the help of the children to help track down his wife and the remaining tiramisu.

With so many people on her trail, Annie was soon found. Hannah discovered her, sitting on the floor of the coat cupboard. She was in the dark, in the lotus position, feeding herself with a huge serving spoon, which she was having trouble getting in and out of her mouth.

Dave came, along with the rest of the guests and having rescued the remaining two thirds of the pudding and handed it to Debbie, pulled Annie out of the cupboard, mumbling apologies for his disgraceful wife.

As she emerged, a small amount of tiramisu still around her mouth, Annie started to giggle. "That big shpoon reminds me of a funny shtory," she slurred. "Do you remember Dave, when we went out to dinner with Chaz and Margaret?" Dave smiled. He remembered it well. "When it was time for pudding, Chaz ashked the waiter for a teashpoon," Annie was spluttering with laughter, it took her a few moments to continue. "He shaid," she laughed again, "it'sh just me wife'sh go' a very shmall mouf!"

This time they all laughed until it hurt. The thought of the voluminous Margaret needing a teaspoon because her mouth was so small, was, very funny.

When the laughter died down, Dave said, "Look guys, thanks for everything. It's been a great evening, but, bearing in mind that the wife's as pissed as a parrot and has eaten a rather large helping of tiramisu, I think I'd better get her home, before she disgraces herself further!"

Everyone said goodnight as Dave put his arm firmly around Annie's waist and headed out of the door, relieved to see that it had stopped raining. Lois was feeling exhausted and would happily have gone home too. But Debbie had put a huge amount of effort into making desserts and with Annie having messed up one of them, she felt she must stay and show her appreciation.

Lois found herself sitting next to the hostess when they returned to the table. Having served out dessert, Debbie asked her where she was planning to have the baby, then immediately jumped up and said "I've got something for you, I'll be back in a minute!" and disappeared.

"I wonder what it is," said Mel, who'd overheard their short conversation. "Must be something to do with birth or babies." She thought for a moment. "A DVD on childbirth perhaps? A pair of forceps?" Mel and Lois started laughing. "Some maternity clothes that will *so* not fit you?"

"Thanks!" said Lois, as Debbie reappeared through the door and handed her a well-read book.

Lois looked at it. "Mamatoto," she read, "A Celebration of Birth."

"I found it really useful," said Debbie. "It discusses the history of pregnancy and childbirth and different cultural beliefs and customs. My favourite chapter is about a tribe, which uses a two-storey birthing hut. The labouring woman stays on the ground floor, holding a rope; her husband is on the upper floor with the other end of the rope tied around his testicles. Every time she gets a contraction, the woman pulls on the rope!" There was a gasp from the male end of the table as they overheard Debbie's crescendoing voice, and giggles from the female end. Debbie continued, "So he can share in the pain of the contraction!"

"What a good idea!" said Mel.

"What do you think Pet? You could sit at the top of the spiral staircase?" said Lois, smiling. Tom did not look amused.

"Anyway, moving on," said Richard, and in a failed attempt at diplomacy, said, "when do you think you'll be up to more mountain biking Tom? I'm thinking we could get a Saturday morning group ride organised." He looked across at Adam.

"Yep, I'd go for that, I need something to stimulate me to get out on the bike regularly. It cost me a small fortune and I've hardly used it."

"Well I think it'll take me a while longer before I'm ready," said Tom, who could see Lois scowling out of the corner of his eye. "Um, and before I'm allowed out? Perhaps in the New Year, when our lives have settled down a bit?" He winked and smiled at Lois, who, he could see was looking exhausted. The men chatted for a few more minutes about the possibilities for cycling in the area. Then, Tom declared that it really was time for him to take Lois home, before she fell asleep on her dessert plate.

They both thanked Debbie and Richard for a great evening and for their gift. Richard, to Tom's great relief, offered to barrow the willow down to them the following day. "I suppose neither of you are in a position to plant it either!" said Richard; with the realisation dawning that he was going to end up planting the thing too. Adam came to his rescue, with an offer to do the planting; all Lois and Tom needed to do was to decide where to put it.

Richard and Adam, true to their words, arrived on Sunday morning, with Mel in tow and the little tree in the barrow. Adam dug a large hole in the middle of the front lawn, relieved that the rain from the previous night had softened the ground considerably. He put a bag of Bill's horse manure in it and planted the little willow.

When he'd patted down the soil to finish off the job, Adam said, "Now don't expect us to be looking after you two forever, okay?"

"Okay," said Tom, "we owe you one. Talking of which, we do owe you, for the roofing work. How much is it, did you give Dean an invoice?"

"Oh forget it, all part of the welcoming committee!"

"Are you sure Adam? That seems very generous."

"My pleasure. Consider it my gift. I don't do stuffed animals!"

Lois brought coffee and some slightly squashed cakes into the front garden for everyone. Tom told her about Adam's gift and as they both thanked him, Charles Black shuffled his way past.

"Morning Charles," shouted Richard, "lovely day!"

"For some it might be," Charles grumbled to the ground, barely acknowledging any of them.

Lois, Mel and Tom exchanged glances. When Tom thought Charles was probably out of earshot, he said, "Ah, so that'll be the delightful Mr Black, then."

"Yup," said Richard, "laugh a minute that one. Right, where do you want this turf and topsoil?" he asked, as he went to retrieve his full wheelbarrow.

"I'll chuck it over the road on the manor scrubland if you like," said Adam, "that's what I do with most of my garden rubbish; nobody notices, amongst the brambles."

"That would be great, thanks," Tom said and he followed Adam, through a hole in the hawthorn hedge on the opposite side of the road to see where he meant. As they emerged on the other side of the hedge, Tom was amazed to see a collection of ramshackle barns, which he had never noticed before, partially hidden behind a mass of brambles. Having emptied the barrow, Adam followed his gaze.

"They're great aren't they? Belong to the manor. Been lying dormant for a very long time, I expect at some point the board will opt to apply for planning permission, who knows what monstrosity they'll try to put here. In the meantime, come with me."

157

Adam picked up a large stick and having walked around to the front of the barns, started to lever the brambles back to create a pathway wide enough to walk along. Once in front of the main barn, he pushed one of the heavy wooden doors open and took out his phone to shed some light on the dark, gloomy interior. As Tom followed him in, they both heard a loud squeak and a rustle from the far corner. "Rats, making a quick getaway," said Adam.

Amongst the cobwebs and grime, Tom could just make out some large oak beams, a couple of wooden gates and a pair of old oak doors. "Wow, this place is amazing!"

"Yup, and I don't think anyone ever comes here, except me."

"So, when we eventually do our extension and put in an inglenook fireplace, I'll give you a shout, Adam?"

"That's the spirit Tom. I can see you'll soon settle into the foraging culture of the country! By the way, are you free on Wednesday night? Richard and I are planning to have a couple of pints at the Flintstone Wall."

"Well, it would be churlish not to join you, wouldn't it?"

18

Tom arrived at the cottage at six o'clock on Wednesday evening, having managed to leave the office early. He'd been staying at the flat since Monday and was astonished to walk into a clean, tidy house. The carpets were laid and the curtains hung. Lois heard the front door shut and emerged from the kitchen with a half bottle of champagne; flutes and a very broad smile on her face.

"What do you think?"

"Lo, it's amazing, you've done wonders in the past few days. You must have worked none stop!"

"So, a celebration. Hold these." Lois passed Tom the glasses, then expertly removed the cork from the bottle and poured the champagne very carefully. "To our perfect house!"

"Our perfect house!" repeated Tom.

They toured the cottage, with Lois asking Tom his opinion of each room and Tom responding that he thought it all looked fantastic. They finished the tour in the nursery. Lois had bought a stick on border with a cartoon baby elephant design, mounted it a metre up the pale yellow walls and hung matching curtains. Tom paused as he walked through the door, turning pale with shock. The reality of them soon, actually having a baby, suddenly hit home. He leant against the wall and slid down into a crouching position. Lois joined him. They both sat in silence for several minutes.

So many contrasting thoughts flooded into Tom's brain, that he found tears welling up in his eyes. The past year had been so busy for both of them; working long hours, house hunting, and then renovating the cottage. When they'd made the decision to try for a baby, he had not expected it to happen so quickly. There was the initial shock, a brief moment of wanting to run away, then, the excitement of something that was going to happen many months in the future. And now, here it was, their baby's nursery. 'Oh my God, how scary is this?' he thought. 'Am I really grown-up enough to be a dad?'

"What do you think, not too twee is it?"

"No, Lo it's…" Tom wiped his eye with the back of his hand, "it's perfect. I can't believe there's going to be a little person in here soon, a real little person."

"It's bizarre isn't it?" Lois said, looking down at her belly and giving it a stroke.

"It's wonderful," said Tom, resting his hand on Lois's. "I've missed you. I can't wait to be settled in here properly." He gave her a kiss on the cheek. "Anyway, I put in enough hours this week to be able to have tomorrow and Friday off, so all is well. Oh, by the way did I mention that I've been invited out for a drink tonight?"

"No. I thought we'd be having one last night of romance on the blow up mattress."

"Don't worry, we can still do that, you smooth talker you! I won't be out long. Literally just popping to the village pub for a pint with Adam and Richard. We're going at seven, so I'm sure we'll be back by nine."

"Oh, go on then. But don't you go leading these country folk astray! And remember, we've a fairly early start tomorrow to meet the movers."

A moment later there was a knock at the door; Tom made his way downstairs and opened it to find Richard and Adam waiting for him.

"You're a bit early aren't you?"

"Well we thought, as we were all home, best to pop out now, be back earlier?" suggested Adam, grinning at Lois who was propping herself up against Tom.

"Tom, do you want to grab a sandwich before you go?" asked Lois.

"No thanks," said Tom, taking a shiny new front door key for the replacement lock that Dean had fitted, "I'll probably grab a bite there. Thanks love." He gave Lois a peck on the cheek, and the three men strode purposefully away.

Lois went to the kitchen to concoct a meal for herself. She felt a bit flat. She'd been looking forward to Tom coming home. Having been on her own in the cottage for the last three days, she'd envisaged them having a nice romantic evening together. "Still," she thought aloud, "nice for him to get to know some of the neighbours better."

Just as Lois sat down on the rug with a plate of pitta, houmous and salad, there was a knock at the door. She hauled herself up to standing; the baby seemed to have increased in size a lot this week … or was it the mini chocolate rolls and flapjacks on BOGOF at M&S that were making bending movements feel so much more cumbersome? She opened the door to find Debbie, Lycra-clad, red faced and sweaty, standing on the doorstep.

"Since the men folk are out boozing for the night, I wondered if you fancy coming round to me for a little something?"

"Out boozing for the night? Tom said they were popping to the pub for a pint."

"Mm, well, if Richard and Adam's 'popping to the pub for a pint's of the past are anything to go by, we won't see them this side of midnight."

Debbie saw a brief look of disappointment in Lois's eyes, before she said, "Yep, that would be great Debbie. I'll just eat my supper. See you in about fifteen minutes?"

"Great, see you then!" Debbie said, and turning, jogged away.

Lois finished her meal, refreshed her make-up and wrote a note for Tom to let him know where she was, in the apparently unlikely event that he was home before her. She changed into her 'holiday' cotton trousers with handy expandable drawstring waist and a clean vest top. The evening was hot and humid; Lois wondered whether there was a storm brewing. She made her way up to Debbie's, feeling a slight pang of guilt as she walked past Bert and Betty's; she hadn't been back to see them yet. She made a mental note to visit them during the early part of the following week.

Debbie answered the door with hair still wet from the shower. She'd made a non-alcoholic fruit cocktail, a glass of which they each took out onto the patio. They settled themselves onto sun loungers with a bowl of Bombay mix on the table between them.

As they chatted, Debbie became more and more relaxed and Lois saw, on following her into the kitchen to top up the drinks, that she was adding a generous shot of gin to her own glass. "Do you want a spot?" Debbie asked, having noticed Lois watching her, "It won't hurt; mine were all introduced to gin early and it never did them any harm. I do mean in moderation of course!"

"Oh, go on then. Just a drop!"

Lois felt somewhat in awe of Debbie; she had so much experience of both giving birth and bringing up children. But, as the gin warmed its way through her body, Lois began to feel less self-conscious and decided she was feeling brave enough to ask Debbie how her deliveries had been.

"Lois, let me give you one piece of advice. Never ask people how their deliveries were. Fortunately I don't have a horror story to tell you, which is probably why I've got four children; but plenty of people will have, and hearing them will heighten your anxiety to such a point, that your likelihood of a natural birth will be doomed!"

"Oh," Lois felt somewhat belittled. She took another slug of her cocktail and said, "but yours were alright?"

"Yes, they were, well, not too bad. Have you had a chance to read the Mamatoto book yet?"

"No. Too busy organising the house. We pack up the flat tomorrow and move in on Friday."

"Fantastic! Well, as soon as you've got time to, if I were you, I'd read that book. It gave me confidence in making my birthing decisions. Of course, being married to Richard helped. He'd done a six-month stint in obstetrics as part of his GP training and reassured me that I was very capable of having a natural birth. He encouraged me to get really fit," Debbie giggled, "He used to say that I needed to prepare for the biggest marathon of my life, and he was right."

"So, I ought to be going running?" Lois asked, sceptically; bar dragging herself around the 400-metre track at school, she had never 'been running' in her life and the thought of starting now was, at the very least, unnerving.

"Not necessarily running, no; but getting fit, yes. Use whatever form of exercise suits you. How about walking or swimming? There's an antenatal aqua aerobics class at the sports centre, that's a bit of a laugh. I nearly gave birth to Lisa in it actually." Debbie started to giggle again. "Fortunately, Richard's practice was not far away and he came and picked me up. Just got home in time and had her on the living room floor." Lois raised her hand to her mouth in amazement. "The midwife arrived ten minutes after the event, by which time Lisa was dressed and so was I. Oh no, that's a lie," Debbie paused, smiling, "I wasn't dressed because I was having a bit of trouble delivering the placenta, bloody thing just wouldn't come out!"

"MUM!" Shouted a voice from an upstairs room. Debbie and Lois both glanced up, shielding their eyes from the sun reflected on the open window. "Would you please stop talking about my placenta, it's embarrassing! You do it all the time!"

Debbie put her hand to her mouth and said, quietly. "Bless her! She's very sensitive that one. And by the way, I don't do it all the time!"

"So, I need to get fit and read Mamatoto. Anything else?"

"Well, when you've read the book, try and decide on the sort of birth you want to aim for. You're welcome to come round anytime and we'll chat about it some more."

Lois and Debbie continued talking, with Debbie going into the house to shout the occasional instruction at one or other of the children. By nine o'clock the sky beyond Debbie's garden started to darken and they could hear some rumblings of thunder.

"That's what we need, a good storm to clear the air, I'm sweating like nobody's business here," said Debbie. Just then, they saw the first flash of lightning, followed by another, then another. As they sat, mesmerised, they witnessed the most incredible lightning display either of them had ever seen. The clouds slowly moved towards them, the thunder grew louder and the time between lightning and thunder grew shorter. Lois and Debbie were picking up their glasses to go inside,

163

when they felt the first drops of rain. By the time they'd reached the back door, the heavens had opened.

"Mm, looks like the boys might get a bit wet then," smirked Debbie.

"So, will they be very drunk when they get back?" asked Lois.

"I think the expression is 'completely ratted!' Unless Tom is going to be such a good and persuasive influence on them as to make them change their ways. What do you think?"

"Um," Lois paused, "no. No, I think I can safely say, if they plan to drink heavily, he will be joining in."

"Ah well, the walk home in the rain should sober them up a bit. Richard will probably invite Tom back here for a bite to eat, there's the remains of a fish pie in the oven, so he'll sober up a bit; unless they get the whisky out, that has been known."

"I don't think Tom will come here, he'll be exhausted after the pub and the walk back, he's still not a hundred per cent after his accident, but thanks for warning me, I was expecting him home by nine. We're supposed to be at the flat by ten tomorrow morning to meet the packers."

"Well that'll be fun! Richard's got his first private patient coming to the house tomorrow morning, that'll be interesting too!"

They continued to chat until Lois noticed the time on the kitchen clock to be just before ten. With the realisation that she was probably going to be doing most of the organisation at the flat tomorrow, she decided it was time to go home and get some sleep. She thanked Debbie for her hospitality, borrowed a waterproof coat and made her way.

The thunder and lightning had stopped, but the rain continued to hammer down. The road was so dark that Lois walked straight through a number of puddles between Debbie's house and her own. Another disadvantage, she realised, to living on an unmade road. She could just make out the sound of Doreen calling to Ellie, through the noise of the rain, as she walked past Bramble Cottage.

By the time she reached Honeysuckle, Lois's cream trousers were splashed to the knee with clay coloured dirt and her pumps, ruined. She struggled to get the key into the lock because of the lack of an outside light, (one of many oversights in the renovation, no doubt). Once inside, she looked for somewhere to hang Debbie's coat to dry, only to find no coat hooks, so she hung it over the dining room door to drip onto the floor tiles. She took off her trousers and put them, along with her shoes, into the kitchen sink in hot water and washing up liquid and then found a scrap of paper and a pen and started the RO (renovation oversight) list.

Lois's heart sank as she thought through washing her trousers in the machine on Friday. They hadn't even considered plumbing for the washing machine or venting for the dryer. She sat for several minutes on the bottom stair wondering what else she'd forgotten; then shrugged and added washing machine etc to her list; after all, the renovation had gone remarkably well so far, and Dean had said he would come back and do any extras for her next week.

Lois had a shower and made her way to bed. She lay, wondering what kind of a state Tom would come home in. Generally he wasn't a big drinker, two or three pints was usually enough for him. It seemed unlikely he'd be too bad when he got home.

Having fallen asleep within a few minutes of lying down, Lois was woken by a bang, which, in her sleepy state, she was unable to identify. Then she heard the front door close. She glanced at her phone to see that it was twelve thirty, felt relieved that Tom was safely home and rolled over to go back to sleep.

A couple of minutes later, she thought she heard the front door open and shut again. This struck her as a bit odd, but she stayed in bed and listened for the sound of Tom coming up the stairs.

When, after ten minutes or so there was neither sight nor sound of him, she got up and pulled on some leggings and a T-shirt to go and investigate. Opening the bedroom door, she was hit by a foul, unidentifiable smell, which made her retch. There was absolutely no sign of Tom downstairs. Well actually, that was not strictly true; there were muddy footprints, leading from the front porch, over the brand new, beige carpet and the newly laid dining room and kitchen tiles and back again. And the stench downstairs was horrific! He had clearly been sick somewhere. Lois followed the footprints to the kitchen sink, where she nearly vomited herself. The sink, where her trousers and shoes were soaking, was now topped up with the most disgusting-smelling puke!

Lois felt her hackles rising as she opened some windows to help get rid of the stench. She had never lost her temper with Tom, but she was tired and they had a couple of busy days coming up; how could he do this to her! Anyway, where the hell was he, he wasn't in the house. Lois opened the front door and peered out into the blackness. She couldn't see a thing, but above the sound of the driving rain, she thought she could hear somebody laughing. She grabbed Debbie's raincoat, put it on and ventured outside in the direction of the laughter; the door, assisted by a strong breeze from the open windows, slamming itself shut behind her.

"Oh no!" said Lois, realising she was now locked out of the house. "Tom, where are you?"

"I'm here my precioush!" Tom slurred. "Ouch! That hurt! You jusht kicked my head!"

"It's lucky I didn't fall over you! What are you doing lying on the grass? It's pouring out here, you must be completely drenched."

"I was shick my special, oh … " And Lois had the pleasure of hearing Tom being sick again, and then, he laughed! How could he find it funny? He was lying in the front garden, in pitch dark and pouring rain, puking up something that smelled like it had died and rotted inside him and yet he was finding it hysterically funny.

"God, it smells terrible Tom! What the hell have you been drinking?"

"Beer my pet, lovely beer. But I think the problem might have been the fisch pie, and the, oh, what'shit called, the shtuff the Pope drinksh? You know, Billy Connelly, green?"

"Crème de menthe, oh my God, not a pint, please tell me it wasn't a pint!" The thought was enough to set him off again. Lois held her nose with one hand and half-heartedly rubbed his shoulder with the other until he'd finished and had once again started chuckling to himself.

"Only a half my pet," he laughed again, "only a half. Richard had a pint though, jusht like Billy Connelly!"

Lois realised there was absolutely no point being cross with him, the impact would be lost. She helped him into a sitting position; onto his knees, then his feet; then she remembered about the door. "Oh my God, I think I might have locked us out!" said Lois, feeling something close to despair.

"Don't you worry my little angel, I've got a key right … " Tom groped around, trying to find the opening to his front trouser pocket.

"Let me," said Lois, feeling for the pocket, and then slipping her hand inside.

"Oooh, cheeky! We should probably wait till we get upshtairs, my little shex pod!"

"Oh p-lease!" said Lois in disgust, as she removed the key and waved it in front of his face. She supported Tom to the front door, opened it, let him in as far as the doormat, where she made him stop, and he leant on her back as she removed his shoes. She then took off his soaking, sick splattered clothes as Tom made suggestive comments, which made Lois feel extremely queasy. She left him naked, shivering and giggly on the mat, under strict instructions not to move, while she hurried to get a bin liner. She bundled his clothes and shoes into it and threw it out of the front door.

Tom registered the footprints on the carpet from earlier. "Who did that?" he demanded in a gruff, serious voice.

"Who do you think?"

"Oh my precioush, I'm shoo shorry! I'll get a cloth and wipe them up." Tom raised a wavering finger in the air as he contemplated his next move and started chuckling to himself again.

"No, you won't. You'll go to the bathroom, clean yourself up and if you promise not to be sick anymore you can get into bed, otherwise, may I suggest you sleep in the bath?"

"Goodjidea. The barf. Yesh, shleep, inna barf. I might barf in the barf!" Tom chuckled, as he made his way up the spiral staircase, hanging onto the banister and heaving himself up by it, as if the staircase was almost vertical. Lois followed, but not directly behind. If he was to fall, she didn't want him to take her out too.

Once upstairs, Lois got Tom to sit down in the shower and tied a plastic bag over his plaster cast. He was so cold and wet already that he barely noticed that the water started off cold, which, Lois admitted to herself, was a touch disappointing. She squirted some shower gel into his hand and ordered him to wash, which he duly did, humming to himself. Lois showered him off, ordered him out, helped him to dry and loaded a toothbrush with which he scrubbed at his teeth. She then allowed him to settle on the blow-up mattress and went back downstairs. She took one look at her trousers and shoes in the sink and decided they were probably ruined anyway, even before the addition to them that Tom had made. She pulled on a pair of rubber gloves, let the plug out and, while looking the other way, breathing heavily and deliberately through her mouth, she wrung them out, double bagged them and threw them out of the back door. The footprints, she decided, could wait until tomorrow.

19

The next day Lois's alarm went off at seven; she reflexly hit the snooze button, a total of three times. At half past, she dragged herself out of bed, grumbling as she went. She never coped very well with lack of sleep. The house smelt disgusting which didn't help matters. She just managed to refrain from kicking Tom's feet, which were poking off the end of the mattress, as she passed.

Lois got dressed into her leggings and T-shirt that she'd brought to wear that day and realised that she had worn them the previous night to find Tom. The top stank; it had a smear of puke on the shoulder. With no other clean clothes to choose from, she swore quietly; angry with Tom, then went through to the bathroom and scrubbed off the sick the best she could using his damp flannel, which she deliberately didn't rinse out.

After bleaching the kitchen sink to try and get rid of the smell, Lois made herself a cup of tea and some cereal. Having eaten, she examined Tom's footprints and decided they were best left until they were completely dry and then hopefully the hoover would suck them up. She organised the things they needed to take to the flat and put them by the front door and was just about to take Tom a cup of tea in an attempt to prize him out of bed, when there was a hard knocking at the door. Lois opened it to find Adam, looking very out of sorts. Lois was about to make a witty quip related to last nights drinking episode, when she realised that he was upset about something.

"Ellie, have you seen Ellie, Jack's dog? She's disappeared."

"No, I haven't been out yet. When did she go?"

"Last night. Doreen let her out in the garden. The gate must have been left open. She's so greedy, she probably went off rummaging for food and never came back, which really isn't like her."

"Oh God, I bet Jack's beside himself!"

"I can't tell you, I've never seen him so upset. Anyway I must carry on with the search. Please keep your eyes open."

"Adam, I'll help. Which way do you want me to go?"

"Well, I'm going to the barns opposite and round the back. Would you knock at the rest of the houses and ask everyone to check their gardens, maybe you check Bert and Betty's? I've seen Dave already."

"Sure!"

Lois went upstairs and woke Tom. She pretty much ordered him out of bed, thrusting the cup of tea into his hand. Then told him that she had to go out and when she returned in twenty minutes, it would be time to go. She grabbed a fleece and her old shoes and set off.

As soon as she left the house she heard Jack calling for Ellie, the tone of his voice sounding uncharacteristically despondent. The thought of how Jack would react to the permanent loss of his dog sent a chill down Lois's spine. Despite hardly knowing him, she had picked up very clearly that Ellie had transformed his life beyond recognition. As she turned out of the garden gate and onto the road, she could see Jack leaning forwards as far as he could in his wheelchair, his paralysed hand flopping down towards the ground. He was checking under the hedges.

Jack looked up when he heard Lois approaching and pulled his limp arm back onto his lap. He looked so upset and worried, a lump rose in Lois's throat. He was about to speak when his gaze moved past Lois and he let out a mournful cry. Lois looked around to see Adam, with Ellie lying flaccid in his arms. She was soaking wet, with blue foam around her mouth and blood on her tail.

"Jack, I'm so sorry," said Adam. "Rat poison. She is still alive. I'll take her to the vet."

Jack shook his head and beckoned to Adam to bring Ellie to him. Adam lay her on Jack's knee with her head resting in the crook of his paralysed arm, his good arm over her to prevent her slipping off. Ellie looked up at him and wagged her tail, and then, went limp. Adam felt her chest for a pulse, there was nothing. "Jack, I'm so sorry." Jack bowed his head down towards the lifeless dog, stroked her tummy and began to sob. Adam put a hand on his shoulder and crouched beside him. Lois, feeling at a loss as to what to do, thought the best thing would be to go and find Doreen.

The door was answered in seconds. Doreen looked at Lois expectantly, then seeing tears welling in her eyes, knew. They embraced each other; their sadness for the death of such a wonderful dog, exacerbated by the thought of what this loss was going to do to Jack. Eventually, Doreen let go, put the door on the latch and the two of them went to find him.

Jack and Adam were exactly as Lois had left them. Doreen crouched down in front of Jack; she gave Ellie a stroke and, through her tears, thanked the extraordinary dog for all that she'd done. Then, without saying a word she wheeled Jack back to the house with Lois and Adam following. When they arrived, Adam suggested to Jack that he took Ellie to the back garden, but Jack clung onto the body and for once, Lois thought his words "Oh bugger off!" were exactly what he wanted to say. Doreen put her hand on Adam's arm, "Don't worry Adam, can I call you in a while, he needs some time." Adam nodded and, with Lois, quietly left, as Doreen tearfully wheeled Jack round to the back of the house.

Lois felt completely flat as she walked back to the cottage. It had been going to be such an exciting day; packing up the flat for the big move tomorrow, but she felt unable to raise any enthusiasm at all. Opening the front door and remembering her hung-over fiancé didn't help; now, she *really* wasn't in the mood.

Fortunately, Tom was surprisingly well on the way to recovery. He had showered, eaten, drunk several pints of water and found some Alka Seltzer tucked away in his wallet. A vague memory of some of the events of the previous night, made him sufficiently aware that he needed to make a major effort to make things up to Lois.

"Where've you been?" he asked, giving Lois a hug. She was tempted to push him away, the smell of alcohol was still seeping through his pores, but as he had clearly been trying to recover himself, she hugged him back.

"I'll explain in the car. We're late, let's get going. We don't want our man with a van to give up on us."

Tom had already loaded his car with everything Lois had left by the door. She did a quick check of the list she'd made the previous day, and then took the keys from Tom; there was no way he'd be driving anywhere today. And off they went.

Lois filled Tom in on what had happened that morning. She'd put some tissues up her sleeve before they left, knowing it would be difficult to tell him without crying. Lois dabbed her eyes surreptitiously; she'd never been good in sad situations, often crying her way through emotional films and books. "Jack's days are going to be so empty without Ellie, she's been his constant companion. And poor Doreen, having seen Jack through his stroke, to see him now, no doubt sink into another depression. Plus her own grief at losing Ellie; it's just so sad."

"Where did Adam find her?" asked Tom.

"I'm not entirely sure, but I know he said he'd go and look in the barns, and 'around the back', whatever that means."

"That must have been the barns he showed me the other day, opposite our house. Lots of rats over there; but who would have put down poison without using a safe container? That's just bloody stupid. We ought to find out who's responsible. Presumably the groundsman from the manor's the only person who would have done it."

"It's a bit late now Tom, she's dead."

"What about the other dogs. I've seen Annie and Dave's two go through the hole in that hedge, imagine if they died too!"

Lois agreed that he had a valid point and asked him to phone Annie and make sure she knew what had happened. When Tom had put the phone down, Lois asked, "So, how was the night out with the boys?"

"Do you know, strangely, I can't remember much about it. I'd been told they did a great range of locally brewed beers in the pub, but I hadn't planned to try them all! I remember getting very wet on the way home and that's about it."

172

"You said, or should I say, you slurred something last night about fish pie and crème de menthe." At the mention of which, Tom became tinged with green.

"Oh dear, no wonder I'm feeling a tad under the weather!"

The traffic going into London was predictably slow, so they didn't arrive until ten thirty. There were no parking spaces within two hundred yards of the flat, and no sign of Ed or his van in the entire street. Lois gave a sigh, thought briefly about Jack and Doreen and decided that missing the packing man, or having him not turn up, was not such a disaster.

They went into the flat, collecting the mail from the doormat on their way, and then Lois rang Ed. He was coming, but had got caught in traffic and hoped to be there within fifteen minutes. That gave them time for a cup of tea and a soft biscuit. "So," Tom said, reaching for Lois's hand across the table, "was I very sick last night?"

"Very sick? Yes Tom, I think that would sort of cover it." Lois thought for a moment, "But hang on, very sick, then very sick again. That would describe it better. Or even, producing copious volumes of vomit. How about that?"

"Okay, okay, I get the message. Please stop before I do it again!"

Lois looked up from the bank statement she'd been pretending to concentrate on and smiled at him. "I'm not sure our little willow tree will survive the experience and you might have to go and rescue some turf to replace the patch of lawn which will almost certainly die! Still I suppose it's a good thing you were ill, think what you'd feel like now if you hadn't been." She thought for a moment, "Tom, you could have died. Half a pint of crème de menthe! What were you thinking?"

"Funnily enough, I can't remember, but probably something along the lines of, 'wouldn't it be funny to drink half a pint of crème de menthe!'"

"I wonder how Richard is. I went round to theirs for a drink with Debbie last night. She said he's got his first private

173

patient going to the house this morning. That could be interesting."

The doorbell rang and, to Lois and Tom's relief, there stood Ed and Co., fully laden with packs of flat cardboard boxes, tape, packing paper, coloured stickers and marker pens. Lois breathed a sigh of relief; it looked like they were going to be really well organised. "What shall we do?" Lois asked Ed, as he started taping boxes together.

"Well, every box we pack, you seal and write wos innit and which room t' pud i' in at the uvver end. And anyfink delicate tha' you don' trust us wif, you pack yerselves. Okay? And, any chance of a cuppa?"

By one forty-five, to Lois's amazement, the packing was finished and Ed was eager to load the van. "We could do the 'ole fing t'day if yer wan'. Plen'y o' time," Ed said to Tom, who felt as if Ed was talking in a foreign language. Ed could see that Tom, who stank of booze, couldn't understand. He wondered what a nice woman like Lois was doing with this alcoholic idiot.

"Move, today?" Ed said very slowly, in an attempt to help Tom get the message, "To Buck-in-am-shire?" Fortunately Lois overheard this as she was coming into the room. Tom looked as though he'd glazed over, his lack of sleep and alcohol consumption catching up with him.

"That would be brilliant Ed! Do you think there's time?"

"Yeah, easy."

"Go for it then!" said Lois, feeling excited for the first time that day.

At ten o'clock in the evening, Tom slumped onto the sofa and Lois sat on his knee and hugged him. "Home sweet home!" she said, with a broad grin.

"Luxury isn't it? Sitting on a sofa," said Tom, eyes closed, feeling exhausted and hungry.

Lois felt completely drained, even though Ed and his three helpers had done practically all the work. They had been absolutely brilliant, really well organised and very efficient. It was so lovely to see the cottage with their furniture in, making it feel real at last.

There was a quiet knock at the door. It was Dave and Annie, with a bottle of sparkling wine and sandwiches.

Annie gave Lois a huge hug. "What an emotional day!" she said, smiling and trying to blink a tear away at the same time. "Welcome," she hugged Tom, "and may I take this opportunity to say how delighted we are that you're here! Oh look, what luxury, chairs to sit on!"

Dave opened the wine. "Just a spot for me please Dave," said Tom, suddenly feeling queasy at the sight of alcohol, "Not feeling quite myself."

"Ah yes, I heard you popped out for a pint with the lads last night. Thought you were looking a little green around the gills old boy!" Dave slapped Tom on the back, "You'll know what to expect next time! Anyway, let's raise our glasses. To Harewood Park!"

"To Harewood Park!" the others choroused.

Annie, being forever practical and seeing how tired Tom and Lois were, asked if their bed was made up. When Lois said no, Annie found the bedding that had been dragged, with the deflated blow-up mattress into the baby's room and made up their double bed. Annie and Dave then drained their glasses and said they would leave Tom and Lois to get to bed.

"Any news on Jack?" asked Lois, as they got up to leave.

"Mm, not good apparently," said Dave. "I saw Adam earlier; he'd been round to offer to bury the dog. Both Doreen and Jack were very upset; the organisation that provided her for Jack, want to come and collect the body and have a post-mortem done, which really doesn't help."

"Life can be so unfair, can't it?" said Lois.

"It certainly can," said Annie, with Dave nodding in agreement behind her. "Anyway, we'll leave you to it, see you over the weekend no doubt?"

"I hope so. Thanks for everything," said Lois, as she and Tom waved their goodbyes. Having closed the door, they went straight up to bed, in luxury.

175

20

Lois and Tom woke late on Friday. Lois felt very relieved that the move had been completed the day before and that they had the next three days to get the house straight, before Tom returned to work. She went down to make breakfast and while waiting for the toast to pop, in an actual toaster, and the water to boil, in a real kettle, phoned Dean.

When Lois mentioned the lack of plumbing for the washing machine, Dean laughed. "There is plumbing for it, have you not noticed?"

"Apparently not," said Lois. She had looked for it. Oh dear, this was embarrassing.

"It's in the little outhouse," explained Dean, "Oh look, I'll pop over, I've got nothing on today, well clothes obviously," Lois laughed weakly, "but no work. I'll come and do any odd jobs you want doing. You okay to be on shopping standby, if necessary?"

"Yep! No problem."

Lois went and looked in the outhouse. She'd only been in it once before, seen that it housed a rusty old fridge and a do-it-yourself brewing kit, then, noticing it was full of spider's webs, had backed out quickly. The outhouse was a narrow building between the small porch-way containing the back door and the outside loo. When Lois stood outside looking at the arrangement, she couldn't believe they hadn't thought to knock it all into one, so they had a utility room and an internal downstairs loo. Oh well, too late now, she couldn't bear the thought of more dust now that the furniture was all in place. She opened the door to the outhouse and stepped in cautiously. Yes, still lots of cobwebs, but also, plumbing for a washing machine and a small window through which they could stick the vent for the dryer. Fantastic. Lois returned to the kitchen and ticked those two items off her list, with a satisfied grin.

The day passed quickly. It transpired there was very little for Dean to do. Not only had Lois not noticed the plumbing, but also, much to her embarrassment, she had failed to spot the outside sensor light that George had mounted by the front door. The override switch simply needed to be turned on from inside the house.

Dean and Tom cleared out and cleaned the outhouse. Lois refused to help, exaggerating her fear of spiders a little as an excuse. Then Dean, with minimal help from Tom, removed the old fridge and carried the washing machine and drier through from where Ed and co. had left them in the middle of the kitchen. Once Dean had connected the machine, Lois was relieved to get some washing done; the delightful smell of stale sick had been lurking in the house since Wednesday and she hoped that washing all their clothes and bed linen would help to clear it.

The remainder of the day was spent unpacking the boxes that the movers hadn't had time for, mainly books, some office files and kitchen equipment. Dean put up two lines of coat hooks, one by the front door and one by the back and mounted their pictures and framed photos on walls throughout the house, as instructed by a rather pernickety Tom. Lois ordered a lawn mower online, they needed one that would be delivered quickly, so, without giving it a great deal of thought, she ordered something big, green and moderately expensive.

In the early evening Lois and Tom walked to the pub for supper. On the way back, they could not resist going to Richard and Debbie's to see how they'd managed the previous day. Richard opened the door and smirked at Tom like a naughty schoolboy. He invited them in and offered tea or coffee, adding with a chuckle, that he wasn't allowed alcohol at the moment. They were just sitting down at the kitchen table, when Debbie came in from the garden with a huge washing basket full of clothes from the line. Richard leapt up from his seat at such a rate, that Tom thought there must be some impending disaster.

"Let me help you with that Darling!" Richard said, taking the basket from Debbie and disappearing through the kitchen door.

"What was all that about?" Lois asked Debbie.

"Ah, he's trying to wheedle his way back into my affections after his bad behaviour on Wednesday night." They smiled at each other.

"Come on then, tell me how he disgraced himself and I'll tell you what my lovely fiancé did," said Lois.

"I think I'll go and give Richard a hand with the washing!" Tom said, making a hasty exit in search of comradeship.

Debbie picked up Richard's tea and began to sip it. "Well. I'd left fish pie in the oven for them, as you know, Richard was bound to invite Tom and Adam back here. They came in at about eleven thirty and were making so much noise that I came down and told them, in no uncertain terms, not to wake the children. Richard said they would be quiet, that the lads were just having a bite to eat, and would then be off home. I noticed the whisky bottle on the table, at which point Richard said, like a five year old doing something he shouldn't, 'I was just showing them the bottle, the label, we're not going to drink it.' And Tom and Adam stood behind him, trying to look serious and nodding their agreement. It was very funny; I wish I could have filmed them really.

"Anyway, I took the whisky away, shut the kitchen door and left them to it. When I woke at two in the morning to find Richard still not in bed, I came downstairs to see what was going on. I went into the kitchen first and found an empty bottle, crème de menthe of all things, and three half-pint glasses with a shade of green lurking in the bottom. Then I went and looked in the rest of the downstairs rooms until I found him, in the study."

Lois, covered her eyes in preparation for what disgusting description was to come, she knew it was going to be bad after Richard's response earlier, two days after the event.

"Oh Lois, you cannot imagine the mess!" Lois thought she probably could, but left Debbie to continue the story. "Blood and puke all over the carpet!"

"Blood! Why on earth?"

"Well, having been sick, in a heap, on the carpet; I don't know how he piled it up; I imagine he was lying down on his side perhaps?" Lois wrinkled up her face and groaned. "Anyway, he then decided that the easiest way to clear it up was to excise the carpet!" Lois looked quizzically at Debbie. "Yes, he got a scalpel and tried to cut out the effected area of carpet; brand, new, carpet!"

"No!"

"Yes. In the process he sliced into his knee without even noticing *and* his finger. When I went in, he was flat out on the floor, asleep. Well, I thought he might be dead at first. But then he did an enormous burp and, I think I was relieved to see that he wasn't."

"Oh my God, how did you sort it all out? No wonder you're so cross with him."

"Well, I got him out of the way first, mainly because he was so eager to help clear up the mess. I stripped him off, made him sit in the shower and hosed him down."

Lois laughed, "Sounds familiar."

"I put a couple of Steri-Strips and several plasters on the finger, that cut was quite deep. The knee wasn't so bad. Slicing through his jeans first offered a bit of protection. I then left him to sleep on the bathroom floor." Debbie laughed. "Well, I didn't want him in bed with me!"

"Then I bagged up the sick, which smelt just awful!"

"I know!" said Lois. They both laughed and said at the same time, "Fish pie and crème de menthe!"

"I was stifling retches the whole time. Anyway, once I'd removed as much of it as possible, I scrubbed and scrubbed and scrubbed."

"Had he done much damage with the knife?"

"Only to himself. No, he was so drunk he made very little impact on the carpet. But, since it's now stained a hint of green, it's going to have to be covered up with a rug anyway."

"Hey, perhaps you can make an insurance claim."

"That would be funny wouldn't it, making him fill out the claim form. I think he'd rather shell out for a new carpet."

"Didn't he have a patient coming on Thursday?"

"Oh yes!" said Debbie, getting up to make more tea. "So, having scrubbed the carpet to within an inch of its life, I got all the scented candles from around the house and left them to burn through, what was left of the night."

179

Lois laughed, "I thought you were going to say, 'to burn through, what was left of the study!'"

"Wouldn't have been a bad idea! Anyway, I got up at six and opened the study windows and the front door to try and circulate some air. I took the rug from the living room and placed it strategically over the stain ... even though the carpet underneath was still wet, I felt it would stop any more of that terrible smell coming out. Then I got air freshener and squirted it everywhere! It wasn't until I went to take the kids out, that I realised he'd puked up the garden path as well *and* trodden in it. So when I got home I had to pressure wash the path, despite the fact it had been raining. Oh yuk, I don't even want to think about it!" Debbie said, raising her hand to suppress the thought, as she grimaced.

"Anyway, I woke him up before I went on a mega-shop and told him he'd got an hour to sober up before his patient came. He had two hours actually, but it gave him an extra incentive to get going."

"It might not have been him on the garden path. Richard wasn't the only one to be sick."

"Go on."

Lois proceeded to tell Debbie about finding Tom in the garden in the pouring rain, how the little willow tree may not see adulthood as a consequence and the necessity to jettison her shoes and trousers. They were both laughing when they heard Richard and Tom coming down the stairs.

"So Richard," said Lois as he was putting the kettle back on, "how did you get on with your private patient on Thursday?"

"Oh God, don't ask. I felt like death. She looked slightly perturbed when she walked into the house; presumably it still smelt a bit? I'd drunk about a gallon of water before she came, so I had to go to the loo twice in the hour! Fortunately she was able to give me a very clear and concise history, which pointed very directly to a particular remedy AND I was able to remember the name of it AND write it down legibly for her to order from the pharmacy! So, it wasn't all bad. She's coming back for a follow-up next week, so fingers crossed."

"And, no sooner had she driven away than he was sick again."

"Debbie! Don't tell them that! Oh I get it, you two have been sitting down here comparing notes, have you?"

"We might have," smirked Debbie, "By the way, has anyone heard how Adam was the next day?"

"I saw him. You know, the Ellie saga," said Lois.

"What Ellie saga?" asked Debbie.

"Oh God, you've not heard?" Lois went on to tell them what had happened.

"Crikey, we'll have to keep a close eye on those two," said Richard, shaking his head in dismay, "poor old Jack will really struggle with this."

"I thought I'd pop round tomorrow morning," said Lois, glancing at her watch. "Gosh it's late, we'd better make a move." Lois pulled Tom to his feet. Debbie told Richard that Hannah needed help with learning lines for a play and sent him off to look for her.

On the walk home, Lois asked Tom if he knew why Dave hadn't been invited to the pub. Tom's response, much to Lois's amusement was, "Apparently they did invite him, but he said he'd rather not go. He was worried he would have too much to drink and embarrass himself!"

21

On Saturday morning Lois dragged herself out of bed at eight thirty. It was a stunning day. She had breakfast, put a load of washing in the machine and had a quick tidy up. Then she sat in the living room for five minutes, because she could. The sun was streaming in through the front windows making the world a happy place. She had realised during the night, on one of her seemingly numerous trips to the loo, that if she and Tom were actually going to get married before the baby was born they were going to have to get organised pretty quickly. To this end she took out her laptop and started to make a list of what they needed to do.

She gave up after ten minutes; her mind was not clear enough to concentrate; partly due to lack of sleep, but also, she couldn't stop thinking about her proposed visit to Doreen and Jack's and what she was going to say.

With Tom still fast asleep, Lois decided the best thing to do was to go for a walk and try and clear her poor addled brain. As she made her way up the lane, Rupert and Reaver appeared from Annie and Dave's garden and followed her for a short distance, then trotted back home. Lois felt it was a shame they didn't come with her; she liked walking dogs. In fact, she thought, wouldn't it be great if they had a dog of their own? It would encourage, no, force her to exercise, which had to be a bonus. She also felt it was good for children to be brought up with pets; her family had never had any and she'd always felt she'd missed out. Now, this really was a good idea. In fact, it would be almost criminal to live in a place like Harewood Park and not have a dog! By the time she had completed her thirty-minute walk, she'd decided that her priority for the day should be to find her and Tom a nice puppy.

Lois made Tom a bacon sandwich and a 'proper' coffee and took it up to him in bed. "I've had a great idea!"

"Oh yes?" said Tom, a little suspiciously.

"I think we should get a dog!"

"A dog," Tom repeated slowly, "We're getting a baby in a matter of weeks; don't you think you'll be busy enough?"

"You know me, the busier the better! Come on, up you get, let's go and buy a puppy!" she said, half jokingly.

"Lois, you cannot just go out and buy a puppy! It needs careful thought and research. We've got a wedding to organise, there's also plenty to get ready for Pumpkin's arrival. We've still got loads to do to get the garden straight. Presumably you need to sell your car and get something a little more child friendly!"

"Sell my car? I'm not selling my car!" Lois sat and thought for a moment. Of course, she hadn't even contemplated how she would fit baby, pushchair and God knows what other paraphernalia in the MG. "Okay. Yes, I've got to sell my car, I'd thought of that!" She looked at Tom and they both started laughing. "Ahh, a puppy would be nice though wouldn't it?"

"Come on!" said Tom, almost leaping out of bed. "Let's get on with some of these jobs."

They spent several hours researching wedding venues on the Internet, resulting in Harewood Manor becoming their number one choice, mainly due to its location. The two of them walked down to the manor before lunch and the duty manager gave them a quick tour. The room that would accommodate them best was much more traditionally furnished than the areas of the hotel Lois had previously seen, and she was quite taken with it. The wedding was only going to be small and simple; a ceremony and a buffet lunch was all they wanted and surprisingly, the manor was able to accommodate them at a not unreasonable cost; even offering a five per cent residents' discount. The manager also said that the hotel would be able to organise the flowers … 'One less thing!' Lois thought, thankfully.

There was availability for either of the first two Fridays in September, so returning home they did a quick ring-around to family members and the close friends they planned to invite. With only four or five weeks before these dates, they wanted to make sure that the important people could come. It transpired that the best date for the majority of the guests was the first one, so they took the plunge and booked it;

subject to being able to arrange the registrar, which would have to be done on Monday. Tom put down the phone, gave Lois a hug and muttered, "Job done!" into her ear.

After lunch Lois decided she really ought to go and see how Doreen and Jack were getting on. Doreen seemed really pleased to see her, welcoming her with a hug. "Come on in Lois. Cup of tea?"

"That would be lovely, milk and two sugars please." She followed Doreen into the kitchen; there was no sign of Jack, but Lois noticed Ellie's basket was still sitting in the corner of the room. Doreen saw her glance at it.

"We're not ready to get rid of it. Not yet."

"Oh Doreen, I'm so sorry. You must be having a really tough time."

"Do you know, I'd never had a pet before. To be honest, I didn't really want her; it was only in the hope that she would benefit Jack." Lois could see tears welling-up in Doreen's eyes as she poured the boiling water into the teapot, "Gosh, I do miss her."

"Where is Jack?"

"In bed. He hasn't been up since Thursday. I can't get him up if he won't co-operate. He's barely eating or drinking anything." Doreen handed Lois her tea. "I suppose it's going to take time. I think I'll ask the doctor to come and see him on Monday if he's no better, not that he'll be able to do anything."

"If you need me to help in any way Doreen, please do give me a call. I could get shopping for you, or stay here with Jack while you get out, if you like."

"Oh Lois, would you? It would be great to go out, it's so depressing just staying here, but I worry about leaving him alone at the moment."

"Let me give you my phone numbers."

Doreen passed Lois her address book and a pen. When she'd finished writing, Lois asked, "Would you like to go out now?"

Doreen's face lit up. "You're an angel," she said, almost immediately grabbing her coat from the peg on the back door. "Are you sure you don't mind?"

"Not at all. How long do you think you'll be?"

"Half an hour at the most. You're a gem!" smiled Doreen, picking up her bag and keys. She was gone before Lois had an opportunity to change her mind, or indeed to ask her if she should do anything for Jack.

Lois spent the first five minutes or so pottering around the lounge and kitchen, looking at photos and some cards on the mantelpiece. The cards were all 'sorry to hear of your loss' types. One was from the charity, which had supplied Ellie for Jack. It had a beautiful photo of a black Labrador on the front. Lois wondered what Jack had thought of that, if he'd seen it.

Feeling at a bit of a loose end, Lois decided she would take Jack a cup of tea, even if he wasn't going to drink it. She found a tray and headed up the stairs with it fully loaded. She squeezed herself past the seat of the stair-lift, starting to feel quite nervous about what she would say to Jack. Not knowing which room he was in, Lois struggled to hold the tray and knocked on the wrong door to start with, going into what must have been the guest room. The next door was ajar, that turned out to be the bathroom. Third time lucky, she thought, now feeling ridiculously nervous. She struggled to knock again and pushed the door. Jack was lying on his side in the bed, looking totally miserable. Lois saw him only briefly before tripping, managing to regain her footing, just in time to prevent herself falling flat on her face. However, the entire contents of the tray flew across the room, the majority, including the teapot landing on the bed.

"Oh Jack!" she grabbed the pot in one hand and the lid with the other. "The lid didn't come off, thank God for that!" Lois was by now in such a fluster, she could see that tea had leaked onto the bed, so pulled the duvet up to see if Jack was getting burned.

"Oh bugger off!" said Jack, as Lois peered into the bed. His voice sounded wobbly, as though he was on the point of tears, sending a pang of guilt through Lois. The tea

185

fortunately hadn't gone right through the duvet and even if it had, the jug-full of milk that had landed close by, would have cooled it almost instantaneously. As Lois lowered the duvet and started to apologise again, she looked at Jack and was amazed to see that he wasn't crying at all, but laughing! She must have looked astounded, because he pointed at her and laughed more, and more. Then he pointed at the doorway, gesticulated a somersault with his hand, chuckled an "Oh bugger off!" and continued to laugh until tears were pouring down his face.

Lois pulled up a chair to sit facing him and joined in the laughter. She looked to see if she could tell what had tripped her up, but there was nothing there. Looking at Jack's smiling face, she began to wonder whether it had been a 'fall of fate'.

Lois picked up the biscuits from the bed and floor, blew on them before returning them to the plate, and then offered one to Jack. He accepted with a chortle.

"I'll go and make more tea," said Lois.

"Oh bugger off!" said Jack, pointing to his wheelchair.

"You want to get up?" said Lois in surprise. Jack nodded. "I can't really lift you Jack."

"Oh bugger off!" Jack pointed to a board by the side of the chest of drawers. Then he pressed a button on a remote control to lift the head of the bed. Between them, Jack and Lois managed to transfer him from bed to wheelchair, wheelchair to stair-lift and stair-lift to his electric wheelchair, just as Doreen arrived home.

Doreen was staggered, "Lois, how on earth?" Jack started laughing.

"Well it's a funny story actually!" Lois looked at Jack and smiled, "I'm afraid I've made a bit of a mess of your bedroom! I'll make some tea and tell you what happened."

22

The next week, Lois was determined to get organised in the hope that, if she could get the wedding, nursery and car changeover sorted, Tom would let her have a puppy. She had to laugh to herself when she thought this through, she sounded like a ten year old, 'If I do my homework every night can we get a puppy?'

Anyway, it worked well as a motivating factor. She designed, printed and posted the wedding invitations on the Monday. On Tuesday morning she bought a dress for the wedding, which she was thrilled to find On Sale in House of Fraser. In the afternoon she part exchanged her car for a slightly newer estate with a five star safety rating, (and room for a dog). Having called her insurance broker, she gave her beloved MG a little pat on the bonnet to say goodbye and climbed into her roomy purchase. "How times have changed!" she mumbled to herself, smiling as she drove off.

When Tom got home that night, he was surprised at her choice of car. "Why the estate? I thought you'd go for a five door hatchback type, Lo."

"There's a lot of gear goes with a baby you know, Tom."

"You got it for a dog, didn't you?"

"No, of course not!" He looked her in the eye. "Well okay, maybe I did, just in case?"

"Well, as it happens I had a chat with one of the girls at work today and her mum breeds Labradors. Really nice ones apparently, working dogs, field trials champions and all that."

"Oh really? Has she got any puppies?"

"Not now, no. She's just sold the last one." Lois felt a pang of disappointment. "I've just got to go and get my phone, I think I left it in the car," said Tom.

He came back within a minute, carrying a cardboard box.

"Did you find it," asked Lois, "your phone?"

"No." Tom put the box down, "But I did find this." He reached into the box and pulled out a sleepy, black puppy.

"Oh my God! I don't believe it!" Lois carefully took the little bundle, sat down on the sofa, rearranged her hands and raised it up so she could see its face. "Tom, it's so sweet! Is it a he or a she?"

"A she. Elsa. Helen's mum had already named her; she was planning to keep her, but Helen managed to persuade her otherwise."

"Elsa, ah that's so sweet. Oh Tom, she's gorgeous, thank you so much!" Lois put the puppy on the sofa and gave Tom a hug.

"Careful Lo!" There was a yelp from the puppy as she rolled off the sofa and onto the floor.

"Oh God, is she all right?" asked Lois, picking her up again.

"I expect she's fine, but I hope you'll be more careful with Pumpkin, I don't want him or her being left to roll off the sofa! In fact perhaps getting a puppy has more of a positive side to it than I'd thought, perhaps it'll give you a bit of training for motherhood!"

Lois put Elsa down again, this time on the floor. The puppy scampered around the room for a short time then squatted and did a poo on the new carpet. Tom looked knowingly at Lois, "You wanted it. It's all yours!"

After clearing up the poo and the puddle that arrived shortly afterwards, Lois asked Tom if Elsa had come with any gear and instructions, she was quickly realising that she knew very little about how to look after her new companion.

"Oh yes, I've been to Superpets and bought half the shop. I'll go and get it from the car." He arrived back with an enormous cage full of toys, bowls and beds, then went out to the car again and came back with a large sack of dry puppy food.

"Blimey! Where are we going to put this lot?"

"Don't know pet, it was…."

"I know; it was me who wanted a dog! I thought it was you who said it needed careful thought."

"Well, it seemed like too good an opportunity to miss, a well bred puppy like this, from somebody I almost know."

Lois took one of the toys out of the cage, removed the label and tried to entice Elsa to play with it. The puppy,

188

however, was unimpressed; she waddled over to the doormat and started chewing on Tom's best work shoes that he'd just taken off.

"Okay, well, I see the purpose of the cage!" said Lois as she scooped the puppy up with one hand and picked Tom's shoes up with the other and put them on one of the dining room chairs.

Lois went around the downstairs of the house removing anything that she deemed chewable. The kitchen was far too small to have the cage in, so after thinking it through and having a chat with Elsa's breeder, Lois decided the best thing was for Elsa to sleep in the outhouse, in the cage.

"Apparently puppies don't poo on their beds, so if the bed fills the cage, they don't poo," said Lois, slightly dubiously, as Tom returned from setting things up in the outhouse. Tom raised an eyebrow in scepticism. "Well I guess it's worth a try," said Lois, giving Tom a hug and adding, "Love you!"

Taking Elsa out to the garden every forty minutes or so, in the hopes of all her business being done outside, seemed to work well, and it was very entertaining watching the puppy jumping through the grass. At ten o'clock Lois settled Elsa down in her cage and made her way to bed, feeling completely drained.

23

The rest of the week saw Lois becoming more and more exhausted by a combination of an advancing pregnancy, a puppy that seemed to take up a ridiculous amount of her time and preparation for her parents' first visit to the cottage, which had been arranged for Saturday.

By Friday morning, Lois was so stressed she was beginning to feel quite nauseated. It was almost impossible to keep the puppy in the tiled area of the kitchen and dining room; every time the door was opened she would manage to run through; the result being several stains on the living room carpet, which needed proper carpet shampoo to shift them. Lois needed to do a supermarket shop; she'd barely left the house all week and they were low on almost everything. She also had an antenatal appointment booked; before which she'd intended to read Debbie's Mamatoto book, so she could discuss her plan for the birth, but she hadn't had time. And the puppy was supposed to have been to the vets for her first vaccination.

Lois took Elsa out onto the front lawn for a wee before heading out. "Come on Elsa, hurry up, I'm in a rush!" Elsa just carried on sniffing at a spider she'd found on the path, then did a huge leap and a twist, squashing her arachnid toy on landing, sniffing it again and proceeding to eat it. As Lois went to try to catch hold of her to remove the spider from her mouth, she raced off as fast as she could, tail tucked down between her back legs, around and around the little willow in the centre of the lawn. She only stopped when she misjudged a leap onto the front doorstep, crashed into it with her chest and rebounded, heels-over-head. A few days ago, Lois would have found this behaviour incredibly endearing. Today however, the puppy's lack of cooperation when she was in such a hurry was quite frankly, getting on her nerves.

Lois was close to tears as she finally managed to pick Elsa up, deciding that she would just have to clear up a puddle from the cage when she got home. A click of the garden gate latch made her jump. "Oh Lois!" Doreen came through the gate and into the garden. "Is it yours?"

"Yes." Lois felt embarrassed, being stressed out by the puppy when Doreen and Jack were so upset about losing Ellie. "Her name's Elsa." Lois paused, "Sorry Doreen, I bet the last sort of dog you and Jack want to see is a black lab. Tom bought her as a surprise."

"Oh nonsense! She's absolutely beautiful!"

Lois offered the puppy to Doreen to hold. Delighted, Doreen carefully lifted Elsa into her arms and started tickling her behind her ears, instinctively avoiding the razor sharp teeth, which were seeking a finger or watchstrap to chew.

Lois thought for a moment, then decided that 'you don't know if you don't ask,' and said, "Doreen, I don't suppose you could look after her for me for a few hours could you? I've got so much to get done in town and she needs to have her lunch at twelve."

"Ah, I'd be delighted to. I don't know what Jack would think though. It might be a bit early for him to see another dog in the house."

"No, you're right, it wouldn't be fair." Lois felt a pang of guilt for making such a selfish suggestion. "How is Jack?"

"Oh, you know, not brilliant. He is getting up now though, thanks to you. I tell you what, let's take her and see what reaction we get. You come with me."

Lois grabbed her keys and shut the front door. They found Jack sitting in the kitchen gazing into space. "Jack. Look what Lois and Tom have got."

Jack looked up and saw what Doreen was carrying. He immediately turned his wheelchair to face the other direction, muttering a very disgruntled "Oh bugger off!" as he did so.

Doreen took Lois into the living room, saying, "I tell you what, you go and get the puppy's food and whatever else she needs. I'll just have to keep her out of his way, that's all."

Relieved, but still feeling somewhat guilty, Lois went back to the house. She decided the cage would be useful, so loaded it into the boot of the estate, along with the food and various other bits and pieces. She scribbled some brief instructions, drove the thirty metres or so up the road and unloaded it all

191

into Doreen's living room. She gave Doreen a hug of thanks and made her way to town.

The supermarket was packed. Lois felt as if she was walking through a fog of exhaustion. Additionally, not yet being used to the layout of the shop, it took her ages to find everything she needed. She eventually joined the queue for the checkout and glanced at her watch. She couldn't believe it; she'd been in there for two hours. Her appointment with the midwife was in five minutes; there was no way she would get there in time. She decided she had no choice but to abandon her full trolley; the last thing she wanted was for the midwife to think she was too disorganised to get to an appointment on time.

About to leave the shop, Lois had a sudden change of heart. The midwife was bound to be running late; last time she'd had to wait half an hour. Having spent two hours doing the shopping; if she returned after the appointment, the trolley may have been tidied away; she couldn't bear the thought of starting the shopping process all over again. She did an abrupt turnaround, almost crashing into an elderly lady, and re-joined the queue she'd left.

As soon as there was enough space, Lois started loading her shopping onto the conveyer belt, piling the goods up high in an attempt to save time. On several occasions items fell onto the floor, including a bag of apples, which she abandoned to the back of the checkout; she didn't want to buy them bruised. Making very obvious glances at her watch from time to time and sticking out her bump as far as possible, Lois tried to give the impression of being about to give birth, in the hope that it would hurry the cashier and customer in front along. Her mannerisms had no effect; in fact she was sure that they were going deliberately slower. It was the last straw when the customer started protesting that one of the items she was buying was on special offer but had gone through at full price. Lois was so stressed by this time, standing there, huffing and puffing, waiting for the runner to go and do a price check, that she took a two pound coin out of her purse. "To make up the difference. Please take it, I'm in a terrible hurry!" she said, as she offered the money to the middle-aged, very well dressed lady in front of her. The woman looked so doubtful that Lois, in desperation and without any forethought, whispered, "My waters have just broken!" in the hope that she would just get out of the way.

"Oh my lord!" The woman shouted, "Quick, get an ambulance! This lady's waters have just broken!"

"Oh no!" mumbled Lois to herself, turning very red. The cashier lent over her till to see if there was amniotic fluid all over the floor. Lois put her hands over her face; this really wasn't going at all well. The manager appeared with a chair for Lois to sit on, which she was grateful for, despite it being under false pretences.

"I'll just go and call an ambulance for you," Lois grabbed the manager by the arm as she turned to walk off.

"No need, really. I'm due to see the midwife at the surgery, right now in fact. If someone would just help me get the shopping through the checkout and into the car."

"Well, if you're sure, dear?"

Having had reassurance from Lois that she was fine, the manager and another shop assistant packed the shopping for her and returned it to the trolley. As they left the till to head for the car, Lois called after them that she hadn't paid. The manager waved her hand back at her, "Our treat my dear, shop policy; when your waters break in here you shop for free!" Lois could feel her cheeks, once again, flushing red with embarrassment. Then she had another alarming thought, where was she going to shop for the remainder of her pregnancy?

When Lois arrived at the surgery, the midwife was just picking up her messages from reception, before leaving. Lois walked up to the desk and gave her name, awkwardly. "I'm so sorry to be so late, I got caught up," she paused, and then decided to leave the explanation at that. The midwife looked at her watch, said she would just have time to see her before her next visit and took Lois through to a consulting room.

"So Lois, I'm Hattie, we've not met before. How's it all going, any problems, worries?" The young midwife checked Lois's blood pressure as she chatted.

"No, I think I'm fine. I would like to talk through the possibilities of a home birth though. I realise with me arriving so late you won't have time today, but"

"A home birth, great! Yes, so long as you're fit and healthy throughout the entire pregnancy, go for it. It will be a truly magical experience for you and your partner." Truly magical? That sounded a bit over the top; presumably it was still going to hurt like hell!

"Wee specimen, Lois?"

"Oh, gosh, sorry, I completely forgot!"

"Don't worry. Look, I tell you what. You seem a bit flustered today. How about I come for a home visit on Monday. I've just had a cancellation, so I can fit you in at eleven o'clock. We can talk through a home birth and check the specimen then?"

"Great!" said Lois; then the thought of the puppy poo stains on the carpet and how the midwife would respond, flashed through her mind. Should she suggest meeting at the surgery? No, she would just have to get rid of them and make sure young Elsa was safely away during the visit.

"Just pop up on the bed, we'll have a quick feel of baby now."

Lois jumped as the midwife put her cold hands on her tummy. "Mm, thirty six weeks. Plenty of movement?"

"Oh yes, especially at night!"

"Always the way. Let's just measure." Lois prepared for the cold of the tape measure. "Oh yes, good size. And heart beat?" Lois loved this bit of the proceedings. She listened intently while the midwife slid the gelled monitor over her tummy where she expected to pick up the beat and smiled happily when she heard it. "There we are, everything appears to be going well." Hattie passed Lois some tissues to wipe the gel away and helped her into a sitting position. "Right, see you on Monday."

"Monday, eleven o'clock. That's great; see you then." Lois walked out of the surgery repeating to herself, Monday eleven o'clock, Monday eleven o'clock.

Lois was completely exhausted by the time she'd got home and unloaded the shopping. The last thing she felt like doing was going to collect Elsa. But, having already been much longer than she'd intended, she got back in the car and drove up the lane, wondering how the hell she was going to manage a puppy and a baby; had she been completely mad thinking she could do this?

She knocked at the front door, trying to look enthusiastic at the thought of an evening of visits to the garden and running round keeping Elsa in check, when all she actually wanted to do was sleep.

Doreen opened the door. "Lois! You're early. I thought you'd be ages yet." Lois was surprised at this response; she'd been almost four hours. "Come on in, I've got a surprise for you."

Lois followed her through the kitchen and into the garden. Jack was asleep in his electric wheelchair, his functioning hand wrapped around a sleeping Elsa. Lois stared in amazement, tears starting to pool in her eyes.

"They've bonded!" smiled Doreen, "The puppy wouldn't leave Jack alone, as if she knew that he needed something to distract him. She started off tugging at his trouser leg, which he ignored. Then she chewed at his slipper a bit, which he tried hard to ignore. Then she desperately tried to climb up his legs, making little whimpering sounds. She kept falling over backwards in her efforts, but would just come back and try again. Eventually he pulled her onto his knee and she jumped up to his face and started licking him. At this point, Jack started to chuckle and for the rest of the afternoon they've been entertaining each other. Cup of tea?" Doreen turned to Lois and was surprised to see her with tears running down her cheeks, reaching into her bag to try and find a tissue.

"I'm so pleased Doreen!" Lois sobbed.

"Lois. What's the matter?"

"It's just so sweet," Lois wiped her eyes and blew her nose, "I'm sorry Doreen, I'm an emotional wreck at the moment; ignore me!"

The two of them went into the kitchen. Lois sat at the table; she'd been desperate to take the weight off her feet. As Doreen made the tea, Lois realised that there was a great possibility here. She wasn't coping well with the puppy and the baby hadn't even arrived yet, and Jack, well, having a little dependant creature might be just the thing for him.

"Doreen,"

"Yes?"

"Would you like to keep her?"

"Sorry?"

"The puppy, Elsa, would you like to keep her?"

Lois explained how she'd been struggling to manage over the past week and was beginning to have serious concerns that she wouldn't be able to give Elsa enough attention when the baby arrives.

"Well Lois, that's very kind," Doreen paused, "Can I think it through and talk to Jack?"

"Of course."

"Tell you what, leave her here for now, she's fast asleep, I'll pop her down later. Now are you sure that's what you want. I don't want to raise Jack's hopes for something that may not happen, no offence."

"None taken," said Lois; it didn't seem appropriate to be defending her integrity so soon after the 'waters breaking' incident. "I think it would be important that you pay for her though," she added; not that she was worried about the money as such, but it seemed appropriate to handle this potential agreement in a grown-up fashion, "so she is really yours, her paperwork all transferred into your names."

"Yes, absolutely." Doreen smiled broadly. "This could work out perfectly, Lois. Thank you."

Lois returned to Honeysuckle, lay down on the sofa and fell asleep. It was Tom arriving home and gently rubbing her shoulder that woke her, several hours later.

"What have you done with our little black ball of fur?"

Lois was feeling a bit disorientated and had a brief moment of panic, that she'd lost the dog or let her loose to roam around the house, chewing and pooing! Then she remembered and filled Tom in on what had happened with Elsa during the day.

"So, let me get this straight. You desperately want to get a puppy. Then, against my better judgement, I buy you one, as a gift and within a week you've offered to give her away!"

"No, no, not give her away. If they have her, they'll buy her."

"Oh well, that's something I suppose! But it wasn't the money I was worried about."

"Oh, don't be cross! I've had such a bad day." Tears, once again, started to well in Lois's eyes.

"Oh don't be daft, I'm not cross, in fact it's quite funny. So why was your day so bad?"

Lois recalled her traumatic shopping trip as Tom hugged her. "Blimey Lo, you do manage to get yourself into some awkward situations! Life was much easier when you were just going to work everyday. What are you going to do when you've got a Pumpkin in tow?"

"Oh it'll be easy, I'll be organised by then!"

There was a knock at the door. It was Doreen, without Elsa. Tom invited her in and offered a glass of wine, which she refused on the grounds of needing her wits about her, in regards to both Jack and Elsa. "Now," she said, followed by a brief pause, "are you both absolutely sure you're happy to let Elsa go?"

Lois glanced round at Tom, who said, "Doreen, if you and Jack would like her, then we are more than happy; I don't think either of us had realised the time commitment involved in taking on a puppy, and you having her would seem like the perfect solution."

"Well," said Doreen, grinning broadly, "in that case, it's a yes please from us! I can't believe how quickly Jack's taken to her, I saw it taking months, if not years for him to take any interest in another dog. But they are practically inseparable already! She's such a dear little thing and seems very intelligent. Jack's already taught her to sit to a hand gesture. Oh Lois, he's so elated, I can't tell you."

Lois glanced at Tom again, beaming. Tom could hardly believe that changing two people's lives so positively could be as easy as buying his fiancée a present on a whim.

"We'll call round tomorrow, shall we Doreen?" asked Lois, "See how she's settling and sort out the paperwork?"

"Perfect," said Doreen, her face beaming with delight.

They said their goodbyes and closing the door, Lois said, "Blimey, she looks about ten years younger than she did a few days ago!"

"That is amazing. So Lois, do you believe in fate?"

"Me, yes, why do you ask?"

"Well, it seems quite a coincidence doesn't it? You deciding you desperately need a dog just after Jack and Doreen have lost theirs. Jack wouldn't have let Doreen get another dog under normal circumstances, not for a long time anyway."

"Mm, funny how these things work out; as you say, it must be fate…or the hand of a greater force?"

24

Lois woke with a jolt on Saturday morning, the realisation that her parents were coming in a few hours hitting home and shocking her into an unwelcome early start. The house was a pit; the kitchen hadn't been cleared for days, the washing needed doing, the poo stains on the carpet had to be scrubbed out and she had been hoping to tidy the garden a bit more before they came for their first visit. She woke Tom in the hope that he would help her to get organised. To her surprise, he was very keen to get up and help; the new lawn mower had arrived and he was eager to take it for a test run.

"I'm not sure it'll cope with the grass the length it is Tom, it's grown a lot since your Mum and Dad were here. I think maybe it needs to be strimmed and raked first. I had a quick look at the instructions yesterday and they indicated that grass over six inches would cause the blades to jam."

"What have I told you about reading instructions? I'm able to rely on male instinct and a scientific mind!"

"Oh dear! Okay, whatever. But remember it cost a lot of money!"

Tom finished his cereal and coffee and disappeared out of the back door, grinning. Lois loaded the dishwasher, another luxury she had really appreciated over the last week, then got on with washing up the pans. She'd always got very nervous about her parents visiting; wanting desperately to give them the impression she was a capable and organised woman.

With the kitchen, old fashioned as it was, looking clean and tidy and having put the washing on, she moved on to scrubbing the stains off the carpet. She heard Tom come in through the back door; he'd apparently jammed the new mower within the first five yards of using it and was not at all happy. Lois bit her lip to prevent a very eager 'I told you so!' escaping. Instead saying, "Oh Pet, I'm sorry to hear that. What are you going to do now then?"

"Use the strimmer, like my clever girlfriend suggested in the first place!" Tom said, giving her a hug. "What are you doing anyway? Scrubbing the house to within an inch of its life to impress your parents?"

"I might be!"

"Lo, you ought to relax with them. Do you really think it's going to make a difference to the way they are with you, whether the house is gleaming or not?"

"Well, it might actually."

"You've spent your life trying to get them to show you more affection. I think you should give up, relax. They are not lovey, huggy people. From what you've told me they never have been and probably never will be. Your dad's only interest is money and your mum's spent most of her life too pissed to know what's important to her."

"Tom, you make them sound really awful!"

"No, not really awful. Just…oh, I don't know. No, I think they have a lot to offer, it's just that I don't like seeing you getting yourself stressed over the state of the house when they probably won't notice what it looks like."

"Okay. I might still scrub the poo stains off the carpet though, eh? Oh, talking of poo stains, why don't we pop up the road to Doreen and Jack's and see how they're getting on with young Elsa?"

"All right, quickly though. I've got a lawn to create. I'm trying to impress my in-laws!"

There was no answer from Doreen and Jack's house and nobody in the garden. Lois chose to take this as a good sign, maybe Jack had gone out in the car. If he had, it would be the first time since losing Ellie. As Lois and Tom came out of the gate, they saw Adam about to turn into his garden having been for a run. Lois explained that they'd come to check on puppy progress, but there was nobody at home.

"Oh yes, you're a bit of a miracle worker by all accounts. Jack was desperate to get Elsa down to the vets to start her vaccination program, so he can take her out for walks as soon as possible. I couldn't believe the change in him. Quite incredible!"

"That's good news," said Tom. "Incidentally, did anyone clear up the issue of the poison?"

"Yeah; it was a trainee groundsman from the manor, apparently. He'd been sent to collect something from the barns and seen a couple of rats, so he decided to take matters into his own hands and put down a load of poison, just out in the open...bloody idiot!"

"God, that's appalling!" said Tom.

"Well, he is now on an extremely tight rein, not allowed out of the groundsman's sight. The manor are going to compensate Jack financially; the manager was hugely embarrassed about the whole thing." Adam thought for a second, and then shook his head, "Poor Ellie, of all the dogs, really terrible. Anyway, can't stop now. I'm picking up your mate, Mel, from the station at eleven. She's coming to stay for the weekend." Adam glanced at his watch and realising how late he was, started to back up his garden path. "Would you two like to come for lunch tomorrow? I'm thinking of doing a barbecue."

"Sound great," said Lois, relieved that tomorrow would be much more relaxing than today.

"Good, see you at twelve thirty!" and Adam turned and ran to his house.

By the time Geoffrey and Irene arrived, Honeysuckle looked reasonably presentable, apart from the back garden. Tom had mown the front lawn successfully, as it had never been left to grow overly long. He had even trimmed the edges. Lois had picked some roses and put them in a vase on the dining room table and the cottage was fairly clean and tidy.

Lois spotted her parents climbing out of her father's sparkling, vintage Mercedes convertible. She called Tom in from the garden, gesticulating at him from the back door as he hacked at the lawn with the strimmer, petrol fumes pouring out of it. Tom came in through the back door and marched through the kitchen as Lois welcomed her parents at the front. He went to shake hands with Geoffrey, his hands covered in oil.

"Oh Tom!" Lois squeaked in panic. But Geoffrey was delighted.

"Working on an engine are you Tom?" he chortled. "Great! Like to show me what it is you're doing? Tom said a brief hello to Irene and the two men went out to the back garden, where Geoffrey insisted on having a go with the strimmer. He never did any gardening at home; they'd had gardeners ever since Lois could remember, but now he looked as though he was in his element.

"Well Lois, this is lovely. So quaint!" Irene looked surprisingly animated. "Are you going to show me around then darling?" Lois gave her a tour of the house and started to relax as her mother gave some unexpected compliments about the cottage, the décor, her choice of curtains, the setting, even the garden. By the time Lois had finished showing her mother around, she felt as though she'd received more positive feedback from her in the last fifteen minutes than in the last fifteen years. The only negative comment was that the upstairs was very small, with only the two bedrooms; but that was a fair point.

They lunched in the garden on the picnic rugs. Lois couldn't remember ever seeing her father more relaxed. He lay on his side supported by his rotund belly, propping up his head with his hand as he chatted and ate. He had insisted on drinking beer out of the bottle and swigged his way through several, which Lois had never known him do before; she couldn't even remember him drinking beer. At one point, Irene, much to Lois's amazement and horror, lay with her head in his lap. "Jesus, have you seen them? What the hell's going on?" she said to Tom, when they were alone in the kitchen. "They never show each other affection!"

"It's nice isn't it?" Tom responded. "Reassuring to think they might still be in love after thirty-five years of marriage."

"Yeah, maybe," said Lois still feeling uncertain about the whole thing.

Lois was even more surprised when, later in the afternoon, her father insisted on having a conducted tour of the cottage and positively cooed over the baby's room. He started reminiscing about Lois and James as babies. He said what a gorgeous little girl Lois had been and how she had developed into a beautiful and sophisticated woman. Lois was so astonished by this remark she didn't know how to respond. She had always felt that she'd been a huge disappointment to her father; she'd never really excelled at school, wasn't sporty and had shown no interest in going to law school as he had suggested. He'd never really complimented her before, or not that she could remember anyway. So this comment rendered her speechless and a little wobbly on her feet.

"Are you all right my dear? You're looking pale."

"Um, yes thanks, I'm ... fine."

Geoffrey continued talking as they walked back downstairs. "Another thing I want to discuss with you and Thomas is the wedding. Delighted to hear you're going to tie the knot, my dear. Now, your Mother and I would obviously want to bear the expense of the event, I hope that suits you both."

'Blimey', thought Lois. She hadn't woken up this morning expecting the day to go like this! Tom was in the dining room, showing Irene photos of how the cottage looked when they first took possession.

"Oh Geoffrey! Do come and have a look at these photographs. It's remarkable the improvements that Lois and Thomas have made in such a short space of time," said Irene excitedly.

As her father sat down next to his wife, Lois said, "Tom, Dad has very kindly offered to foot the bill for the wedding."

"Gosh, that's extremely kind of you! We really weren't expecting you to contribute to that as well; you've been more than generous already!"

"Oh please, take the offer Thomas; we can't take it with us, can we Irene? And I'm damned if the tax man's going to get his hands on it." Geoffrey took his chequebook out of his wife's handbag. "How much?"

Tom looked at Lois. She shrugged. "I'm not sure," said Tom, as he saw Lois's father had already started writing, twenty thousand pounds.

"That should cover it." Geoffrey slapped the cheque into the palm of Tom's hand.

"Gosh Geoffrey, that is far more than we ... " he was cut short by Geoffrey raising a hand.

"We'll hear no more of it Tom, it's our pleasure! Now quick cup of tea perhaps, before we head back to the Big Smoke?" Lois went to put the kettle on, Irene following her through to the kitchen.

"You know, Tom," said Geoffrey, giving Tom a gentle slap on the back, "this really is a very special little spot you've found for yourselves. It's making me wonder whether we shouldn't be giving some consideration to moving out to the country ourselves."

"Well, it's early days, but so far we love it."

Lois called through to her father. She had noticed, from the kitchen window, some kites flying close to the back garden. "Dad, come and see what you think of these."

The four of them went out of the back door and Lois pointed out the birds. "Good heavens, what are those? They're not buzzards are they?" asked Geoffrey.

"No, red kites," said Lois.

They watched, in awe, the flying display in front of them. Two birds, searching for food, flying effortlessly, low over the garden and the land beyond, the only apparent movement being the tilting of their tails and turning of their heads. Gradually the birds moved out of sight. "Fantastic aren't they?" said Lois, as she turned back towards the kitchen door to go and finish making the tea.

"Quite extraordinary!" said Geoffrey looking a little dazed.

"Delightful! Oh Thomas, aren't you lucky. You've found a little piece of heaven!" said Irene, taking Tom's hand and giving it a squeeze.

Once her parents had driven away, Lois sat down with Tom on the sofa. "Well, I didn't expect that! Were they actually my parents, so chatty, so interested, so relaxed, dare I say it, so happy?"

"Na…your parents were abducted somewhere between the North Circ. and the M25. Those were aliens!" Lois gave Tom a gentle nudge in the ribs and smiled. "Still, I liked them. Perhaps we should see more of them Lo, that was a really nice day."

"Yes, it was wasn't it!"

25

On Monday morning, Lois set herself four goals: visiting Bert and Betty; tackling the flowerbeds in the front garden; ordering a new nameplate for the cottage and reading the book that Debbie had given her. The weekend had ended up being full on, with her parent's visit on Saturday and Adam's barbecue lasting until well into the evening on Sunday. She decided she would tidy up the breakfast things later.

Lois felt very embarrassed that she hadn't been to see Bert and Betty sooner. She knocked tentatively on the back door, which was ajar. She pushed the door open slightly more and called, "Cooee, Bert, Betty, it's Lois!"

"Is that Lois?" came Betty's tiny voice from her chair in the alcove.

"It is Betty, yes. How are you?" Lois walked across the kitchen, reaching for Betty's waiting hands.

"Oh Lois, I'm so glad you've come." Betty was shaking, her voice wavering as she spoke. "It's Bert. I'm so worried about 'im!" Betty reached for a hankie that she had poked up the sleeve of a somewhat grubby cardigan and wiped her eyes. After that she had trouble getting her words out. Lois knelt down and waited until she'd regained her ability to speak.

"I don't know wha's the matter with 'im Lois, I'm sure I don't. 'E keeps talking nonsense! Say's there's little people livin' in the 'ouse. That 'e don't know what to do about 'em, says they won't go away."

Lois was completely taken aback; she'd only popped in for a quick chat. "Gosh Betty, no wonder you're worried! How long has he been like this?"

"Ooh, a couple o' days I think. 'E's not been 'elping me you see, Lois. My, I do struggle to get on without 'is 'elp. 'E's not made any food. 'E 'asn't eaten. I've 'ad what I managed to find in the fridge an' the cupboard, cheese and some stale crackers." Lois's mind was starting to wander as Betty spoke. What was she going to do to sort this out? Who to tell first?

"… burn the 'ouse down!" said Betty, snapping Lois's chain of thought back to the here and now.

"Pardon Betty, I didn't catch that."

"'E said 'e's going to burn the 'ouse down, it's the only thing that'll get rid of 'em."

"Get rid of them?"

"The little people. 'E says it's the only thing to do."

"Bloody hell!" said Lois in astonishment. "Where is he now?"

"I think 'e's upstairs dear. Oh Lois, what should we do?"

"What's your doctor's phone number Betty?"

The old lady directed her to where the address book was kept. Lois found the number and having established that Bert and Betty didn't have a phone, put it in her mobile, then went to find Bert.

She climbed the stairs slowly and cautiously, not really knowing what to expect at the top. Had Bert transformed from a sweet old bloke into a raving madman since she'd last seen him? She reached the landing and called quietly, "Bert, it's Lois, I've come to see how you are." Her heart was racing as she knocked on the bedroom door. She could see Bert's reflection in the cracked dressing table mirror as she walked slowly into the room. He saw her reflection and smiled.

Nervously, Lois repeated, "Bert, it's me, Lois. Just come to see how you are."

"Bloody awful! Tha's 'ow I am. Been invaded ain't we! Pol'ergeists, loads of 'em, livin' in the walls." As Bert spoke, Lois saw his eyes flit across the room. Picking up a walking stick from the bed and shaking it at the wardrobe, he growled, "Go on, get out of it yer little bastard! There, see 'im run Lois? You've got to keep on top of 'em, see. So long as I'm 'ere to chase 'em away, it's okay. But when I go downstairs, well, they all come in. There were 'undreds of 'em earlier. I said to Betty, I said, the best thing is to burn 'em out, then they'll not come back. I've not got time to sit up 'ere all day, I've got Betty to look after yer know!" Lois noticed a box of matches on the bed. "Watch out!" Bert shook his stick again, this time, in Lois's direction. "Cor, you was lucky then. That one nearly 'ad yer!"

Lois wasn't at all sure how to respond, she wanted Bert to go downstairs, away from the matches. Tentatively, she said,

"Oh yes Bert, I saw that one! I tell you what, why don't you go down and look after Betty for a while? I'll keep watch up here."

"Would you love? But do you think you can manage 'em?"

"I think so, I'll give you a shout if not."

"All right, if you're sure." Bert got up, passed the walking stick to Lois and made his way slowly downstairs. Once he was out of earshot, Lois dialled the surgery number and asked to speak to Bert's doctor. She felt the situation was serious, but didn't know whether she should call an ambulance or not.

A familiar voice on the other end of the line said, "Hello, who am I speaking to?"

"Lois Shenfield. I'm a neighbour of Bert and Betty Gibbons."

"Lois, hi, it's Richard speaking, what's going on?"

Lois felt greatly relieved to be speaking to Richard; it made the situation a whole lot easier to explain. She proceeded to tell him about Bert's bizarre behaviour, including his threats to burn down the house; the fact that Betty had been being neglected and that she was very worried about leaving them.

"Lucky you called in, Lois! Now, if you can stay a bit longer, I'll organise an ambulance. We'll get them into the community hospital for a few days or so, I'm pretty sure there are a couple of beds available, that should do it."

"But Bert's gone quite mad Richard! It'll take longer than a few days to sort him out, surely?"

"Well, maybe. But the likelihood is that he's got an infection, chest or urine probably. A course of antibiotics will hopefully put him right."

"Oh. Well that would be great. Okay, so I'll stay here. When would you expect the ambulance to arrive?"

"Should be within the hour, with luck; otherwise I'll call you."

When, a remarkably short time later, Lois saw the ambulance pull up outside, she went downstairs to find Bert and Betty sitting, holding hands over rancid cups of tea. Bert

207

got up immediately and said that he must go and take over the watch. "Don't worry Bert," said Lois, "I'll go back up in a minute." Lois had spent her time upstairs carefully planning what to say to the old man, to encourage him to accept the hospital admission.

"Bert, I hope you don't mind, but I rang Doctor Richard to tell him about the little people." To Lois's relief, Bert nodded with interest. "He said there's a special chemical that can be used to fumigate the house. Apparently it works very well on poltergeists." At this, he gave a hint of a smile. "He suggested a short stay in the community hospital for you both, while the house is fumigated." Bert seemed surprisingly happy with this explanation and when the ambulance crew arrived at the back door, was quite happy to potter off with them. Betty called Lois over, "Thank you Lois, you are a dear. What does the doctor think's wrong, why's 'e gone la-la?"

"He thinks it's likely that Bert's got an infection and with a few days on antibiotics, hopefully he'll be back to his old self. Now shall I pack a few things for you both?"

"That'd be grand. And the cat Lois, can you take the back door key and feed 'im for us while we're gone?"

"Of course."

Lois went up and found a very old, dusty suitcase on the top of the wardrobe, into which she packed a few essentials. She didn't like rummaging through their drawers, worried about invading their privacy, but also, everything seemed so grimy, she quite expected a mouse to run up her arm. The place really did need a good scrubbing. The carpets were almost black and the most enormous cobwebs hung from the ceiling. As for dust, Lois had never seen anything like it; there must have been half an inch on some surfaces. Just as she was about to leave the bedroom Lois heard scratching from above her head; glis glis in the loft; a sound that would no doubt encourage Bert's hallucinations along a treat.

Lois took the case down to the ambulance and waved Bert and Betty off. She breathed a huge sigh of relief and walked back to lock up the house. Making her way home, she was surprised to see a car draw up outside Honeysuckle and as she got closer, a vaguely familiar face came into view. "Oh

208

no, it's the flipping midwife!" Lois mumbled under her breath. "Monday, eleven o'clock. I really must start writing things down, my memory is shot to pieces!" The house was a mess, she hadn't read the book … but then Lois realised, she did have a good excuse, she'd been saving her elderly neighbours from the jaws of death! It took her a few seconds to remember Hattie's name, which, fortunately, came to her just as she reached the car and the vibrant young midwife got out. They greeted each other and Lois led the way into the cottage, which it has to be said, was really not looking its best.

Lois felt quite flustered as she offered Hattie a seat and a coffee. Whilst waiting for the kettle to boil she was able to nip to the outside loo and do the specimen that she had also forgotten about.

When Hattie left an hour later, Lois was feeling surprisingly positive about the idea of a home delivery. She'd been instilled with confidence that she had the ability to successfully have a natural birth. "Being at home, you'll be more relaxed, which means you are much less likely to need any intervention. Of course your pain relief choices are limited and it is possible that you may have to be rushed to hospital in the advanced stages of labour," Hattie had said, earnestly, "but that's very unlikely."

As soon as Hattie left, Lois went online and checked the distances to the hospitals. Three maternity units, all about half an hour away…not ideal, but no doubt the John Radcliffe in Oxford could be reached quicker if one blatted down the motorway fast enough … and then there was the air ambulance. Lois was decided; a home birth was what appealed. That decision made, she booked a birthing pool to be delivered to the house two weeks before her due date.

Lois felt so invigorated by her decision that, having ordered the pool, she went out for a run. This was something she'd never done before and was more of a walk than anything else. Jog ten steps, walk twenty … a jalk. But, nonetheless, it was a move in the right direction. As she passed Chaz and Margaret's house, she wondered how Margaret's weight loss program was progressing and whether

Sicily was still involved; encouraging her to take the decision to jalk to Sicily's for a catch-up.

Arriving at Willow Farm, she wandered around the stable yard looking for Sicily. Seeing the place was deserted, Lois decided to call in at the house in the hope that her friend would be there; apart from fancying a chat, it was a hot day and her attempt at exercise, meagre though it was, had made her thirsty and she hadn't had the sense, or experience, to take a bottle of water with her.

As she sauntered along the driveway that led from the yard to the house, she heard a loud rustling in the huge beech hedge, which surrounded the garden. Her brain was just starting to process the fact that she'd forgotten all about the guard dog, when it flew around the far end of the hedge, hackles on end and teeth bared! Lois froze, her heart pounding in her chest. There was no time to run, there was no time to do anything … except, "SIT!" she shouted, in the most commanding voice she could muster. Lois was astonished, she'd expected to be lying on her back, fighting off the monster of a dog, but instead it was suddenly lying down, wagging its tail like a cuddly lap dog. Lois put her hand to her chest and took some deep breaths. She was just contemplating whether it would be safe to move, when a voice from behind made her jump.

"What did I tell yer about comin' to visit?" Lois spun round to see Sicily standing just behind her. "Lucky I was 'ere, 'e'd of 'ad yer!"

"Oh, I was thinking I'd made him sit."

"No Lo, 'fraid not, that was me gesticulatin' from behind you."

Lois, overwhelmed by shock and relief, felt quite faint. Seeing the colour had drained from her face, Sicily grabbed Lois by the arm and guided her to the house; where she recovered quickly with the aid of tea and cake. She certainly would not come to the house at Willow Farm again without contacting Sicily first.

The two of them spent a very pleasant half hour catching up on each other's news. Much to Lois's surprise, Sicily reckoned Margaret had lost eighteen pounds since she had taken up her post as personal trainer. Though Lois did wonder whether perhaps Sicily was stretching the truth, just a little.

Lois walked home at a much more sedate pace, exhausted by her burst of exercise and the Alsatian incident. She stopped in at Bert and Betty's to feed the elderly cat, which was very pleased to see her. She made a fuss of it for five minutes or so, then made her way home and fell fast asleep on the sofa. She was woken within the hour by her mobile ringing. It was Tom. His brother's wife had just given birth to a girl, Izzy; born by emergency caesarean and weighing in at ten pounds.

"Ten pounds! Bloody hell!" squeaked Lois, "That's huge! Did they realise it was going to be as big as that before Chloe went into labour?" Lois's mind was conjuring up a very disturbing image of being at home, trying unsuccessfully to give birth to a giant baby; the thought making her feel, suddenly, quite sick.

"I've no idea. Anyway, shall we go and see them tonight if I can get home early?"

"Won't she be resting?"

"Joe said it would be fine. He's so excited. He sounds like he's desperate to show the baby off to someone."

It was agreed that, provided Tom was home by five, they would drive around the M25 to St Albans and make a brief visit to congratulate Joe and Chloe and welcome Izzy to the family.

Lois felt very unsettled for the rest of the afternoon. Here she was planning a home delivery, good grief, she'd even ordered a birthing pool. What had she been thinking? An image stuck in her brain of having to go to hospital as the baby was too big to deliver at home and having to walk from the house to the car with the baby's head almost out.

Tom arrived home at four thirty and away they went. Having had his plaster removed from his wrist that morning, he kept itching his arm and picking loose bits of skin from the back of his hand as he drove, which Lois, in her anxious state, found particularly irritating. They called into a superstore and bought a card and a little pale green dress and matching cardigan for Izzy. Lois said nothing to Tom about her latest worries; she felt she wanted to be the one to decide where to have their baby. Not that he would necessarily take the decision away from her, but just in case.

The midwife sitting at the front desk of the ward directed them to Chloe's bed. She was sleeping. She looked very pale, accentuated by the fact that they had never seen her without makeup before. The baby was nowhere in sight and they didn't know quite what to do. They were just beginning to wonder whether their trip had been a waste of time, when Joe walked into the room carrying Izzy.

Lois and Tom peered at the tiny bundle in his arms. She may have been a whopper of a baby as far as giving birth was concerned, but she looked minute to Lois as she put her finger into Izzy's grasp. They all stood, speechless for a while, Lois and Tom processing the thought that, before very long, they would have a little thing like this of their own.

"She's beautiful Joe!" Lois eventually managed to whisper.

"Would you like to hold her?" Joe lifted the baby towards her.

"Oh, I d-don't know," she stammered, "I've never held a baby before."

"Probably a good idea to have a go then?" said Tom, smiling. He gently took the baby from his brother, being careful to support her head. Izzy's dark eyes opened and she squinted up at him and yawned. He gently rocked her in his arms, totally mesmerised.

"Hi," came a weak voice from behind them.

"Hi, how are you feeling?" Lois walked across and gave Chloe a gentle peck on the cheek.

"Like I've been trampled by a herd of wildebeest. But I don't suppose you need to hear that, do you?" Chloe paused; Lois thought she could see tears pooling in her eyes. "Anyway, she was worth it. Isn't she beautiful?" Chloe reached out towards Tom, who walked to the bed and gently laid Izzy in her arms.

Lois handed the present and card to Joe. She felt odd. Not quite faint, but a little wobbly on her feet. Shocked perhaps. She glanced at her watch. "Tom we'd better get going and let Chloe rest." She tugged at his sleeve until he reluctantly tore his eyes away from the baby, having given her a gentle kiss on the forehead, and they said their goodbyes.

They both sat quietly as they drove away from St Albans. Their introduction to Izzy had affected them in such different ways. A feeling of awe had left Tom dazed; he felt that he had never seen anything so wonderful, so miraculous, in all his life. He reached over to Lois, gently resting his hand on her tummy.

Conversely, Lois was feeling petrified. She was silently questioning what in heaven's name had led her to think that having a baby would be a good idea. She had spent almost the entire pregnancy not really connecting with it. When she'd first taken the pregnancy test, she'd sat on the loo for ages, in shock, until Tom had come to see if she was okay. She'd never imagined she would fall pregnant so quickly. But after those initial few weeks, Lois had just been 'living the pregnancy', not really connecting with the huge changes that were about to happen. Meeting Izzy had brought the reality of giving birth and the massive adjustments they were going to have to make, crashing into her mind.

26

Lois spent much of the following week going for walks. She discovered quickly the many benefits that walking, in this stage of the pregnancy, had to offer. There was the fitness aspect, of course, and she was trying to walk briskly and incorporate at least one decent hill each time; very occasionally breaking out of a walk into a pace resembling more of a shuffle than a jog. Then there was the protected thinking time. She'd realised, as she lay in bed unable to sleep, on the night of their trip to St Albans, that the reason for her not being in touch with her pregnancy, was lack of thinking time. With work, the move, the renovations, the puppy, the wedding, the neighbours and so on, life had been directing her thoughts elsewhere and what she needed now was time to focus on Pumpkin and his, or her, impending arrival. Yes, it was only three weeks until the wedding, but this was more important. So, twice a day Lois walked, for between thirty minutes and an hour. She took her phone with her, but had it switched off in her pocket.

Tom was worried about Lois at the beginning of the week. It wasn't like her to be thoughtful. In fact he hadn't noticed her being this thoughtful for the entirety of their relationship. She just got on with whatever life threw at her ... apart from having a bit of a hang-up with regards to her parents. Tom's response to Lois's withdrawn mood was to spend money. Not vast sums, but he bought lots of little things. Cuddly toys, outfits, socks, shoes, hats, for the baby; essential oils, scented candles, flowers and chocolates for Lois.

On the Wednesday, as Lois went for her morning walk, she bumped into Debbie, who was, as she put it, taking time out of the madness that was her home life. They decided to walk together, half an hour around the short wood walk.

Lois was grateful for the opportunity to talk through her newly exacerbated concerns with somebody as experienced in childbirth as Debbie. She told her how Chloe's ordeal had made her feel extremely dubious about the whole home birth thing.

"Have you read the book I gave you yet?" asked Debbie.

"Um, no, not yet," said Lois, tingeing red with embarrassment.

"Well, I suggest you read that first. I am sure you'll find it helps you make your decision. And look, you are not carrying a ten pound baby," Debbie stopped Lois, turned to face her and ran her hand over the Pumpkin bump, tilting her head to the side as she assessed its size. "You've got what, five weeks to go?" Lois nodded, "Well, unless it has a massive growth spurt, I reckon that'll be a seven pound baby, no more. Has the midwife said any different?"

"Uh … no." Lois still sounded dubious.

"Look Lois, the decision to aim for a home birth is a major thing and it is YOUR decision and nobody else's. If you don't feel comfortable with it, then there's no point. You need to be happy with whatever you decide. Okay?" Lois nodded slowly and thanked Debbie for her advice.

They had a lovely walk. The weather was warm, but not too warm. The view towards Berkshire was clear. Lois felt very much more positive by the time they arrived back in the lane. As they parted company Debbie called to Lois, "Oh Lois, I forgot to tell you. Richard went to the hospital yesterday. Bert's got a urine infection, apparently. Same time tomorrow?"

"Great!" said Lois, as she thought, 'Yes Tom, she is a bit scatty, but I like her.'

After the walk, Lois went home and read the book that Debbie had given her, straight through, twice. It was fascinating. Enlightening. Reassuring. The message that came across predominantly was the need to be as relaxed as possible during labour. The more relaxed, the less the likelihood of intervention. As she finished it for the second time, the sun was shining through the open French doors at the back of the living room and all she could hear were the birds singing in the garden. Mm, not too difficult to work out whether the hospital environment would be more or less relaxing than that.

By the end of the week Lois was feeling much more positive again. She was having long chats to Pumpkin when she thought they were alone. She had even put some serious, deep thought into the actual birthing process; becoming more and more confident that it was a home birth that she wanted. Tom was greatly relieved that she was back to her old self and thought that all the little gifts he'd bought must have done the job.

The following two weeks flew by; Mel spent a couple of days in 'The Park' during the first week, splitting her time between Adam and Lois. They made a trip to Oxford to shop for wedding paraphernalia on the first day, finding an exquisite dress for Mel, which made her very happy, and shoes and accessories for them both. Tracking down some sexy underwear to fit Lois proved to be a challenge, but they managed it eventually.

Once all the wedding gear was acquired they dumped it in the back of the estate car, covered it with the boot cover and drove to The Perch for a leisurely lunch. They then made their way to the retail park and managed to spend several hundred pounds in the baby/toy megastore, on baby essentials.

"Gosh, good job I bought such a big car!" said Lois, as they squeezed the last of the purchases in.

"So when are you going to pick up the cot from your mum's?" asked Mel.

"Tom's fetching it tomorrow," Lois was trying to sound positive about the old cot, which she felt she really couldn't turn down without causing offence to her mother. "Lick of paint, it'll look great." They'd just bought the latest, most researched cot mattress to put in it, and some pretty stick-on animals to put on either end. 'It'll look great!' Lois repeated in her mind. "It's a good job I didn't need to buy a cot as well, this baby's costing us a fortune! Of course Pumpkin won't need the cot for a while anyway; Debbie has a lovely Victorian crib, a family heirloom, apparently; she said I could borrow it for the first few months, while he or she is in our room. In fact, perhaps we could go and collect that today. Would you mind giving me a hand?"

"That's what I'm here for!"

By the second week Lois was feeling that the wedding was pretty much organised. It was, after all, to be a comparatively minimalist affair. The guest list consisted of Lois and Tom's immediate family, Mel, Jim, Adrienne and her partner Jane and the neighbours, excluding children. The only adult from the lane not to be invited, was Charles Black. In fact Lois was sorely tempted to deliver a 'Not Invitation' through his door. She actually designed one on the computer and printed it out. 'Mr and Mrs Geoffrey Shenfield DO NOT cordially invite you to the marriage of their daughter Lois Helen to Mr Thomas Arthur Allan, because you are a nasty, small minded little man!' … She felt better for having written it down.

Social services contacted Lois to let her know that they had organised a team of cleaners to go in and give Bert and Betty's cottage a blitz. The pest control people would hopefully arrive at the same time to assess the glis glis problem. They asked if she would please leave the key under the flowerpot by the back door, for the following Monday morning. Apparently Richard had been very firm with Bert, saying that they would only be discharged from the hospital if he accepted some regular help. The plan was for the occupational therapists to bring the pair of them home for a visit on Tuesday and assess what assistance they needed. Then, once that help was in place, they would be discharged, hopefully by Friday.

In the event, Bert and Betty came home on the Wednesday, with support from carers twice a week. Lois called in to see them the first evening and was astounded by how clean and tidy the kitchen looked, and how relaxed and happy Bert and Betty both were. Whilst they sat having a cup of tea, Lois asked, "So, do you think you'll be able to make it to the wedding on Friday? Adam said he'd bring you didn't he?"

"Lois," Betty gave a little giggle, "we wouldn't miss it for the world, eh Bert?"

"Tha's right. Booze and good grub; why d'ya think we come 'ome today? Time t' settle back in, then a nice day out on Friday. Smashin'!"

217

27

Lois woke at seven on the day of the wedding and went to the loo. Outside the bathroom window, rain was hammering down on the roof of the outhouse. It can only have rained half a dozen times since they'd moved to Harewood Park. Why today, of all days? She looked in the mirror at her vast self as she washed her hands, and shrugged. It could all be a lot worse; at least theirs was not to be a huge, white affair. She imagined how she'd feel if they'd booked an open-topped, horse-drawn carriage; now that would be depressing. Anyway she'd heard that many a successful marriage started on a rainy day.

She got back into bed and snuggled up to Tom. She knew he must be exhausted; he hadn't got back from work until ten o'clock the night before. He'd needed to tie up all the loose ends on an important project before going off for his long weekend. But, Lois was feeling particularly rude that morning. This was not an unusual state of affairs at this stage in her pregnancy and Tom was certainly not complaining.

"One last chance for sex before marriage?" she whispered in his ear. He rolled over with a sleepy grin.

"Well, if you insist, almost Mrs Allan!"

It was gone ten o'clock by the time Lois and Tom re-awoke, having both fallen back to sleep afterwards. Lois had completely forgotten to re-set her alarm; it was only the post falling through the letterbox that disturbed them.

"Oh no!" she squealed in panic, seeing the time on the bedside clock. "How can it be so late? Mel'll be here in a minute and I'm not even showered yet!"

Tom did his best to jump out of bed. "Stay calm, my little Pumpkin grower, stay calm, we've got almost a whole hour until we have to be there! I'll do the most important thing. I'll make the tea." He gave Lois a peck on the cheek before she disappeared into the bathroom.

By the time Tom had made tea and toast and brought it upstairs, Lois was showered and half way through drying her hair; dressed in just her enormous bra and colossal pants - the sexiest she'd been able to find. Tom put the tray down, looked over Lois's shoulder at her reflection in the mirror and put his arms around her, resting both hands gently on her rotund tummy. "You are the most beautiful woman in the world and I love you more than pie! And Pumpkin, you are the most beautiful baby in the world and I love you more than pie too!"

"That's lovely Tom, but it is time you were getting ready," Lois laughed. Having finished drying her hair, she tried her best to eat toast and put on a pair of very expensive tights at the same time. She teetered around, almost falling over and getting marmite much too close to them for comfort. Deciding that multitasking wasn't working on this occasion, she shoved the remainder of the toast into her mouth, whole and chewed the best she could. Tom had his phone camera out in a flash and got a photo of her, balanced on one leg, cheeks like a hamster and looking very cross at the sight of the camera.

"Now, there's one for the wedding album!" Tom chuckled, before aiming quickly for the bathroom, out of reach of a slap.

As Tom got into the shower there was a knock at the door. Lois pulled on her dressing gown and went downstairs to find Mel and Jim had arrived at the same time; both looking very smart for their respective responsibilities, Maid of Honour and Best Man.

"You're not ready!" they exclaimed in unison. Mel grabbed Lois by the arm and marched her towards the stairs. "What the hell's going on Lo? You said you'd be ready to leave at ten thirty." The door to the bathroom opened and Tom appeared, dripping wet, with a towel wrapped around his waist.

"It's all her fault. Insisted on ravishing me at the crack of dawn. The woman's a crazed beast!" Lois, arriving at the top of the spiral staircase, reached to where Tom was leaning over the bannister and gave him a loving slap on his wet head.

"I thought sex was supposed to be a good way to induce labour. Isn't that a bit of a risky thing to do today?" said Mel.

219

"You don't believe that old wives tale, surely Mel?" laughed Jim, at the bottom of the stairs. "Imagine all those couples whose babies are overdue, they wouldn't need drugs to start the labour; they'd just be prescribed sex three times a day!"

"Come on, we're going to be late!" Mel said, trying to refocus the men to the matter in hand and away from the thought of having sex with heavily pregnant women. She and Lois then disappeared into the baby's room, where Lois's dress had been hidden, to get her changed.

Ten minutes later, Lois walked down the stairs to where Tom was waiting. "Wow Lo, you look absolutely stunning!" he said, raising his eyebrows. Her dress was cream, three quarter length, in silk satin; it could not have been more flattering.

"It's lucky she's got short hair and doesn't go too mad on make-up!" said Mel.

"Not bad going, all ready by ten forty-five and I have to say, you both look very presentable. How pregnant are you now?" Jim asked, grinning.

"Thirty eight weeks and counting," said Lois, as she picked up the bag she'd bought to match her dress, checked she'd got everything, and walked out of the front door.

The decision was to drive to the manor, time being of the essence and, although the rain had now stopped, there was still a stream of rainwater flowing down the road. They arrived at the front door of the manor, five minutes before the ceremony was due to start. Members of the hotel staff grabbed them as they walked through the door to pin white carnations to Tom and Jim's buttonholes. Lois and Mel's bouquets were thrust into their hands and they were all ushered straight into the room where the ceremony was to take place.

It looked enchanting. There were beautiful floral arrangements adorning the various tables around the room. The sun was starting to break through the clouds, lighting up the spectacular gardens and glistening on the lake that was clearly visible through the huge, panelled glass doors. The seating was arranged in a U shape so that Lois and Tom could be seen by their guests and vice versa. As they walked to their places, one of the registrars was turned away from them, talking on her mobile. The second, whom they'd met previously, shook their hands and explained that Ms Sheila Williams would perform the ceremony and that her own role was to record the details in the register. Lois and Tom took their seats. Both of them glanced around at their guests, waving and thanking people quietly for compliments on their appearances and the beautiful venue.

Mel nudged Lois, commenting with a grin, "Pleased to see the flowers are fresh!"

When the other registrar turned around, a minute or so later, Lois was rendered immediately speechless. She was the woman who'd been in front of Lois at the supermarket checkout when her 'waters had broken'!

Lois turned a very bright shade of red. She could not remember feeling so embarrassed at any point in her life. She desperately wanted to tell Tom, but Ms Williams started to welcome everyone and introduce the civil ceremony, so Lois just started praying silently that Sheila Williams would not remember her.

It wasn't like Lois to blush in this sort of situation, she'd always been socially very confident and Mel wondered why it had happened. Suddenly, Mel found herself overcome by a strong urge to laugh. Unusually, she managed to stop the laughter emerging. However, her shoulders starting shrugging up and down, gradually increasing in speed and momentum. Lois caught this movement in her peripheral vision. She made herself focus extremely hard on her and Tom's hands, mapping freckles and lines to stop herself laughing, and as a consequence, hardly following anything that Ms Williams was saying.

Gradually, as Tom and Lois repeated their declarations, Lois's need to laugh subsided and she managed to refocus on the ceremony, the serious nature of the occasion taking hold. But then, just as Ms Williams recited the words '… my lawful wedded wife,' to Tom, she farted; loud enough for Lois, Tom, Jim and Mel to hear, very clearly. Well that was it for Mel. She was ready to burst at the seams. She bit her lip and closed her eyes tight. The other guests wondered what on earth was the matter with her. Debbie and Annie both fought back their giggles, Adrienne and Jane were not so discreet and their shoulders started to shrug up and down, little titters emerging.

By this time, Lois was beside herself. Tom had managed to complete his vows in a very composed fashion, but as it came to Lois's turn, she didn't think she could open her mouth without laughter escaping. Her bladder was also getting very full, which really wasn't helping!

"I, Lois Helen Shenfield, take thee, Thomas Arthur Allan to be my wedded husband," said Ms Williams.

"I, Lois Helen Shenfield," said Lois, not daring to look at Tom's face, because she knew it would be too much, "take thee, Thomas Arthur Allan," Lois suddenly felt a wet sensation in her knickers and pulled hard on her pelvic floor muscles, "to be my wedded husband. Oh God!" The wetness was now gushing down her legs and onto the floor. The colour immediately drained from Lois's face … she'd wet herself whilst taking her vows.

The guests were aghast, with many hands being raised to mouths. "Oh bugger off!" said Jack, rather louder than he'd planned, when he saw the puddle around Lois's feet. Jim pulled up a chair to sit Lois on before she hit the decks, and encouraged her to put her head between her knees, which she had to splay in a most ungainly fashion, to make space for Pumpkin.

"What's going on?" Betty asked Bert, having heard the sound of pouring water and then the gasps.

"It's Lois Love," he said, in the loud, clear voice he always used for Betty, "she's wet 'erself!"

"Oh dear!" exclaimed Betty.

Debbie and Richard went straight to Lois's rescue. Richard knelt down next to her. "Have your waters broken Lois?"

"Oh my God! I hadn't even thought of that." Lois concentrated on whether her bladder was still full for a moment and yes, it was. "Yes. That's what it was! Oh my God, I'm going to have a baby!" The blood once again

222

drained from her. This time she didn't have to be told to put her head between her knees, as excited rumours spread around the room that it was her waters that had broken.

As Lois re-emerged and brought herself into an upright position, Ms Williams said loudly, "I hereby pronounce you man and wife. Thomas, would you like to kiss the bride?" Tom, who was kneeling next to Lois, looking fairly shocked himself, cupped her face in his hands and kissed her. There was a huge cheer and round of applause from the guests. "I love you Mrs Allan," said Tom, taking Lois's hands in his, "How are you feeling?"

"Well, wet. Otherwise okay, I think. No twinges or anything." Lois turned to Richard. "What do we do now?"

"Well. Let's take you home to change. Call your midwife and let her know. Are you going for the home birth? I can't remember what you decided."

"Yes, I think so."

"Birthing pool?"

"Yes, in theory. It arrived yesterday, but it's not set up yet."

"Okay," said Richard, "well, while your guests start celebrating, we'll go and set up the pool and turn on your hot water tank."

"Oh, I tell you what," said Debbie, "it would be worth Annie and Dave putting on their hot water as well, in case yours can't cope. I'll ask them shall I?"

"Yes please," said Lois, as she got up from the sodden chair. "Look at the state of my dress!" she added, trying to turn to see the back of the skirt. As she did so, one foot scooted away from her on the slippery wooden floor. Tom just caught her under the arms before she lost both feet and landed in a heap in the puddle. He helped her negotiate the walk to dry land. "Now that would have added insult to injury!" she laughed. "Or perhaps the other way around?"

"Before you go..." called Ms Williams in a shrill voice, "you need to sign the Register!"

"Oh gosh, I'd completely forgotten!" said Lois. Tom linked his arm through hers and guided her around to the other side of the registrar's table. A cleaner was now busily mopping up the puddle. "Tom, this is incredibly embarrassing, I'm so sorry," Lois whispered towards his ear.

"Lois, I am delighted! It means Pumpkin's coming. And this is certainly a wedding that won't be forgotten!" he smiled and kissed her on the cheek. Tom, Lois, and their respective fathers as witnesses, signed the Register, and everyone cheered again.

To Lois's surprise her father gave her a hug, "Well done young Lois, you held it together very well, under the circumstances."

"Thanks Dad." Lois felt tears welling in her eyes. Tom, seeing that she was starting to feel emotional, and looking cold, said his thanks to the registrars and started to manoeuvre her in the direction of the door before too many guests wanted to chat. As they turned, Ms Williams took Lois by the hand, "Good luck Lois, hope it all goes well," and in a quiet voice she added, "It was bad luck that, your waters breaking. I hear it's very rare for them to break in the daytime, and to have it happen twice, well!" she smiled and winked at Lois, who squeezed her hand and thanked her for everything.

Debbie came back with Annie and Dave's key and to report that their hot water was already on. She asked Lois if she would like her to come back to the house. Lois was delighted with the offer, Debbie and Richard both instilled a lot of confidence in her and that was exactly what she needed right now. Richard went to fetch his raincoat for Lois to put over her shoulders, preventing the entire manor staff from seeing the sodden dress. The four of them then left, leaving Mel and Jim in charge of proceedings and to inform the guests what was happening, letting them know that Lois and Tom would return as soon as possible.

At the cottage, Lois and Debbie went upstairs and between them removed the dress. "Lucky it was in the sale!" Lois joked. She was starting to feel excited now. When her waters had broken she really didn't know whether to laugh or cry, but now she was on quite a high. They went through the wardrobe for a replacement dress. There was only one that fitted, so the decision was made easy. Lois went for a shower and Debbie made her way downstairs to make some tea.

Richard and Tom had managed to put the frame together for the birthing pool and were just working out how to put in the lining. They had positioned it at the back of the living room, close to the French windows.

"Have you turned on the hot water?" Debbie asked Tom.

"Ah, thanks for reminding me, I'll do that now."

Tom had already rung the midwife and explained the situation. Hattie, having established that Lois had not yet started having contractions, suggested they returned to the reception for now and keep her informed. She promised to call in at some point during the afternoon.

When Lois came downstairs she looked fantastic. The loose fitting cotton dress she was now wearing, had been bought for a holiday several years ago and hardly been worn. Tom was stunned, "Gosh Lo, you look amazing! Really, what's the word? Radiant."

"Why thank you kind sir!"

The four of them drank their tea and the men completed the erection of the birthing pool. When, a short time later they returned to the reception, they were met with an enthusiastic round of applause. Richard insisted that it was fine for Lois to have a glass of champagne, which she sipped slowly as she mingled amongst friends and family.

"Lois darling, you look so lovely in that frock! Oh I am proud of you, you were so brave, sweetie!" Irene gushed. More compliments from her mother, blimey, this was becoming a habit! Then, she hugged Lois, and it was a real, proper hug. "How are you feeling Darling? Any twinges?"

"No, nothing…" Lois was about to say "yet" when she felt a pain in her lower abdomen. "Ooh, just a little twinge there."

At a bit of a loss as to how to respond, Irene said, "I say Lois, some of your guests seem a little unusual. Who are they?" as she looked towards Jack, sitting in his wheelchair.

"Unusual?" butted in her father. "Down right rude if you ask me!"

"No one is asking you Father," said Lois, feeling unexpectedly riled. "Jack has had a stroke, that's all he's able to say. And if you don't shed some weight, you may well end

225

up in the same boat; so why don't you stop being so judgemental and go and have a chat to him, he's a really nice man."

Much to Lois's astonishment, her father said, "Oh, I do beg your pardon. Right-o." And off he went with Irene in tow, to introduce himself and his wife to Jack. Lois went to find Tom, to let him know that she'd had her first sign of a contraction and suggest that, since the buffet was laid out, they should start eating.

As they worked their way through three courses, Lois would occasionally feel small muscular tightenings in her abdomen, but nothing too significant. She ate well; the food was too delicious to ignore. Hattie, the midwife arrived as she was just finishing a very tasty slice of Key Lime Pie.

"Ah, we'll probably see that again later," said Hattie under her breath. "I have to say Lois, I've never needed to visit a patient at their wedding reception before; I'm impressed! How are you feeling?"

"Yes, it's a bit unorthodox isn't it? But there we are, that's me! Anyway, yes, I'm fine. I'm getting a few very mild contractions."

"What do you want to do, go home and I'll examine you there? Or perhaps there's somewhere here we could check you out."

"Well we could OW! OW!" Lois's voice went up an octave and doubled in volume. "Now that hurts!" She grabbed hold of the seat of her chair with both hands, dropped her head down and breathed slowly and deliberately until the contraction was over.

"Come on, let's get you home. Things can speed up quite quickly when your waters have broken."

Tom, having downed a couple of glasses of champagne in quick succession, started singing. "Waters have bro-ken, a-at our we-e-e-dding," to the tune of Cat Stevens' Morning has Broken.

"Very good!" said Lois. "Tom, you need to just announce what we're doing. Encourage everyone to stay on in our absence. To eat drink and be merry!"

"Okay."

Tom held up a champagne glass and tapped it with a fork to get everyone's attention. The chatter gradually died away. "Well, I'd just like to say, thank you all very much for coming. It's been great to see you and, well, sorry our presence here is so brief. But, as I think you are aware, my new wife is about to have our baby, so we'd better go! Please, please stay on and enjoy yourselves, it's all paid for, no point letting any of it go to waste!" There was a rumble of laughter through the room. "Before we go, I'd like to make a toast," Tom raised his glass, "To my wonderful wife, Lois." He turned to her and took her hand, "Thank you for giving me a wedding day I will never forget. To Lois!"

"To Lois!" Responded the guests, as Lois tried desperately not to bend double in pain, as the next contraction arrived.

28

By the time they arrived back at the cottage Lois's contractions felt very strong and were coming every five minutes or so. She went upstairs so that Hattie could examine her on the bed.

"Okay," said Hattie, peeling off her rubber gloves, "well, baby's fine and you're half a centimetre dilated."

"Is that all?" said Lois as she rolled onto her side and pulled her knees up to cope with the next contraction. "Blimey, it's going to get quite a lot more painful then?"

"Well, yes. But you're going to cope really well, I know you are and the pool will help." Lois looked doubtful, "You're going to do brilliantly Lois, trust me!"

Lois eased herself off the bed. "Can I get in the pool now then?"

"We probably should get some water in it first!" Hattie gave Lois a playful nudge.

"Oh, ha ha."

"First rule of having a baby, keep a sense of humour."

"Okay, I'll try and remember that."

"Why don't you and Tom go for a walk while I organise the pool?"

"A walk? Is that safe?"

"Lois, you've got nine and a half more centimetres to dilate, I am pretty sure the baby isn't going to fall out on the lane!"

"Okay, as long as you're sure." The two of them made their way downstairs. "Tom, come on, we're going for a walk." Tom looked surprised. As Lois walked out of the front door she turned to him and said, "Bring some hot water and a towel just in case!"

"That's the spirit," said Hattie, giving Lois a wink. Then, in response to Tom's quizzical gaze, she added, "Sense of humour Tom, an essential ingredient to a positive birthing experience."

"Oh, right," said Tom, scratching his head in bewilderment as he followed Lois out of the door.

Lois didn't feel comfortable to venture far from the house, despite Hattie's reassurance that she was a long way off actually giving birth. So they walked up the lane with the intention of then walking around the back of the cottages, maybe repeating the route several times.

A brand new Audi convertible passed them and turned into Margaret and Chaz's drive. Lois didn't recognise the woman who got out of the car, until she spoke. "Lois, what are you doing? You're supposed to be at your wedding!"

Lois tried not to let her mouth gape in astonishment. "Margaret? My God, I didn't recognise you! You are looking AMAZING!"

Margaret must have lost the best part of a couple of stone in weight. She'd had her hair coloured, so the grey no longer showed and was presumably wearing contact lenses, as she'd ditched the thick-lensed glasses. Lois held on to Tom while she endured another contraction.

"She went into labour at the wedding, that's why we're not there," said Tom.

"Oh my word, how extraordinarily exciting!" squeaked Margaret. "I was just about to go down to the reception. I'm so sorry I wasn't able to make the ceremony; a meeting at work that I couldn't afford to miss! So, are you married?"

"Yes, we just managed that," said Tom.

"Before my waters broke all over the floor!" panted Lois.

"NO!"

"Yes, I'm afraid so."

"Just taking a walk to pass the time," explained Tom. "Do go on down to the reception, it's still going strong. Your mate Sicily's there, but I didn't see Chaz. Ow!" Lois was digging her nails, which she'd grown especially for the wedding, into Tom's arm as she breathed her way through the end of the contraction.

"Sorry Pet." Lois brought herself back to an upright position. "And you've changed your car Margaret!"

"It's the new me, Lois. Since I actually started to lose some weight, I've found myself very much more positive about life. That's why Chaz wasn't at the wedding," she grinned, "I've thrown him out!"

229

"Really?" said Lois, once again astonished.

"Yes. Enough is enough. He was never going to change. He kept saying he'd stopped," Margaret paused, "You know what he does, do you?"

"Um, well, we'd heard rumours."

"And they were all true. Anyway, I've had enough of his lies, scary people hammering on my door and the humiliation of having a criminal for a husband. But enough of me, is there anything I can do to help you, Lois?"

"That's kind of you, but no. We'll just carry on with our walk. Great to see you and well done!"

"Thank you. Good luck, I hope it all goes well!"

Lois and Tom continued up the lane. A few moments later they heard the crunching of gravel on Margaret's drive and the shutting of her gate and when they glanced around, they saw she'd put on some trainers, had her shoes in her hand, her bag over her shoulder and was jogging down the road in her suit.

"Wow," said Tom, "I didn't expect to be seeing that the day I met her in the woods! "

"It's impressive isn't it? I hope she manages to keep it up. It would seem that young Sicily's a bit of a miracle worker!"

Lois and Tom pottered for about forty-five minutes, the main topic of conversation being names for the baby. Over the previous couple of weeks they had drawn up a short list, and as they walked they decided on their favourite combinations. Emerging from the bridleway next to Honeysuckle, Lois stopped and leant on Tom to cope with her next contraction. "Oh great," muttered Tom. Lois was just about to ask what the matter was, when she heard a vaguely familiar shuffling on the road and at the edge of her peripheral vision, she saw the owner of the shuffle stop. Charles Black. Bad timing.

"She all right?" he grunted to Tom.

"She's been better," said Tom, then, to Lois's horror he added, "She's in labour."

Lois emerged from the contraction and looked at Charles with a cold glare. "Well," he said, "good luck with that then." He appeared to be attempting to smile as he spoke. He didn't

230

look comfortable. Lois and Tom tried to stifle their laughter until he was out of earshot, as they watched him shuffling his way down the road.

"Gosh, what a funny old character he is, I wonder what goes on in his brain," said Tom, linking his arm into Lois's and guiding her back to the cottage.

"Maybe we've all got him wrong, maybe he's just sad."

"Hmm, I wouldn't bank on it, Lo. I reckon he's like a strong undercurrent; he looks relatively harmless, then when you're not expecting it, he'll drag you down!"

"Charming, I can't wait!"

Arriving back at the cottage, they found Hattie had managed to fill the pool to about a foot in depth and was waiting for the hot water tank to reheat. Tom went straight round to connect the hose to next-door's hot water supply.

"How's it going?" Hattie asked Lois.

"Painfully."

"Would you like a cup of tea and a biscuit? You need to be keeping your strength up."

"That would be great, but I'll make it; any distraction."

The water started coming out of the hose. "We'll have our tea, then I'll examine you again and if you want, you could get in the pool. And Lois, if you haven't progressed very much I might go and do a couple of visits." Lois looked shocked; "I won't be far away, so you can call me if you're worried." Still, Lois felt anxious at the idea of Hattie not being in the house.

The three of them had their tea and Lois and Hattie went back upstairs for another examination. "Well, you're almost three centimetres dilated now, so things are moving forward." Hattie sounded very positive, but Lois was hugely disappointed. With this degree of pain she had expected to be much further on. Hattie, seeing Lois's doleful expression said, "This is perfectly normal for a first labour, Lois. People are often under the impression that as soon as the contractions are regular and painful, the baby will be born at any moment; but I'm afraid it doesn't often happen like that. Look, why don't you get in the pool, you'll be more comfortable; Tom can get in there with you if you like. I'll go and do my visits. I won't be gone long and you can ring me if you need me back. Okay?"

Lois held on to the banister on the landing for support, feeling like crying as another contraction arrived. She really hadn't envisaged the process being so slow. "Okay, that's fine," she said, blinking away the escapee tears, "When this one finishes I'll go to the loo, then I'll get in the pool. See you later."

Hattie went downstairs and let Tom know what was going on. She suggested that he did his best to distract Lois. Maybe put on a comedy DVD of some kind. Then she collected her bag and left.

When Lois arrived downstairs, Tom was setting up the laptop so that she could watch it from the pool. "What are you doing, Tom?" she asked, accusingly.

"Distraction therapy my Sweet, laughter is the best medicine you know. I thought we could watch some of your favourite stand-ups from the comfort of the pool!" Lois looked very doubtful, but was willing to give anything a try. Having found her favourite comedian on YouTube, Tom went and put on his swimming trunks. "Right, are we going for a dip then?"

"How's the temperature?" Lois asked.

Tom put his hand in, "Perfect!"

"Okay." Lois drew the curtains at the front of the house, took off her dressing gown and Tom held her hand as she climbed into the pool and lowered herself down.

"Do you want me in there now or shall I be entertainments meister?"

"I'm getting a lot of back-pain, any chance of you getting in and giving me a massage? And I'd like to be facing the French doors so I can see the back garden as well as the computer. I think kites might have distraction properties as well."

"Right you are Madam," said Tom, doffing an imaginary cap. He moved the laptop, setting it up on a chair by the French doors and climbed into the pool.

By the time Hattie returned a couple of hours later, the two of them were settled and relatively relaxed. Tom would massage Lois during the contractions, then, if she'd missed a particularly funny bit of a comic's routine, he would play the clip again.

"Hey, you two look like you're quite enjoying yourselves!"

"Well, I wouldn't go that far, but I am feeling more positive," said Lois. "Oh look!" Three red kites could be seen gliding in the sky over Dave and Annie's paddock. "Now I feel very positive. They're my good omen, I've decided." A strong contraction grasped her, but she smiled and breathed her way through it.

Lois stayed in the pool while Hattie examined her again. "Wow! You have been busy while I've been gone. You're at eight centimetres!" A tired but happy smile spread over Lois's face. "Probably a good idea for you to go to the loo now, if you need to."

"Yes, I think I will." Hattie and Tom gently, eased Lois up and helped her out of the pool and into her dressing gown. "It'll be easier to go to the outside toilet, straight through the French windows; nobody's going to see me are they." Tom slipped his arm through hers and walked with her out through the door. As Lois reappeared from the toilet, Tom told her that Hattie was busy bringing the temperature of the pool back up. "May as well take a potter round the garden then," Lois said, finishing the sentence with a grimace as a contraction overwhelmed her. She leaned against the wall of the house and snapped at Tom to rub her back, hard. "No I've changed my mind. I want to get back in the pool!"

"That's fine," called Hattie from the living room, "I'll leave the hot water running in for a while longer, but you can get in, that's not a problem. I've just rung my colleague, Jess; she's on her way. It won't be long now, Lois. Tom, could you shut the French doors please, I want to keep the temperature up in here."

Tom, having closed the doors, climbed into the pool and then with Hattie on the other side, helped Lois to get back in. No sooner had they sat her down than Lois exclaimed that she needed the loo again. Tom looked at Hattie, questioningly. "A wee, or the other, Lois?" asked Hattie.

"The other." Lois winced, breathing heavily through the contraction. "Oh God, is it the next stage starting?"

"Very likely. Let me examine you again after this contraction. It may be nearly time to push." Hattie smiled broadly at both of them. "Have you got the baby's things ready?"

"No, well yes, they're upstairs, in the cot in the nursery, sorry." Hattie ran up the stairs to grab clean towels, clothes and a nappy for the baby. "Ah, I'm going to be sick!" shouted Lois.

"There's a bowl by the pool Tom!" Hattie called, as she ran back down the stairs. Tom was looking completely bewildered. Hattie grabbed the bowl and thrust it in front of Lois, just in time.

"Yuck! I wasn't expecting that," said Lois. Hattie passed her some baby wipes to clean her mouth and took the bowl away.

"Are you okay now?" called Hattie from the kitchen, as she washed her hands.

"Yes I think…who the hell is that in our garden?" said Lois, stopping wiping her face. "I don't believe it Tom, it's Chaz! He's going into the shed!"

Tom stood up in the pool and climbed half out, so that he could reach to quietly close the curtains. He could see Chaz leaning into the shed, reaching for something. "We can't be worrying about him Lois, not for now anyway."

Hattie just had time to examine Lois before the arrival of the next contraction. "Well done Lois, ten centimetres! On the next contraction I want you to…"

"Hattie! Hattie! Ahhh! What do I do?" Lois was overwhelmed by the strange sensation she was feeling.

"You're doing great, Lois! Lean back against Tom, that's it, now push hard into your bottom, like you're having a poo!"

"Ahhh!" Lois shouted, as she pushed with all her might.

"That's it. Well done. Keep pushing. Good!" said Hattie. As the contraction petered away, she added, "Lois, that was great, same again next time, you're doing really well!"

Four more contractions came and went. Lois followed Hattie's instructions, pushing as hard as she could. "Fantastic Lois!" smiled Hattie, "I could just see the top of the baby's head. Now when the next one comes, push, just like you were, and if I say 'pant', then pant." Lois nodded. There was a knock at the door. Hattie went and let in her colleague.

"Hi, I'm Jess," said the enthusiastic newcomer. "I don't know what's going on, but I just saw three police cars lurking about at the top of your road!"

"I expect that'll be something to do with Chaz," said Tom, as Lois started to growl her way into the next contraction.

Meanwhile, as Lois pushed with every ounce of her strength, Chaz was making himself comfortable in their back garden. Having expected all the Harewood Park residents to be at the wedding, he had returned to the shed at Honeysuckle to collect the five kilos of cocaine that he'd stashed in the twist off heads of the garden gnomes. On hearing several cars go by and catching a brief glimpse of what appeared to be a police car, passing Lois and Tom's house, Chaz decided he'd better hide. Unfortunately for him, having had a very large joint as he made his way 'stealthily' along the bridleway towards Honeysuckle, he was no longer in full command of his faculties. So, to avoid detection, he attempted to hide in the shrubbery towards the back of the garden, carefully arranging the gnomes in a semi-circle in front of him, for protection.

The drug squad had been tracking Chaz for the past two days, hoping to catch him in possession of a large quantity of coke. They were unsure as to whether or not he carried a gun, so when he headed for Harewood Park, thinking it might be their golden opportunity and not wanting to ruin their chances, they called in the armed response unit and the dog handlers. The dogs had picked up the scent from Chaz's shed and in no time the canine detectives had pulled their handlers, via the bridleway, to Tom and Lois's house, with four other officers in hot pursuit.

"Ahh, it's coming again," murmured Lois, anxiously, as the next contraction started. Then she screamed, a long, piercing scream, as she pushed with all her strength.

Hearing the scream issuing from inside the house, the officer in charge of the operation ignored the fact that the German shepherds were eager to make their way down the garden. Choosing instead to assume that Chaz was inside the house, doing something unspeakable to one of the occupants. Two of the officers stayed outside the front door, to cut off his escape route, while two more, with guns poised, crept passed the French doors and into the kitchen. As Lois emitted her final scream to help push out her baby's head, they burst through the door into the lounge, guns pointing, one at Lois, one at Tom.

"What the hell?" or a more colourful adaptation of the phrase, chorused from all six occupants of the room. Each individual equally shocked.

The officers let their guns down and both of them instinctively removed their hats as a sign of respect for the poor woman who was half way through delivering her baby, its head in the pool, awaiting the next contraction to deliver the body. They slowly reversed out the way they came, mumbling apologies. As they walked out of the kitchen, still in shock and not quite ready for arresting a potentially armed drug dealer, they saw Chaz being frog marched up the garden by the two dog handlers. The officers from the front of the house also arrived in the back garden; Lois's father had just come and told them that his daughter was inside giving birth, and had demanded to know why on earth her house was surrounded by police officers?

Lois and Tom, so totally absorbed in the imminent birth of their first baby, quickly regained their composure and refocused on the matter in hand. Whereas Hattie, sitting on the floor next to the pool, her heart pounding in her chest, felt completely traumatised. She had focused on the guns and not contemplated the fact that the men wielding them were police officers.

"Hattie, are you okay?" asked Jess, putting a hand on her shoulder. Before Hattie had time to answer the next contraction came. Hattie swiftly pulled herself together. She'd come this far delivering the baby, she wasn't going to give up now.

"Pant Lois, pant! That's it, gently now." Lois followed Hattie's instructions and within seconds the baby was born into Hattie's waiting, slightly shaking hands and lifted gently onto Lois's chest. "It's a girl! Lois, Tom, congratulations!"

Lois gazed in amazement at the little person lying on her; blue eyes open and looking up towards Lois's face. "Oh my God, Tom, look at her, she's so beautiful!"

Tom, who was still sitting behind Lois, reached around her and gently put his index finger into the baby's palm and the tiny fingers clasped it. "Hello, most beautiful baby in the world," he whispered. There was a long pause as the newlyweds gazed in wonder at the incredible creation in front of them. Eventually, Tom said quietly, "Do you think she looks like a Mia? Mia Grace?"

"Yes, she does, that's who she is," Lois stroked her little cheek, "Mia Grace." The three of them stayed in the same position for several minutes, until Hattie suggested that Jess take the baby, check her over and dress her. Hopefully the placenta would deliver soon and it may be more comfortable for Lois, if that happened on dry land.

"Tom, would you like to cut the cord?" Hattie asked, as she fixed a little plastic clamp on it, close to Mia's tummy. Tom looked completely bewildered as he was handed the scissors.

"Uh…oh, right. What do I do?" Hattie guided his hand to where the cut needed to be made between the two clamps. Apprehensively he opened the blades and looked up to Hattie for approval.

"That's it Tom, don't worry, it won't hurt."

He cut the cord and breathed a sigh of relief that he had successfully managed to complete his role in the birthing process, along with being a fantastic support and masseur, of course. Hattie carefully lifted Mia and placed her in the soft white towel awaiting her in Jess's arms. Then, she and Tom, slowly helped Lois out of the pool and onto towels and pads arranged on the sofa, where the placenta was successfully delivered moments later. Tom went and got dressed and brought down some comfy clothes for Lois.

Jess handed Mia, dressed in a little yellow babygrow, to Tom. "She's perfect," said Jess, "seven pounds, one ounce." He gazed at Mia, completely mesmerised as he gently stroked her face and soft, downy hair, breathing in her wonderful smell. He counted her fingers and marvelled over the tiny fingernails.

"Lo, I've never seen anything so beautiful. Thank you." He sat down next to Lois and slowly and carefully passed Mia to her. Lois grinned with delight.

"Ah, she's gorgeous," Hattie said, swapping places with Tom, who went to make some tea. "Blue eyes, just like yours, Lois."

Arriving in the kitchen, it suddenly occurred to Tom that, having had armed officers in the house, pointing guns at himself and his wife, it would be a good idea to take a look in the garden and see what was going on. He gingerly peered out of the back door; the garden was quiet and empty. He walked slowly around the back of the house and through the side gate. As he emerged at the front of the house, he was stopped in his tracks. The garden was full of people waiting quietly. Some were sitting on the lawn, some on garden chairs that had been brought from elsewhere. There was a trestle table with the untouched wedding cake, a pot of tea and what looked like wedding leftovers. The majority of the crowd was made up of wedding guests, but there were also, to Tom's astonishment, the team of police officers, complete with dogs. Then he noticed, sat on the lawn between the two very large German shepherds, Chaz, trussed up in handcuffs, looking completely befuddled by the goings on. On the ground next to him, lay a thick, transparent plastic bag, containing, what looked like, four garden gnomes.

It took Tom a few moments to comprehend the scene, everyone looking at him expectantly. Unable to contain his suspense any longer, Jack piped up, "Oh bugger off?" raising a questioning hand as he spoke.

Tom shook his head, grounding himself. Then said quietly, "Sorry, um, yes, a girl. Mia Grace." There was a huge cheer, and Tom was engulfed in handshakes, hugs and kisses. From inside the house Lois could hear the cheers and asked Hattie to help her to take Mia out to meet her friends and relatives. A chair and cushion were carried into the garden and as she walked through the door there was another cheer, quieter this time, individuals instinctively not wanting to frighten the baby. Lois sat down and the midwife gently placed Mia in her arms. With Tom crouched down next to her, Lois, though utterly exhausted, had never felt happier in her life.

Just then, an Interflora van drew up outside the house. "Blimey, that was quick!" said Lois, as the delivery woman lifted out an enormous bouquet in a cellophane vase and walked into the garden, looking a little surprised by the scene. "Are they from you Tom? They're stunning." The woman, carefully put them on the ground by Lois's feet, made some complimentary noises about the baby and departed.

Tom felt slightly embarrassed, "No, they're not from me." Someone had beaten him to it. He knelt down, removed the attached card from the envelope and read aloud, "Wishing the three of you health and happiness in your life together. Best wishes. Charles Black?"

Lois looked at Tom and grinned, "Well, that nicely wraps up a day of momentous events!"

Acknowledgements

A huge thank you to all of my friends and family who have been so influential in the writing and producing of this book. Most importantly, my husband Martin, whose encouragement, enthusiasm and patience, made the whole thing possible; Helen & Richard for being such helpful and generous friends; John, for his very apt painting; Nitia and Angie, for being such supportive and wonderful friends; Matthew, Branka and Louise M for giving feedback on the pre-edited version; the 'Common Book Club' for giving feedback on the almost edited version; various mistake spotters, including Lucy, Emma and Mel; Helen W, for help with the final edit and last but not least, my three wonderful children, for their help and encouragement.

Printed in Great Britain
by Amazon